BLAC

ALSO BY HOUSTON NEAL GRAY

DIVERTED

BLACK GULF

A NOVEL BY

HOUSTON NEAL GRAY

ISBN: 978-0990465324
Copyright © 2013 by Houston Gray

Published by Lower Coast Media, LLC

Text formatting by Lisa DeSpain of Ebookconverting.com
Cover design by Pam Kennedy of thewordverve.com

www.houstonnealgray.com

For Savannah, Ciera, and Angelis
My world and all that I am

ACKNOWLEDGEMENTS

No matter how vivid my imagination might be the pages would remain blank if not for the help of many friends and family members. This novel in particular would have been fraught with mistakes if not for my long time, good friend, Chef Ed Moise. Ed bailed me out numerous times when I barged ahead oblivious to mistakes being made. Additionally, he contributed unique and delicious recipes, gave moral support, never tired of having coffee when I was stuck and encouraged me to "write a good story". Thanks for your friendship and honesty.

My wife, JoAnn, who was always there for me, kept me on track and encouraged me to persevere. Also, thanks to my advance copy readers Rick Conway, Jennifer Winters, Clyde Thompson, Jacki Bilclough, Barry Bilclough, Dania LaSpada, Andy Lang, Elizabeth Thibodeaux, George Mueller and Debbie Terranova, all who read and helped with the story.

Jim Goodwin and C. J. Christ without who there would have been several inexcusable, historical inaccuracies. Thanks for setting me straight. And my FEMA friends David and Meredith McCue who refused to let me off the hook and take the coward's way out when I wanted to change certain details to be more politically correct.

Sgt. Adam Young of the Louisiana Wildlife and Fisheries Department was particularly helpful in technical details pertaining to his department as well as time line events used fictitiously to advance the story. And for unknowingly providing a plot twist I had not considered.

All of you are a huge part of this and an even bigger part of my heart.

CHAPTER ONE

July, 1942
Chandeleur Island, Gulf of Mexico
74 miles East/Southeast of New Orleans

The twelve year old boy hunched down, huddled under his rain jacket as the summer squall pelted him with large droplets that stung like needles. He tried to scrunch himself smaller, but at almost six feet tall and 160 pounds, he was big for his age and getting out of the rain was not possible. The barrier island was covered in patches of sea oats and grass, small trees, and to him looked uninhabited. The lone building, the old lighthouse at the western tip of the island several miles away was not within the boy's sight.

The rain lasted for an hour and his jacket had given him little protection. He was completely soaked and his knees ached from squatting for so long. When the rain slackened he stood, looked south, the direction from which the rain had come, and saw the light of the sun trailing the squall, as if pushing it inland toward the coast of Louisiana. In five minutes the driving sheets of rain passed and the boy removed his jacket. He shivered as the warmth of the sun bathed him, contrasting with the cold wetness of the rain.

The boy took off his boots, draped his socks over them, tied the laces together and hung them around his neck. The sand was warm from the sun and massaged his soles with each step as he moved west along the water's edge. He had no idea where he was or which way to travel, but instinct told him to keep moving. After walking for twenty minutes he was mostly dry. The boots would take longer. He stopped, craned his neck and his eyes focused on the top of a lighthouse at least a mile away. His hand clasped the canteen hanging from his neck and he thought of the previous night.

"This is the best I can do for you. With some luck someone will find you but remember what I told you. Never use your real name and speak only in French. Be strong, be smart, and you'll survive. If you come with us you won't live to see your next birthday." And then the small boat was gone.

The boat was no longer visible but the boy still looked out into the gulf, focusing on the horizon where the water merged with the sky and said, "Wait, I'm...I don't know what to do." He had sat on the beach and cried.

The walk to the lighthouse took thirty minutes, his pace slowed by the soft sand, his bare feet sinking into it with each step. He rehearsed what he would say, practicing in French so it would sound natural. The lighthouse was about a hundred yards away when he stopped. It was a steel structure of four posts with a center column. The boy guessed it rose thirty meters or so. Upon the top of the structure was the light, glass all around with a canopy top.

A small, single story outbuilding, square, painted white with a black hipped roof was connected to the lighthouse by a walkway made of wood. The walkway was elevated twelve inches above the sand and grass grew up through the spaces between the boards. The boy looked at the small building and before approaching took his boots and rain jacket, walked into the thick grass and buried them under a small tree. He returned to the beach and headed toward the lighthouse.

The screen door opened and the lighthouse tender stepped out onto the porch. He held a mug of coffee in his hand and stared at the boy. The tender moved to the walkway and into the sunlight. The boy stared back, but posed no threat.

"What cha doin out here, boy? You lost or somethin?" The tender was short; about five feet five inches tall, with a paunch gut, unshaven, wore khaki pants and a white undershirt.

The boy stood still and did not answer. His mind raced and he tried to understand what the man was saying.

"Come here." The tender waved his arm in a gesturing motion for the boy to approach.

His bare feet had nestled into the sand and were half covered as he stood looking at the tender. The mid summer sun beat down and his pale skin absorbed the rays, already turning pink from the exposure. A soft wind rippled over the barrier island, rustled the grass gently, but offered little respite from the summer heat. He approached the tender and stepped up onto the walkway.

"What's yore name?"

"Bon jour," the boy said.

"Bon jour? Boy, don't tell me you don't speak English. We got a problem cause I ain't no Cajun and I don't speak your crazy French lingo." The tender took a sip of coffee, scratched his scruffy chin and thought for a moment. "I'm Frank," he said, patting his chest with his fist. He took another sip from the mug. "Coffee, you want some coffee, I mean café au lait? Ain't that what they give you kids in your bottle when you's babies?"

"Oui, café au lait, s'il vous plait," he said, remembering what he was told, speak French and don't use your real name. "Pierre," he said, patting his chest as Frank had done.

"Ok, Pierre. Come on inside and get out the sun. You already startin to burn." Frank turned and headed back into the building, "I might as well be talking to myself, hell, I am talking to myself. Out here all alone for a whole month, finally someone comes along and don't speak no English." He turned back toward the boy and gestured for him to follow. "Come on, Pierre."

The boy followed him into the building and watched as Frank made him coffee with hot milk. On the table was a plate with several rolls and the boy stared hard at the bread. His stomach ached from not eating. Frank handed him a mug, steam rising out of it. He reached for the plate of rolls and handed them to the boy.

"Jelly, it's on the table. I know you ain't got no idea what I'm saying but I don't do no good at sign language." Frank pulled a chair out from the table, motioned for the boy to sit and handed him a butter knife and the jar of jelly. "Here, you'll figure it out."

11

The boy sat and Frank walked to a table by the window where the two way radio was stationed. He picked up the mic, keyed it and said, "Minos, this is Frank at the lighthouse. You out there?" He waited a minute, tried again, and placed the mic down when he got no reply. He walked back to the table and sat with the boy.

Five minutes later the radio crackled and a voice said, "Eh la bas, mes ami. What you want?"

Frank jumped up and scurried to the radio. "Where you at Minos? I think I got a lost Cajun boy sittin here with me. He don't speak no English, talks in that crazy French. You heard of any boys missin?"

"I been runnin my crab traps. No, don't hear nuthin bout no boy missin."

"How far away are you? Maybe you can come talk with him."

"I be there about twenty minutes. I needs me some café. You got some made?"

"Yeah but better hurry before the boy drinks it all and eats all my bread," Frank said.

Twenty minutes later Minos pulled up to the lighthouse dock in his twenty eight foot Lafitte skiff, tied up the bow and walked to the outbuilding. Minos Thibodaux was fifty-two years old, too old to enlist in the army and join those fighting in Europe or against Japan in the Pacific. He was lean, broad shouldered with strong arms from years of pulling shrimp nets and crab traps. His hair was still mostly black, his skin dark from the sun, and he walked with the gait of a man half his age. He stepped onto the porch and then entered the building.

"Frank, you got my café?"

"Yeah, me I got dat for choo," Frank said, trying to sound Cajun.

"You a coo-yon, Frank. That mean you foolish, when you try to be Cajun." Minos looked at the boy who had stood up when he entered. "I see he's a boy cause he don't shave. But he's big." Minos offered his hand and the boy shook it with a tentative grasp.

Minos spoke to the boy in French. Frank watched them as he handed Minos a steaming mug of coffee and hot milk, but not understanding anything being said.

"Where you from boy, and what's your name?"

"My name is Pierre, and I'm from France. I, uh, fell off, I mean I got thrown off a ship, and came ashore here. I don't have any family."

Minos understood most of what the boy said but the dialect was different, not Cajun French at all and he struggled to interpret some of the phrasing. Likewise, the boy had trouble understanding Minos. Frank nodded, thinking they were doing fine and getting to know each other.

"I live alone. I have a shack in the marsh I fish out of. When I catch enough I sell it to the people who haul it up to New Orleans for the restaurants. Then I head home to Cut Off, the town where I'm from, and stay there for a while. You can come with me. I could use some help. We'll figure out what to do with you later. In the meanwhile, you can start thinking about telling me the truth. You're a bad liar."

The boy turned red, hung his head and waited for Minos to continue. Minos turned toward Frank.

"I gonna take him with me. I can find his home; you don't need to worry bout that."

"How did he wind up here, did he tell you what happened?" Frank asked.

Minos hesitated, watching the boy as he answered. "He was poling his pirogue out of the marsh, got caught in a storm and it swamped his boat. He washed up down the beach aways." Minos looked at Frank. "Merci, your café was good, yeah," he said and placed the empty mug on the table. "You seen any more trouble out there?"

Frank looked out the window and said, "I climbed up the lighthouse last night. It's a hundred feet to the top and I saw a burning light way off in the distance. I figure they sunk another one. The navy better do somthin fast or we'll all be speaking German."

"I got to get me gone. I got crabs in the boat and the sun is too hot." He turned to the boy and in French told him, "Come on, Pierre, we need to get going."

Frank waved from the porch as Minos and the boy headed west toward the mouth of the Mississippi River.

CHAPTER TWO

October, 2004
French Quarter
New Orleans

The article in the paper said it was suicide by hanging. The body was female, white, approximately fourteen to sixteen, assumed to be a runaway based on the condition of her clothes, and assumed homeless. There was no identification and no identifying marks or tattoos. The French Quarter has many gutter punks as they are called and she was apparently one. She had been found by a longshoreman in a warehouse along the wharf at the end of Esplanade Avenue. The longshoreman had entered the dark building with a flashlight aimed on the ground, his eyes cast downward, concentrating on each step when he bumped the top of his head into something hanging from above. He looked up, pointed the flashlight toward the ceiling and saw the girl suspended on a thick rope, lifeless, her body swaying after being nudged by the man.

An image, aided by the description in the newspaper, came to my mind and I wondered what her last gasp of breath must have been like. Might she have changed her mind, tried to stop, clawed at the rope around her neck, breaking her fingernails until the tips bled, or did she succumb to her decision? Maybe she expelled her last breath with a contentedness of completion like going home, safe, no more threats and no more danger.

The concept of suicide eluded me and I couldn't grasp the need to end one's life no matter how dire the circumstances, even my own in my darkest times. The newspaper made a soft thud as I threw it on the one foot high stack of papers. Brother Lee brought them daily, reading them while riding the bus each morning to his restaurant.

I moved to the doorway which opened to the alley behind Brother Lee's restaurant. It was early morning, almost seven, and the air was cool. The sun was low over the river and bathed the east side of the French Quarter in a bright orange glow and created random shadows stretching out across streets, buildings, and fences. A crew of street sweepers armed with shovels, brooms, and two gallon sprayers filled with perfumed water followed behind the large water trucks. The fragrance was pleasant and belied the previous night's activities of spilled beer and alcohol infused beverages, half eaten street food, and the occasional weak-stomached tourist leaving the other half of the food in the gutters.

I had placed a small table in the alley, snug against the outside wall of the restaurant and close to the door, no chair, just the table. The plate of food covered with plastic wrap I had placed on the table the night before was still there, untouched. I picked up the plate and looked toward the street, then back up the alley.

"You can't save them all. Boy, I done told you that too many times."

I turned around, holding the paper plate of food, and looked at Brother Lee. When he had first told me I couldn't save them all I thought he was just giving me good advice. But I had begun to realize it wasn't advice, it was a warning. Don't get too involved. The homeless street kids of the French Quarter would always be there and eventually bring me trouble. There was a never ending supply, as young as nine years old but the majority of them were fourteen to seventeen. Most were runaways. Too many were rejects, throwaways.

"Why not?" I said. "You saved me."

"Why not?" Brother Lee said. "Because it was different with you. These kids are running away from somethin. You was runnin to it." He looked at the plate. "That's a big waste of food. And business is slow. We ain't operatin a soup kitchen here."

"It's leftovers, we'd throw it out anyway. Show some compassion old man."

"Compassion? After all I done for you, I'll woop your ass boy. You ain't too old for that. I done it before."

"And I deserved it." I paused then said, "But you still saved me. Now I'm trying to help someone else."

"It won't work if they don't wanna be saved. When you gonna learn?"

I threw the plate of food in the open trash can and walked to the end of the alley and looked up and down Toulouse Street. Andi, sixteen and skinny with dirty auburn hair, was nowhere to be seen. She had been dropped off by her parents almost a year ago after failing the eighth grade for the second time. They threw her duffle bag on the sidewalk at the corner of Decatur and St. Phillips Street, gave her twenty dollars and drove back to their home north of Jackson, Mississippi. It was Andi I had left the food for. The article from the morning paper came back to me. The hair on the back of my neck tingled and a chill ran down my spine. I prayed the young girl was not Andi.

I leaned against the wall of the building, picked my right leg up and placed the sole of my shoe against the wall next to my left knee. My street days returned to me as I thought about what Brother Lee had said, about Andi and the many other homeless people in the French Quarter. My early life consumed my thoughts.

My parents were killed in an automobile accident. It was 1983 and I was five years old. They were traveling highway 90 heading east toward Mississippi, going out for supper in one of the small waterfront restaurants in Bay St. Louis. An old man driving a pickup truck was leaving a fishing camp about two miles from Fort Pike, one of six coastal forts built in the early eighteen hundreds. It was late evening and the police determined he had been blinded by the setting sun and didn't see my parents' car. He pulled out in front of them. No one survived.

My parents were in their mid forties at the time of the accident. They had been married for twelve years when I was born. I was a late baby and unexpected. My mother had no siblings and my father had one younger brother, and it was he who was babysitting me the day they died. I stayed with him after the accident and still today I remember crying, but thankfully I don't remember the pain.

It was a big adjustment for my Uncle Tony. He had never married. His job as a Louisiana wildlife and fisheries agent had him constantly busy, or at least that was what he told me. I think he stayed single to make sure he gave me as much time as he could. He had girlfriends and they all wanted to adopt me. And as soon as they started talking about being my mother he got a new girlfriend.

Uncle Tony was a man's man. He was able to hunt anything and catch fish when everyone else had given up and gone home with nothing to show for their effort except a red, sunburned face. Many times he took me on patrol. It was a violation of protocol but Uncle Tony didn't care much about rules and broke them often and with a smile. I'd sit in the front of his patrol boat, ball cap on backwards so the wind wouldn't blow it off, wearing a bright orange life vest and mirrored sunglasses too big for my face. It all made me feel special.

The back marsh of the Louisiana coast was as tricky as any place on earth, but Uncle Tony knew it better than he knew his name. He would work Orleans Parish from the Rigolets down into St. Bernard Parish all the way to the gulf. Often times he would work the other side of the river in Plaquemines Parish. He confiscated illegally caught fish on a regular basis. The fishermen would get so excited catching fish they would ignore the limit placed on sports fishing by the state. Uncle Tony always donated it to a church or a school, and sometimes to the homeless shelter. The churches were especially grateful to have free fish during lent. But it all changed when I was twelve years old.

They told me he was running through the marsh too fast, hit a sandbar, flipped his boat and broke his neck. I never believed it but mostly because I didn't want to. Uncle Tony was too good and too smart. It made no sense to a twelve year old. Father Billy, an Irish priest who had moved to the U.S. years before, and was from the Catholic Church often the recipient of the illegal fish came for me and told me what happened. I remember crying, and fourteen years later, I remember the pain.

Father Billy brought me to Hope Haven, the orphanage for boys run by the Catholic Church on the west bank of the Mississippi River in Marrero. It was 1990 and I was distraught with having lost the last of my family.

I was difficult. The first couple of months I cried myself to sleep at night and during the day I took out my anger on the other boys and staff. The nuns tried to be tolerant but their patience wore thin. Sister Marie called Father Billy.

He walked into the room I shared with five other boys. I had been bullying the new boy who had come in from Lafitte. His mother had been committed to the state mental hospital not long after his father had died in a squall when his shrimp boat swamped after taking on too much water. Father Billy looked at me and I glared back at him. He approached me, stood tall and erect and said nothing. His big hand like lightning struck the side of my head. My ear rang and my eyes saw white stars as if a flash bulb had gone off in my face. I fell to the floor. The other boys scurried out of the room as if it had caught on fire. My eyes watered and I looked up at him as if mortally wounded. He waited for me to speak.

"That didn't hurt," I lied.

"I realize the other pain is much worse," he said. "But you don't have the right to inflict your pain on the others. And I don't have the right to slap you. It all stops right now."

"What do you know about my pain?"

Father Billy stared out the window for a minute, then turned and looked at me. "Get up off the floor."

I rose to my knees and then up enough to sit on my bed. His eyes watered, he cleared his throat and his face softened. He sat next to me and put his arm around my shoulder.

"Travis, the world is filled with more pain and tragedy than you can possibly imagine or understand. It doesn't need your pain too.

You bully these other boys while they suffer with their own issues. You try to start fights hoping the physical pain will take away the emotional pain you feel. It doesn't work. Your loss is great, and yes it's unfair. But it's time to reach out and help the others. You're here for a reason. Remember, God never puts us anywhere to do wrong."

Father Billy pulled me closer. My head rested against his chest, he didn't see my tears. "I'm sorry," I said. "I lied to you."

He pushed me away enough to look into my moist eyes. "When did you lie to me?"

"A few minutes ago," I said, pausing to wipe my eyes. "It did hurt."

The remorse on his face read like a front page headline. "I'm sorry. I'll never hit you again."

"I...I had it comin. I'll try to do better but some nights are more than I can take. I remember my mother and sometimes, I can still smell her like when she would hold me so close, her skin soft like a pillow, and the clean smell mixed with her perfume. And I think about my dad when he would grab me, and it's as if I can feel his whiskered chin nestled into my neck. I don't remember much but some things I do, and then I feel cheated. Uncle Tony made it all so much better, and then he was taken. I get so angry I don't want nobody or nothing."

"Travis, you must find your purpose, what it is God wants you to do. In the meantime, I have something special for you. I worked it out with Sister Marie's approval."

My face showed more skepticism than curiosity. "What?"

"You have anger, and you let it drive you to physical outbursts, it makes you want to fight. I think it is time you learn to control the anger. Mr. Chin is a parishioner at my church. He has lived in Louisiana for several years. He wants to donate his time to the church, his way of giving back he says. He was a teacher in Korea for many years. Now he's a maintenance worker at the sugar plant. I told him about you and the other boys here at Hope Haven. He wants to teach a special class to all those who want to learn."

"I don't need no special class," I said. "I been taught enough already.

"This class will be different. You need to learn discipline, learn how to control your anger and emotions, how to avoid fighting."

"Fighting finds me. I don't go lookin for it."

"You do go looking for it, and you'll always find it. Travis, you have much to learn, always, and for the rest of your life. Mr. Chin will be here Saturday at eight o'clock in the morning. Don't be late, and don't waste his time."

As promised Mr. Chin showed up the next Saturday morning twenty minutes early. Sister Marie had cleared the meeting room by pushing the chairs and tables against the wall and leaving enough room for two rows of four boys to line up. Mr. Chin sat on the floor with his legs crossed Indian style, barefoot, back straight as a board, his fingers interlaced resting in his lap, and his eyes closed. Four boys walked into the room and I followed behind them.

Mr. Chin sat motionless, eyes still closed as we stared at him. "We're here," I blurted, arrogance resonating in my voice.

He opened his eyes and said, "I know you here. You all move like cattle and smell almost as bad." He uncrossed his legs, and with knees bent, placed his feet flat on the floor. Without using his hands he rose to a standing position. We all took a step back as he turned toward us.

With his arms hanging straight and stiff at his sides, fists clinched tightly, he bowed, bending almost completely at the waist, then rose back up. "Shoes off, then come stand in from of me."

"Why do we have to take our shoes off?" I said. "We didn't get dressed...

"Stop! No talk. Shoes off, put by door, come here."

The next two hours were filled with much exertion and little talk. Mr. Chin pushed and prodded each of us, stretching our bodies, and causing us to fall over, never changing his expression and never losing his patience even when I purposely resisted his efforts. At the end of the session we were lined up, made to stand straight for five minutes, and then told to bow.

I refused to relax my arrogance, but I was also filled with the conflict of intrigue. I didn't trust Mr. Chin, didn't understand why he had come to Hope Haven, and didn't have any idea as to what he wanted to teach us. But as I watched him walk away I wanted to learn more.

The next Saturday I was first into the room. Two of the other boys came with me. The rest had decided to sleep in. I watched Mr. Chin as he sat on the floor, his body still and his eyes closed.

"Still like cattle, and don't smell any better," he said. His eyes opened and he rose to a standing position as he had done before. He was dressed in an all white pajama looking outfit tied at the waist with a black belt made of heavy cloth. He pointed to three rolls of white material each tied with a similar belt but white, not black like his.

"All same size, pick one and get dressed," he said.

"Get dressed where?" I said.

"You get dressed here, this all boy orphanage. You not so pretty, nothing to worry about. Now, giddy up."

We stopped and looked at him. He shook his head and said, "No giddy up, I mean hurry up." He almost smiled.

I stripped to my underwear as did the other two boys and pulled on the too large pants. I tied the string belt tightly and then donned the jacket. It hung open as I held the belt in my hand. Mr. Chin overlapped the jacket, right side first and then the left, showed me one time the proper way to tie the belt, and then helped the other two.

"This Gi," he said. "Always wear to class but wash first."

"How come you brought three uniforms? There was five of us here last time."

"I could tell you three come back. Other boys not interested."

I lined up with the other two boys. John was on my left and Tater was on my right. Tater was a nickname and no one questioned how the name originated or why. He had come from the Irish Channel in uptown New Orleans. I always figured the name had to do with Irish heritage. Tater didn't talk much. John on the other hand seldom shut up. But when Mr. Chin arrived John watched closely and said almost nothing.

Mr. Chin bowed and waited for us to bow in return. He moved toward us and stood directly in front of me. I didn't see his hand as it exploded against my chest, knocking me backward and causing me to fall on my butt. My face flushed red with embarrassment and I jumped up, charging him without thinking. Again I didn't see him move and was unaware of his presence until I looked up from the floor.

"Always control your anger. You get mad, you lose control."

I got back in line with John and Tater. Mr. Chin bowed but offered no apology.

"Today we start lessons in Tai Chi Chuan." The words were fluid and soft, almost poetic. "Learn Tai Chi and learn to be one with world. Learn supreme force."

"I thought maybe you was gonna teach us Karate, or somethin like that," I said.

"You too angry for Karate. You need balance in life first. No balance, then no life, you just exist."

I glared at Mr. Chin, my face red with anger because this man would presume to understand anything about me. He stared back at me but with calmness that disarmed my anger. The aggression he had displayed up to this point was gone, and though I didn't understand it at the time I later realized he was viewing me with respect. My initial impulse to run for the door left me and I concentrated on what he had said. Maybe I was too angry."

Mr. Chin showed up almost every Saturday. He was disciplined and stern, but also compassionate. He treated us with a level of respect equal to our dedication. I watched him closely and learned more about the man than I learned about Tai Chi.

Mr. Chin and I would sit Indian style on the floor after class and talk. He grew up outside Seoul, South Korea, the son of a Chinese father and Korean mother. Being Chinese in Korea caused his father to be an outcast, but he endured the social shunning because of his wife, eventually gaining acceptance. Chin's father worked the farm left to his wife, an only child, when her father died. They raised three sons. Mr. Chin was born first in 1940 making him 52 years old when he came to Hope Haven. Chin had the body of a man much younger but his eyes reflected a life older than his years.

At the completion of the first year I had exceeded the level of John and Tater but marginally so. Still, Mr. Chin treated us the same. He did not show favoritism for achieving levels of competence. He told us, "To learn is what matters, not how fast you learn. You not finished. Keep training."

I continued training. I was gifted with natural speed and quickness. Controlling my anger was not something I was gifted with, and it took much greater effort to manage. Most of the time I was successful, but occasionally the demons rose up inside me and the anger won. I have a few facial scars to show for my anger, but not nearly as many as I left on my combatants.

I placed my raised foot on the ground and walked back into the kitchen, angry Andi had not taken the food, and scared of what might have happened to her.

CHAPTER THREE

The restaurant was clean and all the others had left for the night. I walked out the back door into the alley. The night air of October was turning cooler with each passing day and was similar to wind blowing off a mountain lake, fresh and stimulating. I locked the rear door and turned to head up the alley toward Toulouse Street.

"Where's my food? You fergot didn't you? You're like all them others."

Andi's voice startled me. I had not seen her crouched down between the two large garbage cans by the back door. "I didn't forget noth…, I didn't forget anything. I had food for you last night, placed it here as we discussed, but it was still here this morning. If you don't show up I'm not going to keep wasting food."

"See, you *did* ferget. I *told* you I can't make it last night. You was too busy picking out them carrots and stuff at the French Market to listen to me. I knowed you'd be like the others. I'm a dumb sixteen year old girl, a Mississippi redneck is what you think."

"Hey! Shut up. If you told me, I didn't hear you. I'm sorry. Wait here and I'll go back inside and get some food," I said.

"Why wait here? Ain't I good enough to come into yer restaurant?" She glared at me exuding a spiteful attitude. But she did not stand up. "You afraid I might steal something?"

"Why don't you shut up, get up, and come inside. And knock off the act. If you want to feel sorry for yourself or be angry, save it for someone else." I turned the key in the lock, opened the restaurant door, and flipped the switch for the kitchen lights. Andi jumped up and followed so closely behind she bumped me when I stopped by the large kitchen sink to wash my hands before preparing her food.

"There's soap, wash up while I fix your food," I said while turning toward her. "I can make you some…" I stopped short and stared at her face. Her right cheek was swollen and bruised, and her upper lip was cut. "What happened to your face? And don't lie to me, who did this?" Anger welled up inside of me and my eyes watered.

"It ain't nothin. Things got a little out of control, that's all." She stared at my eyes and then said, "What, you gonna cry? Over this? That's a laugh. I'll give ya somethin to cry about. How about a stinky stepfather, piss sour breath and drooling on your neck, pinning ya to the bed with his hand over your mouth while he sticks his pecker up your butt. That'll make ya cry. But only for the first twenty times or so, then it all goes numb."

"Who did this to you? Was it your stepfather?"

"No, I ain't seen him or my momma since they threw me out on the street and drove back home. It don't matter none. Sides, I got a extra twenty dollars from the guy. He was supposed to look but got mad when I wouldn't let him touch me. He slapped me real hard but I didn't cry, just screamed like I was hurt. He got scared, gave me extra to shut up, then he ran off. Couldn't tell ya who he was. So there. Ya happy? Look, I'm real hungry. If ya ain't gonna give me no food then I'm leaving before the other kids get to the good trash cans."

I was angry but not shocked. I had lived on the streets in the French Quarter for six months. Hope Haven was shutting down the orphanage and moving all the boys to other locations. I had finished high school and was almost eighteen. I ran away. No one tried very hard to find me.

"Sit there for a minute. I think we have some seafood pasta left in the cooler. I'll warm it up for you."

"Ain't you got no French fries?"

"The fryers are shut off and cleaned. The pasta is better for you." I walked into the cooler and dished a heaping portion of the pasta onto a paper plate. I didn't use the microwave often but was glad to have it this night.

Andi scarfed down the pasta, chewing every other bite. "What cha got for dessert? I ain't had nothin but them silly donuts with the powdered sugar, and I ain't had them in a long time."

"Beignets, they're called beignets," I said. Andi did not look up from her almost empty plate. "I might have a dessert I can get for you. Tell ya what, spell dessert, get it right, and I'll fix it for you."

"What? I got to pass a fucking test to get dessert? You think I'm stupid cause I told you I flunked the eighth grade, huh?"

"You told me you failed twice. And no, I don't think you're stupid."

Andi glared at me, her face red with anger. She sat up straight, closed her eyes and said, "Dessert, d-e-s-s-e-r-t, dessert. Two esses, sweet and savory. What's next, I gotta perform for you, like the guy that slapped me?"

"Dessert is next, bread pudding with rum sauce. And don't ever think you have to perform for me, or think I want anything from you." I was angry at her implication and showed it.

"Why not? Ain't I good enough for you? No, you think I'm garbage from the street."

"I lived on the street so stop trying to play me. Besides, I have a lady friend."

"A lady friend?" she said. "Not a girl friend?"

"We have an arrangement," I said. "It's complicated."

"Oh, I get it. You got a fuck buddy," she said with a smirk. "Is she married?"

"No, she isn't married." I stared hard at her then realized I was letting her get to me. "Andi, why don't you try to clean up your mouth a little?"

"Ya know what, keep your fucking bread pudding. I'm leaving."

The sound of a night stick rapping on the back door startled both of us. I had heard the sound many times and opened the door wide. Tater came in, dressed in his police uniform, holding his night stick in case of trouble.

"You called the cops on me," Andi shouted.

"No, I didn't call anyone," I said. "Andi, this is Tater, we were friends in Hope Haven."

"I noticed the light on," Tater said. "Thought maybe you had a problem. This is late for you, Travis." Tater looked at Andi and said, "Who's your friend?"

"My name is Andi and I was just leavin."

"Sit down," I said.

"You want me to run her in?"

"No, Tater, I don't want you to run her in. I want you to watch out for her and keep her out of trouble." I stood with my arms folded across my chest, glaring at Andi, frustrated with her lack of appreciation.

"How old are you," Tater asked.

"I'm eighteen, turned eighteen last week," she lied.

"She's sixteen," I said.

"Travis, are you crazy? In here alone with a sixteen year old girl." Tater looked at her and said, "What happened to your face?"

Andi thought for a moment and then a wry smile appeared. "*He* done it. He slapped me around cause I wouldn't do what he wanted."

Tater looked at me then laughed out loud. "Girl, you must be stupid. Travis is the last guy who would do that to you. But heaven help the guy who did it if Travis finds him." Tater turned toward me. "Travis, you've got to be more careful. These street urchins will get you in trouble."

"I ain't no urchin," Andi yelled. She looked at me and asked, "What the fuck is an urchin?"

"Let me tell you a story about Travis."

"Stop," I said. "She isn't interested in anything about me."

"Yeah, I ain't good enough to hear nothin bout him. I get it Mr. Policeman. I don't need no bullshit stories."

Andi got up to leave. Tater stepped to his left and blocked her way. "Let her go," I said.

"You owe me my dessert. Leave it outside, I'll be back."

Andi purposely bumped into Tater as she made her way out the door. He followed her but stopped in the doorway and watched her walk up the alley to Toulouse Street. "That's another one gonna be trouble," Tater said. "I don't know how you find em, Travis. It looks to me like you got enough to do with the restaurant."

"I don't go looking for them but living in the French Quarter makes it hard to avoid them."

"You don't try to avoid them and that's part of the problem. I understand helping someone out but damn, Travis. You ain't their daddy. Give em a dollar, maybe a sandwich, but don't invite them into your life. You've been ripped off more than once."

"Thanks for the sermon, now turn your collar back around. You look better as a cop."

"Speaking of sermons, you still seeing Sister Dorothy?"

"Her name is Maggie and she was never a nun. They called her Sister Dorothy but she didn't take her final vows." My face was turning red and my chest tightened. Tater stared at me, refusing to let me off the hook. "She decided it wasn't for her, and yes we still see each other."

"How do you do it, sleeping with a nun."

My face flushed even more and my eyes burned like ammonia had splashed in them. "You're out of line, Tater. Again."

"I like getting you riled up. It's always so easy. But you're my best friend. I owe ya and don't want anything bad to happen to you."

"You don't owe me anything," I said. "What are you doing around here this late? It's not because the light was on."

"I made it," Tater said. "I made detective. Twenty five years old, one of the youngest detectives ever on the force. You pushed me through high school while we were at Hope Haven, and then pushed me to finish my degree in criminology at Loyola University. The city paid for it but you pushed me same as Brother Lee pushed you to finish college. Like I said, I owe you."

"Like *I* said, you don't owe me anything. Be a good detective and try to help out these street kids in the French Quarter." I was proud of Tater but wouldn't let him see it. "Let's get out of here," I said. "It's almost two o'clock. I'm supposed to be back here at seven to start the red beans and rice for lunch." Tater turned to leave but stopped when I said, "What division are you assigned to?

"Homicide," he answered.

"You know anything about the young girl they founding hanging in the warehouse on the river?"

"They ruled it a suicide, plain and simple. Happens a lot but most don't make the paper. Not sure why that one did. I'm homicide. I won't be involved. Why?"

"It bothers me. I read about it and can't get it out of my mind."

"Let it go, Travis. It's sad but it don't involve you. Keep it that way."

I placed Andi's dessert on the small table outside the back door of the restaurant and watched Tater walk to his patrol car parked at the end of the alley. It would be impossible to go to sleep after arguing with Andi so I walked to Burgundy Street and knocked on Maggie's door.

CHAPTER FOUR

Maggie had forgotten to set the alarm and I had overslept. It was eight o'clock. "Damn," I whispered as I rolled out of her bed and pulled on my pants and shirt. She turned, looked at me and then sat up quickly realizing I was scrambling to get dressed and leave.

"Travis, I'm sorry. I thought I set the clock alarm," she said. "You're upset with me."

I tied my shoes and turned toward her. The soft blue eyes stared at me, her dirty blond hair unkempt and hanging across her face. We had stayed up until four in the morning, talking about whatever came to mind. Sleep overtook us as we lay together, holding each other, and sex the furthest thing from our minds. She sat up, her breasts lost in the extra large tee shirt she slept in.

"It takes four hours to cook the red beans. At this rate they won't be ready until one o'clock, too late for the lunch crowd. I'm upset with me, never with you." I stood, buttoned my shirt and then leaned over and kissed Maggie on the cheek. "Sorry but I have to run, literally. Brother Lee will be angry with me and rightfully so."

I ran up Burgundy, over Toulouse and down the alley to the back of the restaurant and stopped abruptly. Onions, celery, and garlic all sautéed together and mixed with red beans created an aroma so strong it wafted through the door and filled the alley. I shook my head, embarrassed with my failure. It was time to face Brother Lee so I opened the door but stopped before entering, and looked at the table. The dessert I had left for Andi was gone. Brother Lee was stirring the large pot of beans, not stopping to look up at me.

"You late, boy. I suppose you got a good escuse, but sex ain't no good escuse."

"There are no good excuses, isn't that what you always told me. Maybe a good *reason* for something but never a *good* excuse. Excuses are for people who don't plan, don't take responsibility, isn't that what you taught me?"

"Yep. So, you got a good reason?"

"No, I don't. I'm irresponsible. At least this morning." I nudged Brother Lee out of the way and took the large spoon from him, continuing to stir the beans. "Thanks for starting the pot of beans," I said, too embarrassed to look at him.

"Save your self pity for somthin more important." He placed his hand on my shoulder assuring me all was good and stepped to the sink to fix the large pot of rice.

"Chef T, can I ax you somthin?"

I turned, startled by the familiar voice. "Scatback, what are you doing here this early? There won't be any dishes to wash until at least eleven, maybe later. And you did a great job cleaning up last night." I placed the large spoon on the top of the stove away from the beans.

Scatback had come from the projects. He was eighteen, light skinned but considered black. His mother was Latino from Guatemala and had come to America as an illegal many years ago. She had settled in the Desire Street housing projects and lived with several different men until she met Scatback's father, a black man trying to make the Saint's football team. He had made the practice squad and had hopes of moving up onto the playing roster but was killed when randomly shot while shielding Scatback's mother in a drive by, drug revenge killing. Scatback was born seven months later. The project life was not kind to Scatback but he was trying to break out and make a better life for him and his mother.

"I been here since seven waitin for ya. Brother Lee said I had to ax Chef Tee if I wants somthin. He said you was in charge of this kitchen."

I had no idea what Scatback might want. "What is it? What can I do for you?" I said.

"I wants to be your sooze chef. I promise I'll work real hard and I'll still do the dishes and you don't has to pay me no more monies. I just wants to learn." He hung his head, not looking at me as I stared at him.

"So, you want to be Chef Charlie then? Do you understand how much dedication it takes, how hard you'll have to work?"

"Yeah, I do. I'm willin to do it, too. But I need a chance."

"Why do you want to do this?"

"I seen the way you do things, the way you chop them veg-a-tables so fast, and how people smile when they eat the food you fix. And I see how proud Brother Lee is of you, how good you done."

"Hey boy," Brother Lee snapped. "You best leave me outta this. I'll tell him when I'm proud of him. He's gettin good but ain't good enough, least not yet."

"But another thing, I wants to be Chef Scatback. I like my name. It's different. I like it."

"Why Scatback? Where'd you get your nickname?" I asked.

"I used to sneak around them projects, watch all those bad guys dealing dope and fightin, being stupid. Even seen a guy what got shot dead. They'd catch me and yell at me sayin 'you betta scat back home, boy.' But I always come around again. Pretty soon they took to yellin, 'Scatback' and the name stuck."

"Tell you what, Scatback, we can give it a try but a couple of things have to change. Cooking is a big responsibility..."

"Yeah, that's right," Brother Lee said. "So why was you late this morning?"

"Ok, I get it. No lectures.

"I want you to see Maggie. She'll help you with school, maybe getting your GED. You can..."

"Ms. Maggie don't like me none. I can tell. She thinks I'm some project nigger," Scatback shot at me.

"Let's have an understanding right now. Ms. Maggie would help the lowest of the low if they want the help. She wouldn't turn anyone away. That's why she works at the house next to the old convent on Ursuline Street. She helps all the people, young and old, no matter what color, and does a damn good job of it."

Scatback looked at the floor. "Now I spose you mad with me," he said.

"No, I'm not mad. You're wrong and that's all there is to it. But one more thing, two words you never say in my kitchen, don't ever say nigger again, and don't ever say God Damn. The first word is disrespectful, derogatory and there isn't anyway to make that word right no matter what color you are." Scatback stared at the floor, refusing to raise his head. "Maybe I'm not as religious as I should be and definitely shouldn't be preaching, and what you do away from here is your business, but don't ever take God's name in vain, not in this kitchen."

Scatback looked up. "So what I got to do?" he asked.

"You've got to do your best all the time. That's what you have to do. I don't want to always be looking over your shoulder. Learn fast and work hard. The rest will come."

"You is too damn hard for such a young age," Brother Lee said. "Why don't you ease up a bit on the boy? And you best ease up a bit on yo-self too."

I didn't turn away from Scatback, but I listened to what Brother Lee said. And as is usually the case, he was right. I put my arm around Scatback and turned toward Brother Lee. "Scatback's going to be a great chef. You know why? He wants to make good food and see people smile. And, for you to be proud of him, that's why."

A loud knock on the door startled all of us. It was followed by a high pitched woman's voice, the voice of someone who could not have knocked so loud.

"You hurry up. Agnes got fish. Good fish. Speckled trout, big this time. You like."

A short but hardened Vietnamese woman entered the kitchen. Agnes Vu was less than five feet tall but stood straight, shoulders pulled back. Her hair was still black but a hint of gray was starting to show. She was close to sixty but had never said her true age. She had come to Louisiana in 1974 from Vietnam, part of the throngs of people the U.S. brought to America following the fall of the

South Vietnamese government. Her husband had been a fisherman but was killed fighting the communists. Her three children were lost, presumed killed but she wasn't sure, and seldom talked about them. She settled in south Plaquemines parish with other Vietnamese who had formed their own fishing community. Fishing was all she knew.

"Agnes, you got that license I told you bout?" Brother Lee said. "I told you before I can't be buyin fish from you without the license."

"That why you hurry. I go quick. No trouble."

"Agnes, I've told you before many times, if the Louisiana wildlife and fishery people come around here and inspect the kitchen and see the fish they'll make us produce the paperwork. The paperwork showing who we bought it from and their commercial fishing license number," I said.

"No license, so cheap price." Agnes turned toward the door and yelled, "Peter, bring fish."

Peter, Agnes's live in partner, filled up the doorway holding a large gray tub filled with speckled trout packed in ice. His head cleared the top of the door opening by a couple of inches and his shoulders reached from side to side almost touching the frame. His skin was tanned and blotched from years in the sun and his red hair had golden colored streaks, also from extended exposure to the sun. Peter was big, strong, and weathered, looking at least seventy years old, maybe more. He seldom spoke. Agnes did all the talking and negotiating of price. But when he did say a few words the Cajun accent was evident especially when the few words spoken were intermixed with French.

Agnes and Peter would show up at random, usually after every few months or so. It was always the same. Brother Lee would fuss at her about getting a commercial fishing license and tell her he couldn't buy her fish. She would persist until Brother Lee broke down and bought all she had, paying cash, no receipt, taking a big chance of getting arrested if the state fish and game people showed up. Several of the big name chefs had been arrested for buying seafood from unlicensed fishermen. Brother Lee and I had been lucky but I suspect it was because LeRoy Bertrand, the agent assigned to the French Quarter restaurants had worked with my Uncle Tony and purposely left us alone.

Peter looked at Agnes and spoke to her in French. "Hurry up," he said. "We have crabe and crevette grise to sell."

Brother Lee did not speak French but understood the words for crabs and shrimp. "How much crabs and shrimp you got?" he asked Agnes.

"Plenty, plenty," she said. "Good size, good price. You come see."

Peter put the tub of fish on the counter next to the large sink and walked outside to their truck. Brother Lee and I followed as Agnes scurried ahead, jumping up into the bed of the truck. She threw the tarpaulin back, uncovering the baskets of crabs and shrimp. The crabs sprang to life, their pinchers extended like swords ready to defend against the giant enemies.

"Agnes, I swear you gonna get me in trouble yet," Brother Lee said. "Travis, you and Chef Scatback goin to be makin shrimp Creole and seafood gumbo."

I shook my head and walked back into the kitchen. Scatback was sweeping the already clean floor, staying busy, hoping for a chance to do more than wash dishes.

Peter carried the basket of crabs inside, placed them on the floor next to the cooler and went back to his truck for the shrimp. I watched him walk away and wondered why he was always so stoic, why Agnes did all the talking. Peter returned with the shrimp and placed them on the floor next to the crabs.

"Ok sous chef," I said. "You have pounds of shrimp to peel so better get busy." I turned and looked at Peter. "How long have you lived in south Plaquemines?" I asked as Peter was moving toward the door. He stopped and paused before turning around.

"Long time," he answered. Agnes walked up behind him appearing child-like standing next to Peter.

"Peter, I'm curious. Maybe you knew my Uncle Tony. Tony Guillory, he was a wildlife and fisheries agent, worked Plaquemines parish for years before his accident."

"Tony good man," Agnes said, moving in front of Peter. "Tony help me and Peter all the time. Peter like Tony. Peter make café au lait for Tony all the time."

"Peter, is this true? You used to drink coffee with my Uncle Tony?"

Again Peter did not answer. "I tell you," Agnes said. "All the time. They good friends. Tony die, very sad for Peter. Sad for me too."

I reached into my chef pants pocket and pulled out a twenty dollar bill. "Agnes, Brother Lee bought all your crabs and shrimp so you have nothing else to sell. Here, take this," I said, handing her the twenty. "Leave your truck, Scatback and I will watch it, walk over to Café DuMonde and get some beignets, some café au lait and enjoy the morning. October is one of the best months to be in the French Quarter. Spend some time walking around Jackson Square, maybe go in St. Louis Cathedral, then come back here for an early lunch, red beans and rice. I have a couple of soft shell crabs in the cooler, Scatback will fry them up for you."

"I cain't fry up no soft shell crabs," Scatback shouted. "I don't know how."

"You will by the time they get back. Whata ya say Peter?" I watched Peter, his eyes wide, staring at Agnes. A big man but confused, nervous, struggling for an answer but nothing came. Agnes grabbed his hand and he softened with her touch.

"I think be ok," Agnes said. "We come back for lunch." She took Peter by the hand and walked out the kitchen into the alley.

"What you up to boy? I paid em good for the seafood, why you gave em the twenty dollars?" Brother Lee said.

"I'm not sure. I made many trips with my Uncle Tony into the marsh but I never met Peter or Agnes. She says they were good friends. I wonder why I never heard about them."

"Maybe cause you was too damn young. You was twelve when Tony died. He probly never got a chance to bring you to meet em."

"Maybe so, but if Peter knew Uncle Tony then I'd like to talk to him."

"Don't be chasin no ghosts, Travis. You cain't catch em."

"Yeah, what you know about chasing ghosts old man?" I said, trying to make light of Brother Lee's serious nature.

"I told ya before, I never knowed my daddy. It bothered me for years, but I had to let it go. Ya see, the truth don't always set you free, but it's still the truth."

I had no idea what Brother Lee was referring to but the anguish in his eyes caused me to feel stupid and insensitive. I walked to him and put my arm around his shoulder. His face didn't change but he had a grin in his eyes. "Boy, get away from me," he said as he pushed at me. "You got work to do, specially since you gonna be given away free lunches and all. You know how much soft shell crabs cost us? I taught you plenty but sometimes I think you didn't learn so much."

"Good, you're back to normal, a mean, cantankerous old cuss."

Scatback had not moved while watching the scene with Brother Lee and me play out. He reached down into the basket of shrimp and yelled as the spiny heads pierced his hand. "Damn, dem things got fangs," he yelled.

I picked up the basket, poured the shrimp into the left side sink and threw some ice on top of them. Scatback rinsed his hand under the cool running water of the faucet. He didn't look at me.

"Here," I said, "this long, plastic orange tool is a shrimp peeler. Pop the heads off like this," I said as I showed him the technique to peeling shrimp. "After you have all the heads off, then run the skinny end of the peeler up the back of the shrimp. The shell will break open and the large black vein will come out all at once. It works most of the time but takes practice. You'll be real good at it by the time those thirty pounds of shrimp are peeled."

"Chef Tee learned the hard way, too," Brother Lee said. "But he was angry and hard headed. It took him longer."

CHAPTER FIVE

December, 1945
Cut Off, Louisiana

Pierre sat at the table in the small kitchen finishing his bowl of shrimp stew. Minos had gotten up and walked into his bedroom, but returned almost immediately and handed a present to Pierre. It was wrapped in old newspaper and was about the size of a shoe box. Pierre took the present and placed it on his lap, stared at it for a few seconds and then looked up at Minos. He waited, not opening the present, and then spoke in French.

"No, not in French. Use English, like I been teachin you."

"My English not so good yet. I like French. Ma mère était le français."

"I know you momma was French," Minos said. "You done told me too many times. But you need English, cher, cause you gonna finish school. I spoke to Father at the church. He gonna let you go to the Catholic school. I told him you my cousin's boy, my cousin what died. It's a lie and I feel bad about it but you too smart not to be in school."

"I like to fish with you."

"You still gonna fish with me but school first. Now open them present. It's Christmas. Papa Noelle brung it."

"Papa Noelle read the New Orleans newspaper?" Pierre said. He unwrapped the box, dropping the newsprint on the floor, and placed it on the kitchen table, hesitating before opening it. He lifted the top off the box and looked inside, reached into the box and removed a new filet knife secure in a shiny, leather sheath. Pierre pulled the knife from the sheath and placed the blade flat on his forearm. He gently scraped the blade across the skin removing the hair with one smooth motion. "Good knife, sharp," he said without looking up at Minos.

"Best filet knife there is," Minos said.

"Papa Noelle not bring you a present," Pierre said hanging his head, sadness in his voice.

"Cher, he done brung me you. Best gift I ever got. School come Monday. No sass about it either."

"I like school but long time since I go. Not sure I can..."

"The Catholic school gonna teach ya real good. You almost sixteen so now be best time to go. Those big wars are over. I been worried about you maybe havin to go off and fight but not now, and that's good, real good."

Pierre's eyes went vacant as his mind drifted and he thought back to his mother and where he had come from. "What do I tell them at school? They gonna ask who I am, where I'm from when I don't speak no good English."

"Most of em is Cajun and don't talk so good anyway. You gonna fit in. You see, it gonna be good," Minos said as he put his arm around Pierre.

CHAPTER SIX

October, 2004
New Orleans, Louisiana

Peter and Agnes were back in the restaurant at twelve-fifteen. It was a busy time and hectic with the daily lunch crowd clamoring for tables and service. I had saved a table for Peter and Agnes thinking they would be back around eleven. Reserving the table had cost us at least one group for lunch, maybe two. "No good deed goes unpunished," Brother Lee constantly reminded me. Their free lunch was getting expensive.

Scatback watched them come in, ran out of the kitchen and waved for them to sit at the table he was standing next to. He pulled a chair out for Agnes. Peter waited as if thinking Scatback would also pull his chair out. Instead, Scatback turned and hustled back into the kitchen. "Now, you want me to fry those crabs now?"

"Not yet. They fry up in a couple of minutes and I want them hot and fresh. Let the waiter get them drinks and put some hot bread on the table." I watched him standing by the fryers. He shifted his weight back and forth from foot to foot, anxious, looking like a child needing to use the restroom. His excitement and exuberance was positive and refreshing.

I turned out three tables of food by the time the waiter placed the order for Peter and Agnes. I read the ticket and shook my head. One plate of red beans and rice to share and two glasses of water. This wasn't what I had in mind, but I also understood. They were both of meager means and frugal to a fault.

"Chris," I yelled out to their waiter. He turned and walked back toward the kitchen. "Find the two coldest Barq's root beers in the cooler and bring them to that table with two tall glasses of ice," I said, pointing toward Peter. "Tell them it's on me and no arguing. I'll fix their lunch and Scatback and I will bring it out.

"Scatback, do it like I showed you earlier, dredge the crabs in the flour, then the egg wash, then dredge them in the seasoned corn-meal and drop them in the fryer. When they float to the top they're done but don't shake the basket. Hang it and let the oil drip back into the fryer, because if you shake it the legs of the crabs will break off. You understand?"

"I gots it. Watch me work boss man."

I shook my head thinking this might be a long process. "I'm not *boss man*. Call me Chef, or Chef T.," I said. "And he's Brother Lee," I added, motioning with my head toward Brother Lee. "You got that?"

Scatback didn't answer but the big grin on his face showed he understood. He moved deftly and efficiently, preparing the soft shell crabs as I had instructed and dropped them in the fryers. I fixed two plates of red beans and rice making sure to get several small pieces of pickled pork onto the plates. Scatback watched the crabs float to the top of the grease, waited a half minute and then lifted the basket and placed it gently on the hooks, the hot grease dripping into the pool of oil.

I placed the two plates of beans on the table, one in front of Agnes and the other in front of Peter. Scatback set two smaller plates, each with a fried soft shell crab, in the center of the table and walked back to the kitchen.

"Agnes, Peter, I hope you enjoy this. One day I'd like to talk about my Uncle Tony, but not today. Thanks for being his friends." I turned, and said to Chris, "Tarter and cocktail sauce for this table, please." Chris nodded and I made my way back to the kitchen.

"Man! That's the first thing I ever cooked."

"You did real good. You'll be cooking more than you ever thought possible and soon," I said. "But don't forget our deal. You still have dishes to take care of and the kitchen to keep clean."

"I already on it boss…I mean Chef. You won't be sorry, I promise."

Most people simply need a chance and I was sure I had made the right decision with Scatback. I watched as he worked hard keeping the kitchen clean and the dishes washed. I sent two Styrofoam containers, each with a piece of Mississippi mud pie, to Agnes and Peter. They had eaten more for lunch than usual and wouldn't be able to eat dessert, too. Agnes was shaking a fist full of money at Chris but he refused to let them pay. She looked at me as I stood in the doorway of the kitchen and waved at them. Agnes stuffed her money back into her front jeans pocket, grabbed Peter's hand, waved back at me and walked out of the restaurant.

CHAPTER SEVEN

"You have too much on your mind," Maggie said. "You're twenty six but you act and speak like you're much older." Managing a half smile I looked at her face. She was almost thirty six years old but I often thought of myself as older than she. "I think it was living at the orphanage. I went in when I was twelve and had a sense of having to grow up as soon as I got there. I lost my childhood. But you were always the bright spot. I had a crush on you right away, twelve years old and having a crush on a nun." I looked down at the floor trying to hide the redness in my face. "I was confused and guilty all at the same time. It made me get older too fast. I had lost my parents, Uncle Tony, and wound up being on my own. Guess it's why I needed to grow up faster than most."

"I remember when Father Billy brought you to us. You were a handsome boy but troubled, and in pain. I never realized you had a crush on me. Perhaps if I had dressed in the conventional habit and not relied on the headscarf alone it might have been easier on you. But watching over so many boys and trying to play sports and interact with them, the full habit was not practical. As it was, the long skirt was difficult. Jeans were out of the question so I made do."

"I was very upset when you left."

"It was necessary for me to leave. I like to think I was in the right place but at the wrong time. The orphanage closed before I had a chance to go back. So I ended up here in the French Quarter working with the nuns, helping the young girls and women referred to us by the archdiocese. Most of them need some time away from whatever it is in their lives threatening them. Travis, you had it hard, much harder than most, but some of these women have stories that make those daytime soap operas look like the Mickey Mouse Club."

"Do you regret leaving the order, not becoming a nun?" I asked.

Maggie looked at me as if questioning what I really was trying to ask. "We've been over this before," she said. "I left because I could tell it wasn't for me. The structure was too demanding…I didn't feel worthy enough to serve God as a nun."

"That's not what I asked you. You've told me why, how you didn't fit in and that you realized you weren't able to devote yourself like the other nuns." I paused to look at Maggie, to try to understand what she was thinking. "Do you regret leaving?"

"No, I don't regret leaving. I've done some good work helping the battered and abused women and children. My heart breaks when they enter the shelter. But the irony is they heal my heart. They bring me comfort. Their gratitude is overwhelming. One little girl, her name is Mimi, seven years old, latched onto me and wouldn't let go. All I did was hug her, hold her hand and give her a cookie. I don't think she had experienced true care and kindness. She's been at the shelter for three weeks. Tomorrow morning she'll be waiting at the front door for me. She won't eat or do anything until I get there. So no, I don't regret leaving the order and not becoming a nun. I'm good with God and I trust he has me right where he wants me to be."

"I need some help and…"

"What? Since when do you need help with anything?"

"I did alright taking care of myself, but I had lots of help even if I didn't realize it at the time. Uncle Tony, Father Billy, Brother Lee, and you, everyone helped. I was stubborn enough to make it look like I did things on my own. This is different. There's a homeless girl named Andi who needs to get off the streets. I'm worried. If she doesn't get help soon she'll wind up like most of the French Quarter street kids, maybe stripping in one of the bars on Bourbon Street before she's eighteen."

"I can't go looking for her," Maggie said. "We have rules at the shelter prohibiting us from seeking out people to help. We'd have hundreds in no time. Our budget can't handle it."

"So what do I do?"

"Find her and tell her to come to the shelter and ask for me. I can take someone in if they ask, but I can't go looking. It's the best I can do. No promises either. She might not want help."

"One other thing, I need to find a place where Scatback can get into school. He wants to be a chef but there's more to the restaurant business than being a good cook. You can find a place for him, I know you can."

"You certainly have a lot of requests tonight. So, what's in it for me?" Maggie said her face more serious than usual.

"What do you mean what's in it for you?"

Her eyes gave her away and her feigning seriousness melted into her playful nature. "Are you spending the night?"

"Well I'm not sure. I was thinking it might be nice but…"

"Travis, don't make a lady beg. It's not gentlemanly."

"Ok, I'll stay tonight. I'd like that."

"Good cause I'm starving and have lots of work to do. You can whip me up one of those culinary feasts of yours. You can sleep on the couch. I'll be working half the night."

I was angry, angry for turning red and angry for assuming too much. I watched her turn and walk into the room she had converted to a home office. She was modestly attractive but had a derriere as attractive as any Hollywood starlet, Angelina Jolie included. My anger waned, replaced by lust.

We'd had a mutual understanding for over a year. Maggie had told me she was too old for me and said she was dedicated to her work of helping others. A serious relationship between us would never work. As might be expected, that which you can't have draws at you like a riptide trying to take you out to sea. And the more you fight it the more you lose. I did my best not to think about Maggie and instead checked her pantry for ingredients to cook her supper.

The pantry was sparse but I found enough to fix a pot of my Cajun fried rice which would go nicely with the pork chops she had in her freezer. It took an hour to prepare the meal and I was pleased with the result. Maggie and I sat at her small table and ate the rice, pork chops, and canned green beans. Canned vegetables were never found in Brother Lee's restaurant. But sometimes easy is better than noble. And I like easy, which is why I love New Orleans.

I had cleaned up the kitchen while Maggie had retreated to her small study, more a closet with a table top desk barely large enough for a laptop computer. I slipped out the front door and stepped onto Burgundy Street, inhaled deeply and a rush of cool October night air expanded my chest to almost bursting.

CHAPTER EIGHT

I had walked the streets of the French Quarter hundreds of times, first when I was homeless after running away from Hope Haven. And eight years later I still walk them. I started up Burgundy and turned left on Orleans Street. The Mississippi River was about seven blocks away but I had nothing to do and all night to do it. I walked briskly until I got to Royal then zigzagged a half block and entered Pirate Alley. I stopped for a minute, waited, but nothing came.

It was Pirate Alley where Brother Lee first found me. I was alone, the January night air was cold and I shivered, my back pressed hard against the exterior wall of St. Louis Cathedral. I had been living on the street for six months, begging handouts, panhandling tourists, and gravitating toward the other homeless kids who congregated mostly around the French Market. Some of the food vendors were good for tossing an orange or apple when closing up for the day.

The night Brother Lee found me was my lowest point. I'd come to believe all I had was all I would ever get. Self pity is loathsome and destructive. I should have known better, I was taught better, but I let it eat at me like ants on a carcass, consuming until there would soon be nothing left.

Pirate Alley was a good place to find a tourist who might take pity on a homeless beggar, or a literary scholar searching for the soul of Faulkner or Tennessee Williams. The night air was almost freezing but calm. It was one in the morning and I remember I heard voices, distant yet clear enough to sound close, but nothing was understandable. It was all gibberish as they talked over one another.

47

I strained to understand what was being said. I looked both ways but saw nothing, and yet the voices continued talking. I closed my eyes and leaned my head back against the cold wall. I didn't hear his footsteps but felt his presence.

"What you doin here boy?"

I opened my eyes but didn't move. The black man stared down on me waiting for an answer. "Ain't doin nothing. Ain't botherin no one neither. Trying to get warm is all," I said, drooping my head to avoid his glare.

"I seen you round the quarter before. How long you been on the streets?"

"I don't need no lectures, and I don't want no trouble."

"How long boy?" he said.

"Don't know, six months or so, maybe more." I looked up at him, "I left Hope Haven in July cause they was talkin bout closing it down. So I left."

"Hope Haven? So, you a local boy?"

"Yeah, but so what? I was in Hope Haven cause I ain't got no one else. That's what orphanages are for. Don't you know that?" I said, irritated with his badgering.

"What's your name boy?"

"Travis, Travis Guillory."

"Get up. You can come with me. I got a kitchen needs cleanin. Got lots of leftovers too. How long since you ate?"

"Couple days. Long time since anything good. Why you doin this man? What you want? Look, I ain't like them other boys."

"What other boys?" he asked.

"Them other homeless ones. They let the gay guys blow em for five dollars and a hot meal. I ain't like them."

"Boy, you must be crazy you think I want that. Now, get up."

He didn't offer his hand to help me up so I struggled to my feet, my body stiff from the cold, my legs weak from not eating. "People call me Brother Lee. You can do the same. My restaurant's back this way."

Brother Lee did not speak as we walked the six blocks back to his restaurant. We entered the kitchen through the back door to the alley. The fluorescent lights blinked on instantly as he flicked the switch and the brightness stunned me, hurting my eyes and causing me to turn my head toward the floor, my body slouching as I put my arm across my face. When I looked up Brother Lee was staring at me, shaking his head. He crossed his arms across his big chest and loomed larger over me than before.

"Stand up boy. Jesus, have you had a bath in the last year? How the hell you stand you-self. You too dirty to clean this kitchen."

I stood up straight, fighting the stiffness of the cold and said, "I don't need no shit from you. I can go back where you found me. All I wanted was somethin to eat. And I don't want to eat no shit from you."

"Boy, shut the fuck up. You's one sorry escuse for a white boy, I tell ya that *right* now."

"I'm gonna go. The street ain't as cold as you, old man."

"Awe, you feelin sorry for ya-self." Brother Lee watched me for a minute. "Just as I thought. You ain't goin nowhere. You too hungry to leave. It's amazin what a man will put up with when he ain't ate in a while."

"What you want from me, man? You ain't got to be so mean," I said. "Just let me go. I don't want to bother you none."

"Look boy, I'm tryin to help you but you got to help ya-self first. Stand right there a minute." Brother Lee left the room and I thought about running but I was tired, hungry beyond description, and it was too damned cold outside. "Here, these are clean. You can put em on but first, you got to clean up. Them two big sinks over there, you can clean up in them."

"What you gonna do? Stand there and watch me?"

"No, I ain't interested in watchin you. I'm leavin. It's almost two o'clock. I gots to be back here at seven. But here's what you gonna do. Throw them nasty clothes away in the trash can outside. Clean ya-self real good in the sinks. Put on the check pants, the ones that's black and white, then the shirt. After that ya needs to clean all the kitchen and mop this floor."

"I thought I was gonna get somethin to eat."

"Lots of food in the cooler right there, already cooked, but got to warm it up."

"You trust me old man? You don't even know me," I said, watching him walk toward the door.

"I told you, call me Brother Lee. I ain't no old man, I'm fifty two. And no I don't trust you, but you said you ran away from Hope Haven. I'm bettin they taught ya somethin bout doin good. Guess I'm gonna find out soon enough."

Brother Lee walked out and shut the door. He didn't lock it. I could take some food and leave without doing anything. But his words haunted me. Hope Haven had taught me well and yet I had abandoned my teachings like I had run away from my home. I sat on the floor and tried to understand what had happened to me. The self-pity was gone, replaced by self-doubt. It was a familiar feeling and it ate at me like a guilty conscience. Uncle Tony, Father Billy, Sister Marie, and Mr. Chin had all come into my life at moments like this. Now Brother Lee.

With my elbows on my knees and my head in my hands I thought about praying. I was never good at prayer. I was taught to pray, and I prayed often because I was told to. The priests and nuns at Hope Haven made sure we all prayed. But I prayed because it was easier to go through the motions than resist and listen to a lecture from the nuns. My self doubt had always made me question if my prayers were good enough, question if I was good enough for this benevolent, all knowing, all loving God. I had finally admitted to myself I wasn't good enough for God, and the prayers stopped. No sense in being a hypocrite I had told myself.

Sitting on the cold terrazzo floor of Brother Lee's restaurant, still holding my head in my hands, I asked God to help me. I made no sign of the cross, gave no self diatribe with confession, offered no promises of repentance, nothing more than a simple please. I sat up straight.

I stripped off all my clothes except for the dirty and tattered boxer shorts and threw them in a pile by the door. Opening the cooler door a blast of cold air escaped and covered my bare skin. I shivered like I had jumped into a mountain lake. I grabbed the closest pan and slammed the door shut.

For two hours I cleaned the kitchen and ate cold jambalaya out of the large pan. Every counter top and surface area was spotless and the pan of jambalaya was empty. My stomach stuck out like a women in the early stages of pregnancy. The double kitchen sink was large, but not large enough to bathe in. But I managed. Starting with my hair I used kitchen detergent and shampooed it clean then proceeded to sponge bathe my body while standing up. It took three kitchen towels to dry off. I was exhilarated after the first bath I had had in almost six months. The chef pants and shirt were too big but the fresh clothes next to my clean skin reminded me of being wrapped in a towel by my mother after a playful bath. I had thrown the boxer shorts in the pile of ragged, discarded clothes. Using a pair of large kitchen tongs I carefully placed the smelling heap into the garbage can by the back door of the restaurant.

The dining area of Brother Lee's restaurant was sparse and basic, unlike many of the fancier places in the French Quarter. I counted a dozen tables with four chairs each, and one short bench against a wall by the front door. Using a rolled up kitchen towel for a pillow I lay down, arms and legs hanging over the too small bench and fell asleep almost instantly.

CHAPTER NINE

M y cell phone vibrated and I pulled it from my pocket. I read the text message from Maggie. *Where are you? I was teasing. Not too busy. Please come back* .I walked out of Pirate Alley and into Jackson Square texting as I walked. *Maybe later. I'll text you.* The river was straight ahead, up the levee and over the street car tracks.

Walking to the river had become somewhat of a ritual with me. I did it often, perhaps because the river is always moving, always changing, much like my life. But, paradoxically, the fast moving river would cause me to slow down, think and resolve.

Near the bottom of the levee, four or five feet above the river's edge and extending into the water at least five feet more was a deposit of large, gray, granite rocks. The Army corps of engineers had placed them here years ago to keep the constant flow of water from washing away their levee. I sat on one of the largest boulders less than two feet from the water, and listened to the river gently lap against the stones, belying the swiftness of the current farther out. Old Algiers was across the river and I stared. Shards of lights, cast from the street lanterns, danced across the wind-blown ripples of the river, changing direction constantly, and I recalled once reading the Mississippi river is so wide and deep over a million gallons of water per minute flow past the foot of Canal Street. More than sixty million gallons of water per hour made me feel insignificant.

At night the area close to the edge of the river was dark because none of the street lights were aimed at the water's edge. They were all

52

focused on the top of the levee to give the tourists a secure feeling. For several years I had come to the rocks and performed the Tai Chi exercises I had learned from Mr. Chin. Seldom using the same rock twice I moved up or down river, stopping and perching on a precariously unsettled rock until a feeling of purchase was accomplished. Too many times the rock had momentarily prevailed, but I always found my balance and completed my task. And though the river never slowed down, in my mind's eye I was able to see the swiftness diminished to a crawl, the movement lumbering as if burdened.

An hour later I climbed up the levee and walked back to my small apartment on Governor Nicholls Street. I sent Maggie a text as I walked explaining I would contact her soon. The Tai Chi had relaxed me, given me calm, and I was ready for sleep. I didn't notice Andi following me home.

CHAPTER TEN

The alarm went off at six o'clock, a chirping bird noise but not sounding like any bird I had ever heard. I had already been awake for fifteen minutes, staring at the ceiling fan as it turned, the circular movement hypnotic. The alarm broke my stare and I sat up on the side of the bed.

The apartment I rented was an attached cottage to a much larger French Quarter house. It had been a slave's quarters years before the civil war and common in New Orleans. Originally it was a single room with a dirt floor. Two or three slave families would live together in the single room. Ventilation of the space was poor and summers were as brutally hot as the winters were cold. A small wood burning stove was all they had for cooking. Many of the houses had similar slave quarters. Most had been renovated to be an extension of the main house but some, like mine, were rented either for extra income or because the owner did not need the extra space.

Entry to my apartment was through a small iron gate that fronted Governor Nicholls Street. Through the gate a path runs along the courtyard which is hidden from the street by a seven foot high concrete wall. Years ago the apartment had been redesigned to include a living room and kitchenette with a separate room for the toilet and shower. A second story loft had been added for the bed room with an iron, spiral staircase for access. I had become spoiled with the kitchen at Brother Lee's restaurant and seldom used the small kitchenette in my apartment. But on a day off with lots of time and ambition I can manage to cook a pot of chicken

54

gumbo which pleases my landlords and keeps me in good graces with them.

The landlords are Jerry and Terry, a male gay couple who had been together many years and managed to avoid the AIDS scare of the early eighties. Those are not their real names but they like the rhyme and Terry giggles when someone calls out their names together. Jerry is less amused because he is the more dominant male in the partnership.

The walk to Brother Lee's restaurant is usually accomplished in less than fifteen minutes. I'm guilty, like most people, of walking and being oblivious to all going on around me. Today was no different as I closed the gate, locked it and turned up the street. Terry called out my name before I had taken two steps.

"Yoo hoo, Chef Tee EEE," he called out, turning the one letter abbreviation for my name into two syllables. "Wait, wait, way-*aaate*."

Inhaling deeply, pausing a moment and then gently exhaling, I turned around to face him. Terry was holding a cup of coffee and was quite a sight wearing a pink robe and blue bathroom slippers with fluffy balls covering the toes.

"Yes, the blue clashes with the pink but they're Jerry's slippers and I like wearing them. It drives him crazy and he is soooo cute when he's mad."

"You look stunning as always Terry," I said.

"Oooh, you brute, you. Always trying to get on my good side."

"What, Terry? I've got to get to work."

"Weeeell, I wanted to tell you my niece is coming to visit me for a while," he said. "And...I thought you should know."

"That's it? Ok, I'll keep an eye out for her and be nice when I see her."

"She's real cute and almost your age. I thought maybe you'd show her around on your time off, pleeeese."

"Terry, I hate to make promises. And I don't have much time off, and I spend it with Maggie when I can." He pouted like a little girl. "But I'll try," I said. "Look, I've got to get going. When is she coming?"

"You are such a dear. I'm sure you'll take good care of her. She comes this morning so scoot and get on with yourself. Tata."

A simple distraction and I lost my focus, contemplating the baby sitting chore Terry had coerced me into agreeing to be part of. I shook my head. Seldom do favors work out for the good and I had no reason to expect this one to be any different. The walk to the restaurant became slower this morning as I thought of how I would handle Terry's niece.

I concentrated on the buildings and homes I routinely ignored hoping to put Terry's request out of my mind. The architecture in the French Quarter is captivating when one takes the time to concentrate and study it. Almost daily for more than three years I had passed the house several doors down from my apartment and never noticed the details of the intricate scroll work along the top of the house directly under the roof line.

It was six-thirty and the sun was rising over the French Market bathing the street with soft, morning light. Long shadows accenting the buildings would soon begin to recede. The wet asphalt of the streets, recently swept and washed by the city trucks, produced an odor similar to the aroma of a thick stew but decidedly more pungent. It reminded me of the asphalt covered dock where my Uncle Tony would launch his boat when taking me on patrol. Why, I wondered, had I never thought of it before. And why had I abandoned the marsh, a source of great pleasure with Uncle Tony.

The doors of New Orleans are legendary, at least in New Orleans, and I scrutinized each one I passed this morning. They were more than doors but closures to portals that when entered would expose new worlds. Most were subtle in color and design but closer inspection revealed character as well as uniqueness. One black door on Burgundy Street was so dark it appeared more as a void instead of a door. I stopped and inspected it closely. Etched into the door were numerous and repetitive, intricate carvings of devils standing on crosses, fallen angels, children in chains, women with torn clothes, breasts and buttocks exposed, and beheaded lambs. Jesus, I thought, who the hell lives here? My eyes traveled up the door, and at the top were two eyes carved deeply into the wood, much larger and more pronounced than the other carvings. It did exactly what was intended; it made me feel as if someone was watching me, making

56

me the observed instead of the observer. The door was darker than the black paint.

The quarter is full of them, people trying to be what they are not, and I assumed this was another one. Shaking my head I picked up my pace and made it to Brother Lee's Restaurant, having taken an extra twenty minutes more than usual. As I walked up the alley LeRoy Bertrand, the wildlife and fisheries agent and Uncle Tony's good friend, was standing by the kitchen door. He was wearing his full agent uniform complete with service revolver.

"Morning, LeRoy. Up a little early. And what's with the uniform? Usually you are casual when you come to inspect the kitchen."

"I'm not here to inspect the kitchen because if I was here for that you'd fail," he said. "Want to take a guess as how I know?"

"No because I got a feeling you're going to tell me. So?"

"Travis, you and Brother Lee have been told the black market for seafood in Louisiana is one of our biggest problems. Yeah, sure we have a problem with sports fishermen catching too many fish over the state limit but that's nothing compared to the unlicensed people who use gill nets to catch tons of seafood and sell them illegally. Most they ship out of state and we never catch them. But some hit the local markets and it gives us a chance." LeRoy paused as if expecting me to comment so I obliged him.

"What, is this true confessions time? Am I supposed to fess up to buying illegal seafood?"

"It's more than that Travis. You don't have to confess. I already know. Take a guess on how I found out. It's not complicated," LeRoy said.

"I'm not confessing to anything LeRoy, so clue me in."

"Travis, for Christ's sake. There's one big seafood distributor in the city. You guys usually buy from them on a regular basis but guess what happens when you run lunch specials all week of seafood gumbo, shrimp Creole, crawfish ettoufe, and fried catfish. I'll tell you what happens. I get a call from the seafood vendor asking me how you can run these specials without buying seafood."

"Like I said, I'm not confessing especially since you already have this all figured out. I find it hard to believe these guys are focusing on us when there are over eight hundred restaurants in the city. We're nothing compared to most of those other restaurants. Why us?"

"Wrong is wrong, and breaking the law is wrong," he said. "In the big picture you're right, this is nothing. But someone must be pissed off."

"Are you coming inside?" I asked. "And what do you want from me?"

"I told you I'm not here to inspect the kitchen. I know you bought a load of seafood from Agnes Vu and Peter. What I want is for you to wise up and play by the rules. Talk to Brother Lee and if you don't do anything else place an order for some shrimp or crabs from The Seafood Boys." LeRoy stared at me making the conversation even more uncomfortable.

"I got it. I'll talk to Brother Lee and figure this out," I said. "Why the uniform today?"

"I'm going on patrol today with one of the other agents. I've got enough time served with the state so I don't have to patrol anymore, but I still like to get out on the water once or twice a year. Tell Brother Lee hello and stay out of trouble. I've got my hands full with the black market stuff. It's even bigger than I've told you. And more dangerous."

LeRoy walked down the alley and turned the corner. He had chastised me like a child and it bothered me. The door to the restaurant opened and Scatback walked out. He wore a chef's hat and apron and for a moment I viewed him as he wanted to be, a chef hard at work in the kitchen.

"That be bullshit, man. I been listnin to that line of shit and I call BULLSHIT on him."

"All his bullshit got you riled up, Scatback," I said.

"I maybe not so bright as you but I know when people be making fun of me, Chef T."

"You're wrong, twice. You are bright, and I'm not making fun of you. You need to clean up your language and quit acting like a raggedy ghetto ..."

"Nigger, go ahead and say it. I'm just a ghetto nigger."

"Shut up Scatback. I told you before, don't use that word." I glared at him, my teeth clenched tight, anger crawling up my back.

It took a few seconds to wrestle my temper. "So you're wrong. Raggedy ghetto punk is what I was going to say."

"I ain't no damn punk."

"Damn, Scatback, you make it hard for someone to compliment you. What's bothering you this morning?"

Scatback looked up at the sky, breathing in quick gasps, and a tear rolled down his face. "My momma's sick, Chef. She in Charity hospital and I don't know what to do. I'm scared, T. I brung her there last night. She was *real* bad, man, sweatin and throwin up. I hated to leave her but you told me to be here."

I wondered if Scatback thought I lacked compassion to the point I would not understand him missing work because of an ailing mother. He stared at the ground. I put my hand on his shoulder and said, "The good thing is she's at Charity. It's always been one of the best hospitals in the south. Some of the finest doctors and nurses in the country trained there. A friend of mine is a nurse who's high up the ladder at Charity. She's more familiar with how the hospital works than most of the people there. She used to come to Hope Haven once or twice a month to help with cuts and bruises, guys who were sick, minor medical stuff. She liked me, said I reminded her of her son. Her name is Lillian. I'll call her and see what I can find out."

"Man, you'd do that fo me? Thanks chef. I'll make it right with ya I promise."

"Scatback, you never have to show up if someone is sick. Call and tell me what's happening. Brother Lee and I will make do. You need to get back to the hospital."

"Naw, it won't do no good. They put her in a room, won't let nobody see her. I'll be better here, workin and doing stuff. But maybe if you'd call the nurse she'll be able to tell us what's happenin. Please."

CHAPTER ELEVEN

It was late in the afternoon, the lunch crowd gone and back to work. As typical, Brother Lee sat with me, Scatback, and the two servers, Chris and Becky; all of us enjoying the first break of the day. The phone in the restaurant was by the front door, placed on a small round table with a note pad and pen next to it. It rang loudly and I was first to get up and answered it. For five minutes I talked and listened, not once looking at the others.

"Scatback," I said, "that was Lillian from the hospital. Your mother is sick but not too bad. They think she might have gotten food poisoning, plus she's very run down, dehydrated, and tired. She needs to stay in Charity for another day or so, get her strength back before they release her. Otherwise she's going to be fine."

"How she done got food poison? Man, it makes me look bad, working in a restaurant and all." He looked at Brother Lee and added, "But I don't think it was anything I give her."

"It can happen to anyone," I said. "What's more important is for you to go see her first thing in the morning." I looked at Brother Lee and said, "You need to take the night off. You're falling asleep sitting there. The rest of us can handle all of this."

"What about the supper crowd?" Brother Lee asked.

"What crowd? We'll do regular menu tonight. No specials, close and clean up by eleven. I'll double back in the morning, receive the produce, beer, soft drinks and get lunch started. You and Scatback try to get here by ten and we'll be good. Go, I've got work to do."

"Nope," Brother Lee argued. "I'll open up. Can't sleep much anymore. You come in late."

By eleven o'clock I was locking the back door of the restaurant after having placed another plate of food on the table by the trash cans hoping Andi would find it first. I took the long way home walking to Iberville then over to Bourbon Street. The police barricades were up and two of New Orleans finest dressed in their police uniforms leaned against them, watching the crowd and flirting with the half intoxicated girls ogling them.

Each of the first eight or nine blocks of Bourbon Street had at least one window vendor serving beer in plastic cups. I stopped at the first one, got a large Abita Amber and took my time walking up Bourbon Street to Governor Nicholls. The crowd, noise, music, debauchery, the smell of the spilled drinks on the street, all mixed with the night air was good. It had been deplorable when I was a homeless street kid. But it had become home and I loved it.

The beer was finished by the time I got back to my apartment. The gate was unlocked and ajar. Terry's niece came to mind as I stared at the gate. This is not a coincidence I thought. I walked down the path and stopped. The lights in my apartment were on and the door was open. Terry was sitting on the small sofa watching the television. He jumped up when I entered.

"Travis, she's pregnant!" he exclaimed.

"Terry, you're gay. How did this happen?"

"No, you big goof. It's my niece. *She's* pregnant. That's why my sister sent her here to be with me. But they didn't tell me she was pregnant. What am I supposed to do?"

Huge relief swept over me as I realized I was off the hook and would not have to baby sit the niece. "You're supposed to take care of her, that's what you do." The shine of the floor caught my attention. I turned around in a complete circle noticing the apartment had been cleaned. My place is a typical bachelor pad, a completely lived in, disorganized, and neglected mess most women would run from.

"Terry, you did a great job cleaning this place up. Very considerate of you but I'd have been nice to your niece anyway. Thanks."

"What *are* you talking about?" he said. "I've been soooo distraught since my niece arrived I've not done anything but pace the floor, sit and fan myself, then pace some more."

I looked around the apartment again. "Someone was in here. I never leave it looking this good even after I've cleaned up, and I haven't in a couple of weeks." I ran my finger across the television screen. "Even dusted," I said.

"Travis! What about my niece?"

"Terry, she is not a problem. You'll take care of her, and you'll figure out what to do as the days go by. It's simple. How long is she staying with you?"

"A couple of weeks but maybe a month or so. She's due in January so she's about six months. I *don't* know what to do. I'm beyond distraught."

"This might sound funny under the circumstances but the first thing to do is be a man. She's family and needs your help. So man up." I looked at him as he pouted and stared at the floor. "Terry, it's real late and I'm tired. Brother Lee is opening up in the morning so I'll hang around and meet your niece. Then *we'll* figure out what to do, got it."

"Travis," Terry said quietly, still staring at the floor, "I don't know how to be a man, and that's the problem I've had all my life. It doesn't feel right. Jerry usually handles the manly stuff and even he isn't very good at it."

"In the morning, I'll come over for coffee. Forget what I said about being a man. You're more man than most. You have to be to wear the stuff you wear and live your life so openly. Come on, get going while I try to figure out how this place got cleaned up."

"I guess I need to pay more attention cause I didn't see anyone around here today, but I was distracted," Terry said. "Jerry is upset too, so I need to go patch things up with him."

I watched Terry leave then moved around the apartment looking for a note to indicate who had been there. I picked up my cell phone and called Maggie.

"No, I wasn't at your place today and I certainly wasn't cleaning up," Maggie said. "I'm not good about cleaning my place. Is something wrong?"

"No, but I don't understand why someone would clean my apartment and not leave a note or anything."

"You didn't come back last night. I thought you were mad at me. It's late but since I'm still up…"

"Thanks, but I'm tired and worn out. I'll see you tomorrow before lunch. And no, I was not mad with you."

CHAPTER TWELVE

"You know what a whore is? I mean, really what a whore is?"

I stared at Alexis, Terry's niece, my mouth agape. It was a rhetorical question and she didn't want an answer, but instead wanted to tell me.

"It's a woman usually paid for sex, one so promiscuous she would just as soon make money screwing someone than do it for free." There was pain in Terry's face and anger in Alexis's. "My mother," she said, pointing at Terry, "his sister, thinks I'm a whore."

Terry stared at the floor as silence echoed in the room. I'd been here for less than twenty minutes, long enough to get a cup of coffee and meet Alexis. And long enough to become uncomfortable and confused. It had started cordially but as soon as Terry stumbled over the mention of Alexis being pregnant the conversation had taken a turn for the worse. And the more Terry tried to correct his faux pas the angrier Alexis became. At this point I didn't understand why I was standing in Terry's living room. I wondered if I was here to meet Alexis, or more likely to bail him out.

"That's a laugh coming from her," Alexis said. "She's a product of the hippie era, the free love generation. And she has the nerve to call me a whore." She looked at Terry and said, "He knows. Don't you Uncle Terry." Alexis's face flushed almost crimson but then she calmed herself. "Momma was at Woodstock. I found some old pictures of her and they were less than flattering. She bathed in the communal pool. I assume you saw the movie," she said, looking at me. "Then again, maybe not. You're rather young. Anyway, I'm sure it's not the only communal thing she did. And it was all ok back then. But today, I'm a whore."

"Lexie, dear, please. I invited Chef T to meet you, told him what a nice girl you are. Must you be so uncivil?" Terry said. "I didn't know you were pregnant until you got here."

I'd had enough. "Why are you telling me this?" I said.

"Because, I can see it on your face. You've got the look. The 'what the hell am I doing here' look. I was watching through the window last night. You got it as soon as Uncle Terry told you I was pregnant."

"This is the look I was born with, take it or leave it. I'm here to meet you, welcome you to the city. Maybe show you around when I have some free time. But maybe that's a bad idea…"

"You know why my momma's mad as hell? It's because I told her I don't know who the daddy is. I told her it was a group sex thing and it could be one of five or six guys."

"OH MY GOD!" Terry shrieked.

Alexis and I stepped back at hearing Terry's reaction.

Alexis recovered first. "Relax Uncle Terry. It was a lie, but momma had it coming. She was acting all high and mighty, telling me what I was going to do, demanding I tell her who the father is and how we would make him pay, make him marry me. She never one time asked me if I was ok and what I wanted, never asked if I needed anything. She took over and started yelling orders and making demands so I made it all up. I know who the daddy is. And the first thing he is," she said, "is a big mistake. He's married, and I don't love him."

"Married? How did this happen?" Terry exclaimed. "I mean, I know how it happened but HOW did this happen?"

"I'm twenty-five and I look in the mirror and already see the difference. Men don't care, but women see the aging process daily. We panic and our minds race, we think we're running out of time. Can you believe that? All the men my age are carefree and non-committal. Then you meet a guy who is stable, mature, responsible, and takes an interest in you, a guy who can actually hold a conversation that doesn't include sports or cars. So I took a chance. And before you say anything, I was on the pill but apparently not the right one for my body. At least I tried to be careful." Alexis paused, put her hand on her belly and her face became calm. "I've told him about the baby but he can't do anything to help. Did I mention mature and responsible?" She looked at me and said, "So Mister Chef T, don't worry about me. I'll be fine. Uncle Terry will take care of me and be a better mother than his sister." She walked to Terry and put her hand on his shoulder. "Ain't that right?"

"Isn't that right," Terry said. "You are a refined lady, at least use proper English, especially since you have a degree in American Literature from Vanderbilt. One I financed, and was the best money I ever spent, my dear."

Alexis leaned down and kissed Terry on the forehead. "So tell me, if you're a chef how come you aren't fat?"

"Because he works out at the gym on North Rampart Street," Terry answered for me. "Does all the Chinese stuff." Terry looked at Alexis and added, "T is a fighter, not a lover."

"Well, maybe we can change him," Alexis said. Patting her belly she said, "Or maybe he can change me."

"I'm not changing anyone, me or…"

"Chef T, what does the T stand for?" Alexis said interrupting me.

"My given name is Travis. My mother…"

"Travis? Are you from Tex-ass mister Travis?" she said with an exaggerated southern twang.

I shook my head having been asked the same question too many times. "No, I was born in Louisiana. I was about to say my mother liked Travis McGee, from the novels by…"

"John McDonald. I *do* read."

"Yes, I imagine you do," I said. "I think it's about time I left."

"Look, I might need to make a few dollars before the baby comes so if you want to get rid of the maid I saw cleaning your place yesterday I'll take over for her," Alexis said.

"I don't have a maid. What are you talking about?"

"I was in the courtyard yesterday when she came out of your apartment. I stopped her and she said she was the maid and had

66

been cleaning your apartment. She's a real scruffy looking thing, hard to tell but looked real young and not clean at all."

I described Andi to her and she said, "Yeah, that's her."

"I'm not getting rid of her anytime soon, but if you need to earn some cash I'll see what I can do. There's always a restaurant in the Quarter looking for a dishwasher."

Terry looked up, about to protest my suggestion when Alexis said, "I'll do practically anything for some cash. Ask my mother."

CHAPTER THIRTEEN

I took my time walking to Maggie's place. The air was cool and fresh, the humidity unseasonably low and I was reminded of late summer in the Smoky Mountains in Gatlinburg. I'd made a trip there with Mr. Chin to help his cousin open a restaurant. This air was similar and invigorating. I made a mental note to call Mr. Chin later this day. I didn't remember any Tai Chi instructions especially good for pregnant women but I was sure he would. Alexis needed balance and harmony, but more importantly her unborn baby needed it.

"Use your damn key," Maggie yelled after I knocked.

I unlocked her front door, pushed it open and yelled before entering, "How do you know it's me?"

"I don't get visitors," she said walking to the door. "There's lots of foot traffic, the tourists and all, but seldom does anyone stop to visit." She stretched to kiss my cheek. "You're later than I expected.

I told her about meeting Terry's niece, that she was pregnant, and the awkwardness of the conversation. Then I asked her if she could help in any way. She stepped back and stared at me, her mouth open.

"Jesus, Travis. How do you get yourself into these situations? First you want help with the homeless girl, then Scatback at the restaurant, and now Terry's niece. You give Mother Theresa a run for her money."

I turned away to consider what she had said, her words bothering me. I was conflicted and feeling guilty, but had done nothing wrong.

First Brother Lee's warning, then Tater cautioning me, now Maggie questioning me. "I'm not sure. These things continue to happen."

"Travis, it's a good thing but slow down. Maybe you should have worn a collar and I should have been a chef."

"Not a chance. I don't look good in a collar and besides, I've eaten your cooking."

"Well maybe if you'd share some of your *secrets* my cooking would be better!"

"Come on, let's go for a walk," I said. "The air outside feels great and I need some right now."

We walked for several blocks until we got to the black door. I stopped, forcing Maggie to stop when I didn't let go of her hand. "What do you think about this? I asked, staring at the door.

"A black door? Not so unusual in New Orleans considering..." Maggie stopped speaking as she looked closely at the door. "Damn, those carvings look terrible even for New Orleans. Halloween's in a couple of weeks, but this is a permanent door. Why would someone make a door like this?"

"They're obviously not looking for company. The eyes at the top are too spooky, and they alone are enough to keep a sane person away."

"I've seen all I want to see," Maggie said. "Time to move on."

The door opened before we moved. A lone man stopped short, pausing in the open door as he looked at us. We exchanged stares, his face emotionless but his posture defensive, as if awaiting confrontation. I nodded at him and got no response. I guessed him to be in his late thirties, average build on a frame about five foot ten, bespectacled and with long reddish brown hair combed straight back.

A late model BMW pulled up along side of us and stopped in the middle of the street. "Interesting door," I said to him as he pulled it closed and locked it.

"Yeah, well all places have them."

"True, but not like this one, what with all the carvings and all."

He walked past me toward the car waiting in the street.

"I was wondering about the significance of the carvings, why..."

"Excuse me," he said, "but do you know what I'm doing?"

I was taken aback with the curtness of his question. "No, guess I don't."

"I'm minding my own business," he said getting into the car and slamming the door.

Maggie tugged at my hand, gesturing for us to move on. I stared at the car as it accelerated away and noticed a Tulane Medical School parking sticker on the back glass.

CHAPTER FOURTEEN

It was late, after eleven at night and I was busying myself by cleaning up the restaurant alone. Both lunch and supper had been less than half the usual crowd so cleaning was quick and almost not necessary. Scatback had done a great job and the wait staff had also helped. I putzed around wiping down the counters and thinking of new recipes. The knocking on the back door was expected.

"Come on in Andi," I yelled, making sure she heard me.

"Suppose it wasn't me?" she said after opening the door and sidling across the floor toward the walk in cooler.

"I wasn't expecting anyone, plus you're becoming predictable. After a couple days or so you get hungry," I said. "And I think you like my food."

"Yeah, I guess your food's ok," she said looking at the walk in cooler door.

"Better than the trash cans?"

"Sometimes."

I threw the cleaning towel on the counter, crossed my arms and stared hard, challenging her response. She looked back and her eyes softened, but she didn't smile. "Man, you worse than a girl," she said. "What, you looking for a fucking compliment?" The hardness in her eyes was back.

"Are you hungry?" I asked.

"Yeah, that's why I'm here."

"Good, I'll fix you some food and you can tell me why you broke into my apartment the other day."

"Well if you had a better lock it wouldn't be so fucking easy to break into your fucking apartment. Geez, how fucking stupid can you be?"

"If you're going to eat with that mouth you might want to clean it up a little, maybe cut down on the F word," I said as I entered the cooler.

"You ain't my f…, my daddy. And if you lived on the street like you said you did then what's the big deal? What you expect from a street urchin?"

I came out of the cooler carrying a small pan of leftovers and placed it on the counter. "A street urchin? I'm surprised you remember that name, especially since you didn't know what it was a couple of days ago."

"Cause you think I'm stupid, huh?"

"I don't know what you are; smart, stupid, liar, thief, full of self pity, whatever. Maybe you ran away from home because you didn't get what you wanted. I don't know if your step father abused you or not. You've been talking a good game but…"

"Fuck you and your fucking food!" Andi slapped at me and turned to run out the back door.

I grabbed at her, catching the collar of her shirt. It was crusty in my grip, dirty and thin from wear without washing. Andi pulled hard and the shirt ripped down the middle of her back and fell off her right shoulder as she moved away. She was not wearing a bra and moved to cover her breast with her arm. She stopped, dropped her arm and turned, exposing herself to me and then looked at the floor. Her hardness dissolved with her exposure.

"Take a good look," she said as she removed the rest of her torn shirt. "Is this what you want?" She paused, "It's what all the other guys want," her voice a mere whisper.

"Turn around and cover yourself," I said. There were blotches of dirt caked on her neck and her back was full of pimples and red marks. Her shoulders drooped as if in defeat, waiting for me to take advantage of her. "When's the last time you bathed?"

"I ain't had a bath since I don't remember when. But I clean myself off in the public restroom at the French Market when the workers ain't around. They don't like us street kids and call the cops, always trying to run us off. But mostly they too lazy so I go when they ain't there. I wash the important parts. You got any idea what a woman's pu…private parts smell like after a couple of months of not bathing?"

I was uncomfortable and it showed. Andi seized on this and stood straight, turned and looked hard at me and took control of the moment. "So you gonna give me a bath? Is that what you want? Come on, we can do it right here in them big sinks."

I thought back to my first night in Brother Lee's kitchen, re-membering how dirty I was, my stench as I undressed, and how badly I needed a bath.

"You wouldn't be the first to bathe there," I said. "Here, put this on." I handed her a chef's shirt I had taken off the rack where the clothes, aprons, and towels were stored. "Andi, I believe what you tell me but I can't know if it's true or not."

Andi held the shirt up to cover herself. "I might be trash but I ain't never lied to you Mister Chef T. Never, all I done told you is true." She placed the shirt on the counter and moved toward me. I stared into her eyes, refusing to look at her breasts. "Look," she said, lifting both small breasts up, exposing the underside. "Go on, look."

Reluctantly my eyes moved and focused on Andi's chest. Almost a dozen small, circular scars about a quarter inch in diameter were revealed. A couple were still slightly pinkish in color, a sign they weren't as old as the others. It was obvious what they were. I'd seen the same on a boy at Hope Haven who had been taken from his parents. My teeth clenched so tightly my jaws ached. Andi released her breasts and the scars were again hidden. She stepped back, fear evident on her face as she focused on my ire. All she had told me was true.

"Cigarette burns," she said softly. "That's what he would do when I refused him. He'd light one up, hold me down with his hand over my mouth, puff it till it glowed red hot and place it against my tit." A tear rolled down her cheek as she spoke. "He'd push so hard on my mouth I couldn't hardly take a breath of air. Then he would hold it there till it went out."

I picked up the chef's shirt and handed it to her. Andi slid the shirt over her shoulders easily, it being much too large for her small-framed body. She tied the bottom of the chef's shirt in a large knot, taking up the excess fabric hanging loosely on her small frame.

"I got a baby sister. She'd be eight by now. I'm scared for her. I was ten when he started with me, twelve by the time he first raped me. With me gone it won't be long for he gets after her. I'd kill him if I could."

"Write his name and address on this," I said, handing her the pen and pad I had taken from the dining room as she fixed the shirt. "I need to notify the authorities in Mississippi."

"Are you stupid or what?" she said, the softness again gone, replaced by her familiar rough exterior. "They *been* told. But my momma denied it, said I made it all up, said I was a liar and hated him. Said he was a good man what took care of us. That's why they drove me here and left me. Said I caused too much trouble."

"Different authorities, so write it down. And stop feeling sorry for yourself," I said, my own demeanor changing. "I can't save you Andi. You have to save yourself. Brother Lee didn't save me, but he gave me a chance at the right time and it's what I needed. I made a decision to do better and make my own way. I had an advantage over you because I had lived in the orphanage. I got better care, and I finished high school. You have it harder, but I'll help you."

"How *you* gonna help *me*? You gonna give me a job or some-thin?"

"No, I don't need any more help here and you're too young. You need to be eighteen to serve beer in New Orleans and Scatback takes care of the kitchen. But, I'll pay you for cleaning my apartment, not much but I'll manage a few bucks here and there. And I spoke to Maggie. I think she can help."

"Maggie, is she your fuck buddy we talked about? Is she the pregnant lady I seen when I was leaving?"

I shook my head. "No, Maggie isn't pregnant. The pregnant lady is my landlord's niece. She came for a visit and he…"

"Hey, I thought you was gonna feed me. That's why I cleaned your stupid apartment cause of the food. What's in the pan?"

74

"This is going to be more difficult than I thought," I said. "It's seafood with tri-color rotini pasta in a creamy Alfredo sauce. Lots of calories and carbs. You need to put some meat on that skinny ass of yours."

She smiled. "You better leave my ass alone. You'll go ta jail cause I'm too young. Tater cop said so."

"Yeah, sixteen going on sixty," I said as I placed her food in the microwave.

Andi ate in silence, taking large bites and chewing only half of what she swallowed. I watched her but took no pleasure in feeding her. The hunger she exhibited was disturbing and replaced the satisfaction I normally receive when someone enjoys my cooking.

"Have you heard anything about the young girl they found hanging in the warehouse?" I asked. "The paper said she was homeless. Tater said it had been determined it was a suicide."

"Girls come and go all the time but I might have seen her around. It weren't no suicide, though. Don't care what Tater cop says."

"Why not? Maybe she was tired of running and decided to kill herself."

"Man, all you people are stupid. You don't run away to kill yourself. You run away to live.

Andi's words chilled me. What she said made sense and I did feel stupid. "Why didn't you tell Tater when he was here the other night?"

"Ain't none of my business. I got enough to do takin care of me. Besides, the cops don't listen to us. We're street urchins, remember?"

CHAPTER FIFTEEN

May, 1952
Cut Off, Louisiana

Pierre sat at the kitchen table, his head drooping and his shoulders slumped forward. The funeral for Minos had been small. A dozen people plus the priest from the church attended. He was alone much like ten years before when the crew from the U boat dropped him on the island. He had eventually told Minos the truth, who he was and how he came to be on the island. Minos didn't care. They formed a father-son bond and never left each other for more than a day or two. Minos would sometimes leave to see a lady friend, and Pierre sometimes to wander the back marsh fishing, crabbing, and occasionally to remember.

Pierre looked up when he heard the knock on the door but hesitated, not wanting to answer, not wanting company. But Minos had raised him better than to ignore a visitor. He rose and walked to the door, opened it and looked out at Father Paul.

"Pierre, I'm concerned about you. I know how close you were to Minos, and that there's no one else here for you. I promised Minos I would look after you if anything ever happened. May I come in?"

"Sure, you always welcome, Father," Pierre said moving to the side, allowing Father Paul to enter. "When did you make the promise to Minos?"

"Minos could tell he was sick. He liked his cigarettes and whiskey, but they didn't like him. He was not scared of dying but he was afraid for you, afraid what would happen and how you'd survive.

So I promised him I would check on you. But as big and strong as you've grown up to be I think you should check on me from time to time."

"I'll be ok. Minos taught me real good. I can fish and get crabs and shrimp, oysters too. And most all the peoples know me. I can sell it all and be fine. But you welcome to visit anytime you want. If the boat is tied up then I be here. Otherwise, I'm out fishin."

Father Paul hesitated, looked around the room and then said, "Pierre, I'm being relocated by the archdiocese. They're sending me to Lafayette, close to where Minos said you come from. They need a new principal at Mount Carmel high school and I've been chosen to go. It's not the kind of thing I can refuse. It's my calling."

"Then you's got to go. Minos always told me about doing what's right. I'll be ok by myself. I think I get to keep all of Minos's things including this here house, right?"

"Yes, Minos left everything to you. It's all yours and all paid for. It's a great start. All we need to do is get you a wife," Father Paul said hoping for a smile from Pierre.

"I dated a few of them girls from around here but they was too serious. Minos needed my help. Maybe one day, but don't need no wife now."

"I'm leaving in a couple of weeks," Father Paul said. "It'll take me that long to get things in order here and tell all the parishioners. I hope you'll come to mass for my last homily."

The next morning at four o'clock Pierre navigated the skiff through Little Lake into Barataria Bay and headed for Empire to the small shack he and Minos had rebuilt. They had claimed an old abandoned fishing camp for their own. Minos was well known in Plaquemines Parish and had no trouble getting a deed to the building.

They had worked off and on over a six month period restoring the shack, adding on to it, building a dock and stairs, and made it weather proof, better than some of the new houses being built in New Orleans. Minos had salvaged an old diesel generator off a sunken work boat and rebuilt it, mounted it behind the camp with a fifty-five gallon drum of diesel fuel, and used it to power the couple of lights and the refrigeration for the seafood they caught.

They could easily last a week working the marsh, bays, even offshore in the gulf catching crabs, shrimp, fish, whatever was in season and keep it from spoiling until they sold it in Empire. But they typically stayed out fishing for three or four days. By then Minos was ready for a good time. He and Pierre would sell their catch in Empire and return to Cut Off. The seafood wholesalers would drive the catch up highway 23 to New Orleans where someone would be eating it for supper the same day.

Pierre docked the skiff at the fishing shack, tied off to the cleats and walked up the stairs. He had been here before by himself but always returning to Minos the same day. They had maintained enough provisions to last several days at the shack. This was a precaution should an unexpected storm kick up in the gulf and make crossing Barataria Bay impossible.

Inside the shack Pierre sat on his bed, elbows on his knees and head in his hands. The tears came and he didn't fight them. Minos had saved him, taught him how to fish the waters of Louisiana and Mississippi to make a good living. He had all he needed but the void in his life felt as big as the Gulf of Mexico. He was alone for the second time in his short twenty-two years. He rose from the bed and stood in the doorway looking out across the marsh. Perhaps this is what God planned for him, to be alone, obscure from the rest of the world.

The morning sun was glowing across the horizon and casting light over the distant bay. The mild, early breeze caused the water to ripple and sparkle in the new sun like diamonds in a jewelry case. Pierre remembered his mother, and the necklace she wore glimmering around her neck as she stood on the train platform, waving goodbye, sending him to be with his father in Germany. He never saw her again, but he never forgot her face, the beautiful smile. And never was he able to rid himself of the loneliness without her.

He had been eight years old when she sent him away, too young to understand what was happening in the world and why he had to leave his mother. She had taken him to temple, prayed with him for his safety and begged God for his return. But it was not to be. His father had little time for him and had placed him in a military barracks when he was ten years old. For two years he had not seen his father. Excitement overwhelmed him when he was told he was being allowed to take a trip on a submarine, a German U boat that would cruise underwater, safe from harm as the war raged. Germany would soon be victorious and he would return to the Fatherland.

Minos had made him see it was all a lie. He was never supposed to return to Germany. The German U boat captain must have had orders to abandon him at sea, make sure he died and did not return. But the sailors had been kind, not telling him the whole truth, and only that they must leave him on the island. They had disobeyed direct orders by not killing him. With Minos gone Pierre was again like the young boy alone on Chandeleur Island.

Pierre walked back to his bed, reclined on the soft mattress and drifted off to sleep. His mother came to him holding Minos's hand and he was comforted in his sleep. He awoke and was at peace. There was food in the pantry and he fixed a meal of grits, canned ham, and crackers. He decided to spend a few days in the marsh, checking crab traps, throwing his cast net for bait shrimp, and fishing for speckled trout to cook for supper. The days alone would help him heal from his loss.

CHAPTER SIXTEEN

October, 2004
The French Quarter

I stood in the doorway separating the kitchen from the dining area. Most of the supper crowd was gone but there were two tables with diners still eating. Seated at a table in a corner were two men. The one facing me was the man who had exited the house with the black door, and who had not so politely told me he was minding his own business, strongly insinuating I should do the same. An off handed remark but one easily understood. I moved back into the kitchen before the man looked up.

"Scatback, go get Becky and tell her to come to the kitchen." I dished two large orders of warm bread pudding and topped them with whipped whiskey sauce. Becky came through the door.

"What's wrong, Chef?"

"Nothing, and why would you assume there's a problem? Never mind," I said. "Take these two desserts to the table in the corner with the two men. Tell them it's on me. Offer them some coffee too."

"Sure, but any particular reason you're doing this? I mean, what do I say if they ask why?"

"I might have been a little rude to the one guy facing this way earlier today. Tell him no reason."

Becky was back in a couple of minutes. "I don't think I handled it so good," she said. "They kind of tricked me into telling them why, so I sort of told the one guy what you said. I hope it's ok but they want to thank you."

Becky had her hands full being a single mom with five year old twin daughters. She seldom stopped to think but charged ahead with whatever task before her. And she was kind, never rude or discourteous to anyone. I'd have preferred she had not told them but was not surprised when she confessed to me she had.

"Uh huh," I mumbled. "Why am I not surprised?"

"Shit," Becky said stomping her right foot. "There goes my raise."

"We don't give raises, and put a dollar in the potty mouth jar."

"Damn it Chef! Is this what I get for doing you a favor?"

"Two dollars!" I wiped my hands on a towel and headed for the dining room.

"That's great," Becky yelled. "My girls won't get McDonalds and it's all Uncle Travis's fault."

I had become the surrogate uncle almost as soon as Becky came to work for Brother Lee. Her twins were two years old, no father or male figure to speak of and it seemed almost natural. I nicknamed them Tick and Tock. When they visit the restaurant they always run up to me, each wraps her arms around one of my legs and we sway back and forth in rhythm while they chant tick-tock, tick-tock. I always get their names wrong and they are quick to correct me. I am powerless when I look into the faces of two five year old girls.

I approached the table, offered my hand and introduced myself simply as Travis to the two men. Both men stood offering their hands. Ray spoke first and thanked me for the dessert. Then the man from behind the black door spoke. "I'm Charles, Charles Du-Pont and I apologize if I was rude today. Please, have a seat."

Becky brought two cups of coffee, placed them on the table and looking at me asked, "Would Mister Chef T like some coffee?" as sarcastically as she could manage.

"Yes, please join us," Charles said.

"Perhaps it was I being rude today," I said. "The door to your place is very interesting and certainly not so out of place in New Orleans. But you don't owe me or anyone else an explanation." Becky

81

returned, placed a cup of coffee in front of me, some of it splashing over the side into the saucer, and retreated back into the kitchen.

"Chef T, T for Travis, I like it," Charles said. "So tell me…"

Here it comes, I thought, the Texas question.

"Is Travis a family name?"

"No, my mother liked the name. It's after a character in a novel. My mother loved to read, at least as I remember. My Uncle Tony told me about her."

"I take it your mother has passed," Ray said.

I spend the next twenty minutes drinking coffee and telling Charles and Ray my brief history. I'm not sure why I was so open with them, but looking at Charles it came easily and the words flowed. I ended my story with Brother Lee finding me and bringing me in to his restaurant.

"That's an amazing story," Charles said. "Especially for one so young as you. I suppose you'd like me to explain about the door, the significance of the carvings. Am I right?"

"I would, but it's getting late and I've got work to do in the kitchen before I leave for the night."

"What time do you usually finish?" Charles asked.

"If I'm lucky I can sometimes get out of here by ten but usually more like eleven."

"You know where I live and I'm a late-night person so why don't you stop by after you get off. I'll fix us a cognac and tell you about the door. Please make it by eleven. I imagine the conversation will last a while."

I returned to the kitchen. Scatback and Becky had almost completely cleaned up and had things in order for the next day. Scatback had chopped up a large batch of mirepoix for the next day's special of braised beef over Jasmine rice.

"Scatback, get the whole grain wheat bread and make two grilled cheese sandwiches while the flat top is still hot. And make a small batch of sweet potato fries, put it all in a take-out container." I looked at Becky and said, "McDonalds? Really? My girls deserve better."

"Let them come spend a week end with you and you'll see how easy it is. Two five year old angels who can *terrorize* an apartment and wreck it in five minutes. I can't *wait* to see that happen."

"*I* can wait. Take the food Scatback fixed and give the twins a kiss for me. No dessert, too much sugar and it's too late," I said looking at the clock. The display read nine-fifteen. "Go, get out of here, you've done enough."

Scatback handed Becky the food and went back to prepping for tomorrow. It had been a week and he had taken to the kitchen with vehemence. He was still slow using the large chef knife but he was diligent. I was sure he would work out.

"Let's finish up and get out of here. I've got someplace to be," I said.

At ten fifteen I knocked on the black door, suddenly uncomfortable as if the two eyes at the top were piercing right through me. I imagined a scene from a movie, waiting for the door to open, a Hitchcock moment. Footsteps sounded as someone inside moved toward the door, a telltale indication of a raised house with wood floors. The door opened and Charles stood there, relaxed, holding a brandy snifter which I presumed contained the cognac he had mentioned. A hint of incense wafted through the door and assaulted my nose reminding me of church during the Christmas and Easter seasons.

"Chef T, please do come in."

"Call me Travis, the Chef T is too formal. I don't suppose they call you Chuck, do they."

"My father tried but it didn't stick. Charles works fine."

As we shook hands I looked around the room. It was a fairly typical French Quarter house, wood floors, high ceilings, two large windows in the front with exterior shutters, and a door opening to the rear of the house. Against the wall to the right of the room was what was obviously a fire place but one which had been closed off. I stared for several minutes, sure of what I was seeing but not sure why it was there. Built around the fire place was a small altar, complete with crucifix, candles, chalice, and bible.

"Well," Charles said, "the little ones did call me Father Charlie, but it always changed to Father Charles by the time they got to high school."

"You're a priest?" I asked.

"A defrocked priest if you will, no longer acknowledged by the archdiocese in Wisconsin or anywhere else for that matter. But in my heart, yes, most of the time. However, I'm working on it and getting better." Charles was almost my height, stared at me eye to eye and said, "Hold that dumbstruck look for a minute, I'll be right back."

Charles returned, handed me a snifter of cognac, and raised his eyebrows waiting for me to speak. "I think I'm at a loss for words," I said, lifting the glass to my lips to take a sip.

"Christian Brother's Brandy, coincidentally appropriate I would say. It's not cognac. The French are so fussy about wine and champagne, what is or isn't, depending on how it's made and where it's from."

"It's fine," I said. "I feel like I should call you Father Charles."

"Don't be ridiculous. Like I told you, I'm not a priest anymore."

"Yes, but not many people have an altar in their house," I said, gesturing toward the fireplace. "Why would you build one if you were kicked out?"

"I wasn't kicked out, well, not exactly, anyway. I left to avoid a scandal, and to avoid embarrassing the church."

"None of this has anything to do with the door, I'm sure, which is what I was curious about in the first place."

"Of course it has to do with the door," Charles said. "But why are you so interested in it?"

"There's a popular poster sold in the gift shops. It's called the doors of New Orleans. It's nothing special except it's always been one of my favorites. It shows many doors from houses around New Orleans, all different but all interesting, to me at least. So when I noticed your door and took a close look I became confused. Why would someone make a door so ominous?"

"To keep nosy people away, to hide from our past."

"Charles, why would you invite me in and bare your soul, so to speak," I said, not choosing my words carefully. "I'm sorry I didn't…"

"It's alright, even rather humorous," Charles said. His priestly mannerisms were evident and I relaxed despite my faux pas. "I think it was because you spent those years at Hope Haven. The priest in me took a liking to you right away. Come, let's sit at the table in the kitchen, the New Orleans way, or so I've been told."

I stopped in front of the altar looking at the crucifix on the wall, not sure if I should genuflect and cross myself or not. Charles had walked by without stopping but turned and looked at me when I hesitated. "Travis, you may if you wish," he said, understanding why I hesitated. "But it's not mandatory. God is always aware of what's in your heart and you will *never* fool him." I bowed my head, did the sign of the cross and followed Charles into his kitchen.

The kitchen was modern and not what I expected. It had been remodeled within the last couple of years. The cabinets looked new and the appliances were late model stainless steel, and all matched. We sat on barstool type chairs, chrome with black leather cushions, thick and comfortable, and arranged around a four-seat, round, high-top table in the corner. Charles raised his glass to toast, a gesture I was not comfortable with but I clinked glasses with him.

"You already shared your story with me and Ray. Now it's my turn," he said taking a sip of the brandy. "I was a good priest. I taught biology at a small parochial school in Wisconsin. The town doesn't matter and is better left unsaid. The school was small but included kindergarten through twelfth grade. I'm thirty-eight and left four years ago." He fidgeted in his seat. "This is more awkward than I thought. I've not told many people this and certainly not someone I just met."

"Charles, you don't have to tell me anything. I was interested in the door, remember?"

"Yes, but it won't make sense if I don't explain why. Anyway, as I was saying, I taught biology. I had parent conferences all the time. But one mother presented a problem. She was a single mother with two boys ages fourteen and sixteen. She developed, let's say, a romantic interest in me. I was aghast at first. She had scheduled the last conference of the evening so we would not be forced to limit the meeting to the allotted time. It was all quite innocent at first but the halls quieted as more people left and we were virtually alone. She was very attractive and leaned across the desk placing

85

her face within an inch of mine. Her smell was intoxicating and the man in me was reacting quickly, beyond my control. I was frozen, mostly in shock when she placed her lips on mine. I jerked back so fast I fell off my chair. Like a buffoon I sat on the floor watching as she came around the desk and straddled my legs. She offered me her hand but I was afraid to touch her. I scooted away, stood up and reminded her I was a priest. She chuckled which I found insulting, as if I were being foolish. I rebuked her then and several more times. She became so insulted and incensed that she threatened me with exposure, said she would go to the archbishop and tell him I made unwanted advances toward her. And then she said, and this hurt the most, said she would tell them I had fondled her sons when they were younger. Suffice it to say, I lost my priestly calling for a few minutes."

I watched Charles as he told his story; the hurt on his face was evident as he relived the experience. He lifted his glass and gulped the brandy, grimacing with the burn as he swallowed. "Charles, you don't have to say any more..."

"Don't be ridiculous, this has a happy ending," he said, but I did not see this in his face. "So, to shorten the story I called her bluff, my big mistake, and went about my life. She tried several times to meet with me, even eventually following me in the evenings. Rejected and furious, she went to the archbishop and told a tale so outrageous I was called in for a conference. This is not the happy part," he said, pouring more brandy into his glass. "The story got out and I was publicly tried and convicted without a day in court. The archdiocese wanted to move me to a remote parish in Montana so this would all go away. I refused proclaiming my innocence. But it fell on deaf ears. The Catholic Church has had too many scandals and the deanery wanted this hushed up immediately. I felt so betrayed, well I left the order. I quit, to put it bluntly. But the scandal never died. Small towns can be cruel. I was so naïve. I expected them to come running back to me apologizing for their mistake. Instead I was ostracized. So I left, moved to New Orleans four years ago."

"What about the happy part?" I said.

"I moved here, one of the greatest cities in the country although I didn't realize it at the time. I was accepted into Tulane medical school and will graduate shortly. Soon I'll get to help people of all denominations, including the Catholics. And the good part is I've dated several women over the last few years. Even fornicated, which is *NOT* overrated I must say. But the happy ending is that the mother tried the same thing with another priest. He was much smarter than I. He set up a trap. Again, long story short she confessed, including how she had used me. I got a nice letter from the archbishop begging my forgiveness. So," he raised his glass again and said, "all's well that ends well. Almost anyway, there are still people there who believe this was all a cover up. Did you know there are women who intentionally try to compromise a priest? As if it's a challenge they can't resist. I suppose much like a man will try to convince an avowed lesbian to have sex with him. As if! Men can be so stupid it defies explanation."

I shook my head in disbelief. Might such a preposterous story be true. But I believed every word of it. "And the door?"

"Oh yes, the door. A bad idea as I look back on it but it did serve the purpose. When I first came to New Orleans I hired an artist to carve the door for me. I wanted it to be gruesome and intimidating. I *DID NOT* want visitors. I had been mortally wounded, yes a bit dramatic, but I wanted to shut myself off. I succeeded. Medical school changed me, and all for the good I like to think. But the door stays lest I forget. It keeps things in perspective."

"The door is a little extreme," I said.

"Perhaps but if you remember history, especially history of the church, much worse things have been done in the name of religion. Oh sure, they would say in the name of God, but no. It was all self serving and they used God to justify it all. The Crusades, Attila the Hun, all too gruesome to think about."

"What about the two big eyes at the top? Intimidating as hell if you ask me."

"Not at all. The eyes of God watching over me. Actually rather simple," Charles said.

I looked up at the kitchen clock. Almost midnight. "I think it is time for me to go. Brother Lee will cover the early morning but he still needs my help. I've had all the brandy, cognac, or whatever for one night."

"My priestly instincts tell me you're a good man, Travis. I have enjoyed your company and hope it wasn't too much to digest."

"What about your parents, any siblings?" I asked.

"No siblings, and my parents died before the scandal took place, thank God. They lived long enough to see me ordained but passed several years before the trouble. They left me well off which is how I was able to afford this house, go to medical school and survive. Like I said, a happy ending."

CHAPTER SEVENTEEN

The night air refreshed me as I left Charles's house and started up the street. I had gotten to the corner when someone tugged on my chef's jacket. I spun, leading with a backward round house kick. Thankfully, Andi was shorter than the typical street thug and I barely grazed the top of her head.

"Andi! What are you doing? Where did you come from?" I yelled. "And grabbing my jacket, I could've knocked you on your ass, hurt you."

"Are you crazy? What the hell you doin comin outta that devil door?" she yelled. "And I ain't following you. I seen you go in the house and I got worried. That place is creepy. Did you even look at the door, all the shit on it?"

I looked at Andi and saw concern, far removed from the usual rough exterior she portrayed. She wore the shirt I had given her and appeared to have bathed since the night in the kitchen. Her long hair was pulled straight back and tied in a pony tail, her slacks dirty and slick with wear.

"Don't you have a jacket? The nights are getting cooler and that shirt isn't enough to keep you warm."

"Quit trying to be my daddy. I never knew my real one and don't need one now."

"Yeah, well I don't need a momma so why are you following me?"

"I weren't following you, dumb ass. I seen ya, that's all and…"her voice softening, "maybe I was curious what you was up to."

"And maybe you were hungry?" I said.

"Everything ain't always about food. Jesus Christ, is food all you think about?" she said, her voice loud, her face defiant.

"What do you know about Jesus Christ? If you're going to use his name maybe you should understand what it is you're saying."

"I learned all I needed to. I went to church plenty. I'd pray and pray and guess what it got me. I'd go home and that son of a bitch step daddy would get my momma drunk and then come in my room. Make me do them things I told you, and if I refused he punched me, hurt me, you seen the scars, and then still climb on top of me. Sometimes he would drag me into their room, make me look at my momma all drunk and messed up. He'd tell me 'why I want a pig like her when I can have you.' He was mean and nasty but..."

"Stop, I get it," I said.

"It don't make it no better just cause you don't want to hear it."

"What are you doing tonight? Where you going?"

"I ain't doin nothing, like always. I thought you said you was a street kid? I stay on the move until late. Then I meet my girls and we find a place to sleep. It's better that way, havin three or four of us together. Don't want no more than four of us cause it draws too much attention, like we are a gang or somethin. Even when them other girls went missin like I told you before, there's always more to take their place."

"I told you I was on the street. You can believe what you want. Look, I'm headed to my apartment. You want to walk with me?"

Andi started walking down the street without answering. I caught up to her and we walked for several blocks before I asked her, "Where do you sleep most nights?"

"Why you ask me stuff?" Andi said, walking without looking at me. "Most of the time me and the other girls walk over the levee and the tracks by the big warehouses on the river. There's one with a broke door. We always get in. But we got to get out by the time the workers show up. Sometimes, if there ain't no ship to unload, they don't come. We can stay there longer. Just depends. They got stacks of old sacks that used to have corn in em. We can make a bed with the sacks and cover up when it gets cold. It's dirty but we feel safe there, cept for the bugs and all, but we make do."

"What about the young boys? I see them walking around, too. Do y'all hang around with them?"

"Not much. They usually try to scam us, get it out of us. You know. But I don't mess with em. Some of the other girls do, especially the new ones. They stupid, thinking them boys gonna help em. They ain't learned yet, you don't got no friends out there."

We walked to Governor Nicholls Street and then headed toward the river in the direction of my apartment. I stopped by the gate but Andi continued on. "Hey," I yelled. "When are you going to clean my apartment again?" She held up her hand high over her head, her middle finger extended, flipping me off, and walking away without turning around.

As soon as I entered my apartment I picked up the paper with Andi's step father's name and address on it and looked hard at the address, ignoring the name. The name I wanted to forget. Tomorrow I had business to attend to. Brother Lee had been told I was taking the next day off, but no one else. There were no questions asked and no explanation given.

Sal picked me up at seven o'clock the next morning and by eight o'clock I had dropped him off at his office and having borrowed his car, I was on the road headed north, alone. The trip took almost five hours including a break to stretch my legs and consider what I was doing and how I would do it. A character flaw, by definition, is not good. My biggest flaw might be the lack of remorse and the lack of guilt after deciding a path, and following it.

I took the long way home driving south into Gulfport after completing the business I had traveled to handle. The casino I stopped at was crowded and offered average food at best, but I was hungry and wanted to relax. The steak was served medium rare and was large enough to fill the plate. Blood-red au jus seeped from the steak onto the plate and made me feel animalistic, and rightfully so. I paid with the only credit card I owned. Before heading back to New Orleans I filled up with gas, again paying with the credit card.

A guy could easily spend the entire day gambling on the Mississippi gulf coast. I was back in my apartment before midnight.

It was one o'clock in the morning and I looked at my cell phone. I had missed a message from Maggie around nine thirty. My phone had been on silent, and as usual I had forgotten to check it during the day. Maggie had left a message asking if I would stop by, but it was too late to respond.

The knocking on the door was faint at first but as sleep left me and my eyes struggled to open the pounding became louder and louder. Seven-eleven showed on the digital clock by my bed, too early for visitors but the knocking persisted. I normally sleep in boxer shorts, no shirt, no pajamas, and sometimes no boxers. Using my feet I kicked the sheet off and sat up on the side of the bed. The knocking persisted. "Wait a minute," I yelled, "and stop banging on the door." I moved downstairs from the loft, crossed the living room wearing baby blue boxer shorts and opened the door.

Maggie stood stoically in front of the door, her arms crossed, and tapping her foot. Behind her seated on a bench in the courtyard was Terry's niece. Alexis was leaning back supported by one arm while she rubbed her stomach with her other hand. She wore a one piece dress, flower print, predominately red with varying shades of yellow and green. The dress stopped at mid calf, exposing nothing even with her legs parted.

"Anything you want to tell me?" Maggie asked. She did not look at Alexis but instead cocked her head slightly toward her. Her lips formed a tight straight line and her eyes bore into me.

"You can't be serious," I said. "I mean you can't seriously think I…"

"I'll tell you what I think," she said while using both hands to push me back from the doorway into my apartment. She closed the door using more force than necessary causing a loud slamming noise to echo throughout the courtyard. I imagined what Alexis was thinking.

"I think you've been avoiding me." There was a pause, and then she added, "That's what I think."

"I haven't been avoiding you but our schedules are out of sync. I'm busy when you have time and you're busy when I'm not. Or you're sleeping by the time I finish at Brother Lee's. You've always told me how important your work is, how much those young women and mothers mean to you, so I stay out of the way." Maggie moved toward me and wrapped her arms around my waist, placing her head against my chest.

"Tell me who your pregnant friend is outside, and if it's even close to what it looks like then lie to me. Don't tell me it's your baby.

I would have stepped back if Maggie had not been holding me so tightly. At a momentary loss for words I cleared my throat and stifled a grin. "I suppose I might have lied to you once or twice but not since I left Hope Haven, and not since we found each other again, so I'm not going to start now." Maggie pushed me away and glared at me. "The lady outside is Terry's niece, the lady I told you about," I said. "She came here from Tennessee because she *is* pregnant, not to *get* pregnant. I've only known her a couple of days."

"Remember our agreement?" she said, approaching me and again wrapping her arms around me. "If either of us wants out or finds someone else we'll tell each other. No regrets and no lies, remember?"

"Yes, I remember." Maggie hugged me tighter and then looked up at me. Her face had a mischievous appeal to it. Her right hand moved from behind me and entered the front of my boxer shorts. She took me with her hand and gently stroked, stared into my eyes and opening her mouth, nibbled my unshaven chin. I grew in her grip and she stepped back without letting go.

"I know your weakness," she said kneeling down and pulling my shorts to my ankles as she did so. Her breath was warm as she teased me, causing my knees to bend ever so slightly.

"Stop," I said grabbing her hand and pulling her to her feet. Without letting go I turned and pulled her behind me, heading up to the loft. She was half undressed as we approached my bed. As I turned around to face her she pushed me to the bed where I fell onto my back. I watched her remove the rest of her clothes. My excitement was still prevalent so without saying a word she straddled me and I was inside her. We thrashed together for almost ten minutes, intensely taking and giving from each other. Her release flooded me and sent me over the edge causing my own climax. There was nothing I could do to prolong it.

"Don't move and don't say anything," she told me. I lay for five minutes feeling the energy drain from my legs, the tingling sensation in my feet subsiding. Maggie rolled off of me onto her back, her breasts rising with each breath as she inhaled deeply.

"There's something I don't understand," she said. "How is it you can be a chef, cooking all that food, tasting it, and still keep the body of a teenager? No fat to speak of, your ass still hard and an abdomen that ripples when you exert yourself. And you did exert yourself I'm happy to say."

"It's genetics more than anything else. But I still go to the athletic club on North Rampart Street, perform Tai Chi, work out and do some kicks on the heavy bag, and follow the routine Mr. Chin taught me."

"Ok, but what about all the food? You're always cooking and dreaming up new stuff and I'm sure you eat it."

"Not as much as you might think," I said. "I taste most of it but it's more like eating five or six small meals in the course of a day. I seldom eat big meals anymore except when I cook for you."

"Well keep doing what you're doing," she said. "It works. And so does this." She grabbed me again and moved her hand softly back and forth until I was hard again. I moved on top of her, entered her and we repeated our performance until collapsing with exhaustion.

The shower was too small for both of us but we managed. It was ten o'clock when Maggie and I walked out of my apartment. Terry, Jerry, and Alexis stood in the courtyard and waved as we walked up the path to the gate. Alexis smiled and I was sure her eyes followed me as I opened the gate and turned up Governor Nicholls Street.

I walked with Maggie toward her office on Ursuline Street. The lower section of the French Quarter, closer to Esplanade than Canal Street, was typically quieter, less people moving around, and more enjoyable than the area of the Quarter where most of the businesses were. Few tourists ventured into the more residential section and a mid morning walk became leisurely, as if miles away from the craziness of Bourbon Street even though it was, in reality, a few short blocks removed.

"There's someone I want you to meet," I said as we approached Maggie's office. "Remember the door with the disturbing carvings, and the man who was leaving when we stopped there? Well, turns out he isn't a bad guy. He was in the restaurant the other night. I introduced myself and we wound up having a long discussion about lots of things. I think you'd like him."

'And why is that?" she asked. "He was rude, not the type of person I want to get to know. Plus, anyone living behind that door is not someone I need to meet."

"It's not what you think. Anyway, keep an open mind. He's graduating from medical school so he might be able to help you with the shelter."

"He's a little old for medical school but ok, I'll keep an open mind." She paused a moment obviously choosing her next words carefully. "I'm supposed to not say anything but I guess you can be told. Scatback came to see me, told me you said he would be able to get some help from me, maybe some 'schoolin'. He said he wanted to be smart like Chef T." She waited for a response but I remained quiet. "I told him it wouldn't take much."

"That's about right, use me for my body, insult me and then kick me to the curb."

"Seriously, he didn't want you to know. I think he wants to surprise you later when he gets into a program. I told him I'd help. There's a GED program I can help him with. He'll have his diploma in less than a year if he works at it."

I thought for a minute and then said, "What about the young girl I told you about? Her name's Andi, did she come see you?"

"No, I haven't seen her." Disappointment showed in my face. "Travis, like Brother Lee told you, can't save them all."

CHAPTER EIGHTEEN

Three days later Tater showed up at the back door of the restaurant and standing outside motioned for me to join him in the alley. Accompanying him was a female detective, short blond hair, five foot seven and maybe a hundred and fifty pounds.

"Travis, this is detective Arnold. She's been with the department fifteen years. Handles mostly domestic violence but also is our liaison to other police departments. Seems she got a call…

"Tater, I can speak for myself," she said. "Call me Julie, unless I have to arrest you." She did not smile nor offer her hand. Instead, she moved back a step and eyed me up and down. Without asking she took my hands and examined them closely. "My guess is he used gloves," she said, still holding my hands.

"Let's cut the bullshit, Julie, and tell me what you want," I said.

"Ok, let's start with the typical questions. Where were you three days ago?"

"I took the day off, drove to Mississippi, the gulf coast, played tourist." The truth, but not the whole truth.

"Did you borrow a black Ford Explorer from Sal Salvo? You are friends with Sal, right?"

"Yes, and yes." Curtness, almost defiance, dominated my tone.

"Travis, you better lighten up," Tater said. "Short evasive answers usually translate to guilt."

"Maybe they mean you guys need to tell me what the hell you're up to," I said staring at Julie even though I was answering Tater.

"Sal told us you borrowed the Explorer Thursday, said he picked you up early and you took the vehicle after bringing him to his office, said you didn't get back until late that night, almost eleven. Then he drove you back to your apartment. Does this all sound about right?"

"Sal's an old friend. I've helped him, he helps me, simple as that."

"Mississippi State police got a call from a lady, hysterical and babbling into the phone about a black car, Louisiana license plate, had the number and type of vehicle. We traced it to Sal and he says he loaned it to you. The thing is, it was about an hour north of Jackson, not on the gulf coast."

"Half the cars in Mississippi have Louisiana plates. People make mistakes with plate numbers all the time," I said, feeling stupid and trying hard to hide my nervousness.

"Travis, your alibi doesn't cover the entire day," Tater said. "You're lucky Julie is my friend. She got the call, ran it down to you having the car then called me. She's been in Brother Lee's with me, seen you cooking, and knows we're friends. But she has a job to do and like it or not, I'm still a cop."

Julie put her hand on Tater's arm to quiet him then said, "It's like this, even though I think you could tell the story better than me and Tater." She watched me for a reaction but got none. "The husband gets home from work about two in the afternoon, works at the dairy and goes in real early. Somebody jumps him in the yard and does a number on him."

Julie paused and Tater spoke. "Somebody beat him unconscious, but that wasn't good enough. Then this "somebody" proceeded to stomp his nuts and dick so hard, so brutally, and so many times it left the guy in a coma. EMS takes him to the hospital. The doctors tell the wife they can't save the guy's testicles. She's sobered up by this time and tells them to cut it all off. The guys a fucking eunuch." Tater took a step closer to me and said, "Anything you can tell us about this?"

"I guess it must have hurt," I said. "A lot."

"The real problem," Julie added, "the guy's still in a coma. Severe trauma to the body can cause it to shut down. The guy might die. Then we have another issue, much bigger than a beating."

I flinched enough to make her smile. I hadn't thought about him dieing, but I needed to make sure he never hurt Andi's sister or anyone else again. Tater took Julie's arm and turned away from me. They spoke softly to each other for several minutes then turned back to me.

"You got proof you were on the gulf coast?" Julie asked.

"Yeah, I got a receipt for gas and a receipt for dinner at the casino."

"You and I need to have a serious talk and soon," Tater said. "For now, stay close to town."

Julie placed her hand on Tater's chest, gesturing him to stay put, then took me by the arm and led me several steps away. Whispering into my ear she said, "I know it was you, and I'm sure I can guess why. If I wasn't into women I'd give you a kiss. You better pray this guy lives, and there better not be a next time. Cover your tracks better. Tater cleared the GPS in the Ford." Julie slapped me on the ass and walked back to Tater. "We'll file the report," she said.

I had been stupid, and I was angry for being so stupid. After beating Andi's stepfather, and doing so with no remorse and no guilt, instead wishing it had happened sooner, my adrenaline had coursed through my body like a freight train on a downhill run. It had consumed me and when I drove off all I thought about was getting to the gulf coast, a casino or two, and calming down. The GPS with the address Andi had given me was far from my mind. Julie had been right about one thing. The gloves had been thrown away in the bathroom of the casino.

CHAPTER NINETEEN

A week had gone buy and it was late October. I had seen Maggie once since our tryst in my apartment. The restaurant had been much busier than usual even with the high tourist season typical of this time of year. It was Monday night, nine o'clock and the restaurant was thinning out.

Brother Lee stopped me from prepping for the next day's special. "Your new friend is back," he said. "Second time this week. He's sittin out there by hisself."

I walked to the door and looked out on the dining room. Charles was seated at the same corner table, a cup of coffee in front of him. I watched Becky place a bowl of bread pudding on the table and as he looked up I waved, turned and walked back to Brother Lee.

"His name is Charles. I think he's a good person. Why'd you tell me he was here?"

"Cause he axed me to, that's why. Guess he want to chat with ya."

I approached Charles and he motioned for me to sit. "What brings you back here? It can't be the bread pudding and coffee," I said.

"Well I don't know why not. It's some of the best in the city, except maybe for the bread pudding soufflé at Commander's Palace."

"That almost sounds like a compliment," I said. "The truth is all of us chefs steal from each other, some more blatantly than others. The bread pudding with the whipped whiskey sauce came from Visko's. I got it from Kirk, a customer who worked there years ago before they closed down. He used to come in and complain about the desserts. One day he gave me the recipe and I made it. It's been popular ever since."

"Well, wherever it came from it's exceptionally good, but you're right, that's not the main reason I came in." Charles stopped, took a bite and said, "I'm curious about your time in Hope Haven. I'd like to discuss it with you and wanted to ask you to stop by, maybe have another brandy."

"It's been real busy lately and I've still got all the prepping to do for tomorrow. I won't be finished for at least another hour and a half. But I've got an idea if you're not in a hurry." I pulled my cell phone from my back pocket and called Maggie. Charles listened to my side of the conversation.

"What did she say?" he asked.

"She'll be here in about fifteen or twenty minutes. I'll introduce you when she gets here."

Maggie walked in and went straight to the kitchen. We talk-ed for a few minutes before I walked with her to the table where Charles sat, introduced them and went back into the kitchen. By eleven-thirty all was ready for the next day.

"I'm leavin. You and them friends gonna have ta lock up," Brother Lee said. "I've had enough and don't want ta socialize. I got the morning but don't go being too late. It's been crazy busy round here."

I joined Charles and Maggie at the table and I would have thought they were old lost friends. They were speaking freely as I approached.

"You sure you two never met before," I said.

"You didn't tell me Charles had been a priest."

"I figured it was up to him if he wanted to tell you. I didn't tell him you were almost a nun, either."

"What?" Charles said. "You were a nun!"

"I was getting to that part," Maggie said. "And I was never a nun," she paused. "But I got real close. The stories I could tell, but then I guess you have plenty of your own."

"I do indeed," Charles said, "but most of them tame. We priests didn't do as much as we were accused of. Big days for us were to dress up in Hawaiian shirts, head to a town far away and act like civilians. I don't think we fooled anyone."

Maggie's laughter was interrupted by a loud banging on the front door of the restaurant. "We're closed," I yelled, turning toward the door. Tater was looking through the glass, standing with a uniformed cop. The flash of the patrol car's blue lights caught my attention. Maggie was close behind me as I unlocked the door and opened it.

"Travis, we've got a situation," Tater said. "I need you to come with me."

"Tater, what's this about?" Maggie asked, her voice rising as she moved next to me.

"Maggie, you and your friend need to go home. Travis, you need to come with me. I'll explain in the car."

"Charles," I said talking over Maggie's shoulder. "Please walk Maggie home. I'll contact you as soon as I can." I turned toward Maggie and said, "Tater's an old friend. Don't worry, I'll call soon."

Tater's unmarked car was parked in front of the police unit with the flashing lights. He opened the passenger front door and motioned for me to get in. We drove several blocks with the patrol car following, lights off, Tater not speaking.

"Tater, what's this about? Did the guy in Mississippi die?" My stomach churned as I asked the question, afraid of the answer.

"No, that piece of shit is still alive. His wife finally told the authorities the truth. What a piece of work. I wish you had killed him," Tater said. "Except I guess it wasn't you."

"Then what's this about?"

"We got a dead body. It's a young girl, maybe fifteen or sixteen, hard to tell."

"And why does this concern me?" I asked.

"Travis, I'd bet my badge this has nothing to do with you but I don't get to make that choice. I'm sticking my neck out a mile for you as it is. My brass wants you downtown. You're a suspect and they want to question you. And they want to do it, now."

"Slow down damn it. Why me, why am I a suspect?"

"Homicide got a call a couple of hours ago. A ship had docked at a warehouse down by the Esplanade wharf. The workers coming in for a night shift to unload found the body. The coroner's office rolled on it thinking it was a run away, most likely an overdose or another suicide. But when they got there it was worse than they thought. The body had been dead for at least two days, maybe more. The river rats had gotten to it. Ate most of her face away, can't even tell if it's a girl except for the body. It's one of the worst I've seen. The coroner called because the girl's throat was bruised and her neck was broken. Somebody strangled her and then made sure she was dead by breaking her neck."

"Tater, what aren't you telling me?"

"She had one of those shirts y'all wear at the restaurant. And this one had Brother Lee's name stenciled on the inside."

My heart started beating fast as I stared out the windshield. "Tater, you can't think I did this?"

"Don't matter what I think. This don't look good, Travis. I saw the homeless girl in your kitchen one time and couldn't say for sure if it's her or not. Looks about the same age, same size, but can't be sure. I work homicide, not juvenile. I see em on the street but don't pay much attention to em. But we got a murder, and I'm involved.

"Well it matters to me what you think. Tater, do you believe I had anything to do with this?"

"I know you didn't. But homicide is looking for someone and it points to you first. I promised to bring you in for questioning. They didn't want that because we're friends, but I insisted and pulled it off. Let me tell you what's gonna happen. They're gonna slam you from all sides, keep at you for hours trying to trick you up. Oh it'll start nice and friendly at first, some small talk then a few questions, but if you don't outright confess at the beginning it'll heat up until they have what they want."

"What about a lawyer?"

"That's the thing, they'll tell you it's just a few questions and you'll go along with it because you want to help. Even the guilty ones try to cooperate at first. But they'll keep pounding away. If you can't produce a rock solid alibi, and you can't because we haven't nailed down the exact time of death, it might be a long time span you've got to alibi up for. So, they'll keep at it."

"I want to see the body," I said.

"No you don't. It's too gruesome. Travis, this is a young girl with-out a face, a mass of bloody pulp and tissue, and the rest of her torso is the same. I'm not even sure she has eyes left. And please don't tell me you'd recognize the body. God *Damn it* Travis, don't tell me that," he said, slamming his open palms against the steering wheel.

"Tater, listen to me. Andi was in the restaurant a little over a week ago. It was late and she came to the kitchen looking for food. You heard what a smart mouth she has. She made a comment, I don't remember what, and I answered back. She made a move for the door. I grabbed at her shirt, it ripped almost completely off. She removed the rest of it and stood there. But then I threw her a chef's shirt and told her to put it on. That's it, all of it. Nothing happened. I ran into her a few nights later on the street. We walked for several blocks, she flipped me off while walking away, and I haven't seen her since."

"We've got a dead body, Brother Lee's shirt, and you. This is ugly." Tater pulled up in front of headquarters. "You dodged a bullet the other day because Julie took a liking to you. I hope you can dodge another one." Two detectives waited for me to get out of the car.

It was seven in the morning when I walked out of headquarters. As I approached the corner of South Broad and Tulane to catch the bus Tater pulled up along side of me. The passenger side window rolled down. "Get in," he yelled.

"You were right," I said after getting in. "They slammed me for hours asking the same questions over and over. Two detectives and they never let up. I told them I wanted to cooperate…"

"They don't give a shit if you want to cooperate, they want the truth and they're used to getting what they want," Tater said.

"Whatever happened to the good-cop, bad-cop routine? They were both bad," I said looking out the side window.

"They're all good cops, and they're all bad cops, depends on what side of the table you're on." Tater glanced at me and said, "You want some coffee or maybe breakfast? You look exhausted. We can do Katie's. I'm buying."

"I am exhausted, but my story never wavered. I told the truth and I'll tell you what I figured out? They have no witnesses and no way to refute my story. It took all night, but thankfully they gave up."

"They never give up," Tater said. "They let you go knowing if you was guilty you'd screw up and they'd get you. You're their only suspect and they ain't looking for another one."

"Tater, can you get me into the coroner's office? I need to see if the body is Andi."

Tater turned the car around and headed back toward the coroner's office. "You ain't gonna like it, but yeah, I'll get you in. Good thing we haven't eaten."

The coroner's office was cold and sterile. The lighting was clinical, no ambience at all, then I figured it out. No emotion. Don't get comfortable, don't relax. We walked into a room with several stainless steel tables. Drain lines ran from the table to the floor and into a square cutout where the body fluids emptied into hazardous waste containers. A large, movable exam light was over each table. There was a tray on a rolling cart with an assortment of instruments of odd shapes and sizes and looked like they were from an old Frankenstein, horror movie. I didn't want to imagine what they were all for. A body lay on the middle table covered by a sheet. I remained still, not approaching the table.

"I tried to warn you," Tater said. "You can still change your mind."

An assistant coroner walked in wearing green scrubs and a white lab coat. She grabbed the sheet, looked at me and when I nodded she peeled the sheet back. It was colder in the room than outside in the hall and even still, looking at the lifeless body on the table my palms were sweating, my breathing increased and I began to sweat as if some volcanic force deep inside was rising up. My face flushed and I tried to swallow, but my mouth was dry.

I stepped closer to the table and looked down on the young body. Andi had always stood next to me. Was this body the same height? The build, at least what was left of it, was similar, hair about the same color but so dirty it was hard to tell. She was young which was about all I was certain of. I was angry at myself for not having paid more attention to Andi. Even when her shirt ripped off in the restaurant I had averted my eyes, purposely not looking at her. I remembered she was thin and small breasted. Then I remembered the burn scars.

The arms had been reduced to little more than bones and ligaments as almost all of the flesh had been eaten away. They lay next to the upper body. The shirt, what was left of it, was blood stained. It was from Brother Lee's restaurant, and definitely the one I had given Andi. But I didn't want this to be her. Please God, I thought, why Andi?

Tater and the doctor said nothing. I forced myself to look at her face. Most of the flesh was missing, eaten by the wharf rats. Her lips and nose were gone and her teeth flashed in the glare of the exam light. The rats had consumed most all of the skin and facial tissue. Tiny patches of flesh remained, but most of the tissue had been eaten away in clumps exposing the high cheek bones. They had eaten around her eyebrows, scratched at the eye lids and destroyed most of the eyeballs. Dark holes, voids, remained where her eyes had once glistened. The face was macabre and would haunt me for a long time.

"It gets worse, but I think you've seen enough," the coroner said. "Much of the upper torso is in the same condition as her face. The rats got under the shirt but didn't get to the lower extremities because of the tight jeans.

"I'm not sure," I said, still staring at the corpse. "I should know. I wanted to help Andi. I thought I cared and wanted to do good, find her a place to stay, get her off the streets. But I can't even tell you if it's her."

"Are you kidding me?" Tater growled. "Her own fucking mother wouldn't recognize her."

I turned away repulsed with myself, looking at the floor, searching for an answer to this. "Who would do this?" I asked looking at the doctor. "Why would someone do this?"

"Let's step outside," she said taking me by the arm and leading me to the hall. "I never get numb to this but I've learned how to deal with it." She paused and then spoke more softly. "The young ones, they're the hardest to handle. We don't see too many of them but then, one is too many. You never hear about most of the bodies we recover because they've either died from exposure or a drug overdose...some are obvious suicides. All tragic, but nothing news worthy I'm afraid. However, this young lady was murdered."

"What about the young girl they found hanging in the warehouse? The newspaper said it was suicide. Why did she make the paper?"

"Like I said, most don't but sometimes the paper will fill up some space. I didn't handle that autopsy but talk around here was straight forward. Suicide," she said.

"Who could do this, murder this young girl?"

"Might have been a sex act gone wrong. Usually there's a reason and almost never are they a random act of unprovoked violence," she said.

I had been so absorbed I had failed to look at the name on the lab coat. Dr. G. Cousins was stenciled in script above the left breast pocket. "Do you mean she was raped?" I asked.

"Not necessarily. A rapist wouldn't take the time to put the clothes back on her. They typically run away as soon after as possible. She was still dressed when they found her. But young girls are targets of pedophiles, rapists, even sadists and it usually involves some kind of sex act. We won't be certain until we finish the autopsy and get all the lab results. We X-rayed the body as you see it. We identified the broken neck and examined the tissue enough to conclude this was murder. I'm ready to disrobe the body and finish the autopsy. Look, I'm sorry if she was your friend. I'll treat her with respect, but I've got a job to do."

While listening I had been able to regain my composure, but it was soon replaced by anger as I thought of what Dr. Cousins had said. "Tater," I said turning toward him. "You *know* I had nothing to do with this." Dr. Cousins stepped back and looked at Tater.

"You mean he's a suspect," she said. "Detective, why didn't you tell me?"

"Because he *isn't* a suspect," Tater paused. "Not by me. We've been friends since Travis and I were young teenage boys. He's not capable of doing this. But he works at Brother Lee's restaurant, and the shirt on the girl came from there. And this big dumb ass keeps messing with these homeless kids, giving them food, trying to help, even quoting the bible to em. He won't take good advice and leave them alone."

"Tater, you better find this guy before me otherwise, I will be a suspect. That is, assuming you find his body."

"I told you he was a dumb ass," Tater said looking at Dr. Cousins. "You just confessed to a possible future crime *and* you did it in front of a witness."

"I've eaten at Brother Lee's a few times," Dr. Cousins said. "The food is good."

"Chef T at your service," Tater said.

"Let me know the next time you come in. You've been very helpful, I won't forget." I looked at her more closely. Although conservative and somewhat plain in appearance, in another setting, another mode of dress she would be very attractive. I guessed her to be late twenties, dishwater blond hair, deep blue eyes and a pert nose. I promised myself to pay more attention. I thought of Andi and cursed myself for not having looked more closely at the person.

CHAPTER TWENTY

I was no good to anyone for several days after the trip to the coroner's office. Maggie had tried to help, Brother Lee told me to take a few days off, and Tater checked on me twice a day. Three days later the real anger settled in and I quit feeling sorry for myself. Andi was gone and I was helpless to do anything about it, but I wouldn't let it go. I'd try harder to make sure it didn't happen to someone else. I wasn't sure how, but I'd try.

Friday morning I awoke after the first good night's sleep in those three days. I showered, standing in the hot water until it turned cool. The shaving cream was smooth on my face, the stubble of whiskers prickly against my hand as I applied the foam. The mirror held my image and I stared back, ashamed of the days I had wasted. Each stroke of the razor brought a fresh feel to my face, changing my appearance and my outlook. At seven o'clock I was leaving my apartment, dressed in check pants and chef's jacket headed to Brother Lee's.

"Travis?"

I turned. Terry stood in his doorway holding a cup of coffee. He wore men's pajamas, blue with red vertical stripes. "No pink robe this morning? Don't tell me you're changing."

"Oh my God, you are better, aren't you," Terry squealed as he rushed toward me. "We have been *soooo* worried about you. And no, smarty pants, I'm not changing. This is for Alexis. She knows I'm gay but the blatant display drives her crazy. You would not *believe* how touchy pregnant women can be. Did you know she sits between me and Jerry on the sofa? And won't move."

"That is not true," Alexis said, walking out the door into the courtyard. "Well, it's true but not like he thinks. I feel more secure sitting between two men, even if they are gay. It's comforting."

"Well why didn't you say so. I thought you were upset with me."

"No, I get it Uncle Terry," she said. "I just don't want to hear the moans and groans from the bedroom, and you two are far more adventurous than I care to imagine."

I looked down staring at the brick pavers of the courtyard, shaking my head and refusing to smile. "I think I need to get going. I've missed too much work this week and…"

"You better start eating some of your own cooking," Alexis said. "You look like you lost ten pounds you didn't have to lose. Your cute butt is disappearing."

"Alexis! What is wrong with you girl? You're pregnant and …"

"I *know* I'm pregnant," she spoke back, louder than necessary. "The hormones are all out of whack and my body is going crazy. One minute I'm cold then the next I'm hot and imagining all kinds of wicked thoughts, thoughts which got me in this condition in the first place. Get out of here Chef Tee-EEE before a really good thing happens to you."

I tried to control it but I turned red. My ears tingled and they blushed with heat. "I think you're complimenting me," I said.

"Don't flatter yourself too much. Even Jerry is starting to look good."

"You brazen hussy," Terry said in a shrill voice while heading back into his house. "I need some more coffee."

I was unaware I had been staring at Alexis's ever growing belly when I heard her clear her throat. "There is no way you find this appealing," she said.

"No, well I mean, I don't…that is…" I composed myself and said, "What I was thinking is it will be nice to have a baby around here. I can't get the image of the young girl who was murdered out of my mind. And well, a new life is growing inside you. It's a nice vision, and it helps. That's what I meant."

Alexis approached me and moving to the side to avoid pressing her belly against me, wrapped her arms around me and hugged tightly. "Travis, sometimes I'm scared, real scared," she said.

I turned up the alley and walked toward the back door of Brother Lee's restaurant. I slowed my pace when I noticed LeRoy Bertrand, dressed in his wildlife and fisheries agent uniform, standing by the door, speaking to someone inside.

"What's going on?" I asked while walking up to LeRoy.

"I got a call early this morning. Agnes Vu is headed up this way with a big load of seafood." He turned his head and looked into the kitchen. "And I'm trying to convince Brother Lee to help me."

"Help you how?"

"Sort of like a sting operation. I want him to buy the seafood from her and then I can walk up, make the bust and arrest her for selling seafood without a state license."

"Why get us involved? Why not stop her on the highway and arrest her?"

"Because she hasn't done anything wrong, yet…and we tried once already. She said she was donating it to a church which was a lie but we couldn't prove it. This way, we catch her, and Peter, too."

I shook my head, disapproval in my face.

"Travis, it's the law, and it's for her own good."

Brother Lee stepped outside, followed by Scatback. "You ok, boy?" he asked. "You ready to work?"

"You been sick?" LeRoy asked.

"Travis knew the young girl what got murdered. He been taking it kinda hard."

"You can do your job, but I'm not going to be a part of it," I said. "If you want to help them get a license, get all legal and such, then I'll help."

"You think I haven't tried? Neither of them wants to get a license. Peter avoids me, disappears when he sees me coming and Agnes doesn't want to be bothered. If they'd cooperate then none of this would be necessary."

"I don't get it, LeRoy. How are they hurting anything?"

110

"Travis, Brother Lee, I've told you we have a black market problem. The waters off south Louisiana have some of the best and most abundant seafood in the world. There are people out there catching it illegally and selling it by the tons. They offload their boats into larger vessels and it's gone within hours. I'm telling you, tons of fish and shrimp, even some oysters. But oysters are harder because they have to be harvested in shallow waters, close to shore. And the owners of the oyster beds patrol them closely, but even still, some of them get robbed."

"Something's fishy here," I said. "And yeah, I'm being a smartass."

LeRoy motioned for me to follow him as he walked away from Brother Lee and Scatback. I looked at Brother Lee, shrugged my shoulders, and followed LeRoy. He stopped at the end of the alley and turned back toward me.

"You're too young to know this so let me explain a few things to you. Back in 1974, when we pulled out of Vietnam, the US brought in thousands of Vietnamese people who wouldn't survive under communist rule. They were spread out all over the country but more than a few settled in Louisiana. Agnes was one of them. Those like Agnes who made a living fishing settled near the water. It's all they had ever learned so it made sense they'd fish here. The problem was they didn't know the laws and didn't want to obey them anyway. They fished where they wanted with no regard to limits, took oysters from private beds, and did pretty much as they pleased. They even used illegal gill nets and were catching too many undersized fish. It got real bad down in Plaquemines. People were getting hurt, were missing, a few were killed. The department had too much to handle so we called in the feds. Eventually it settled down and we got a handle on it. Agnes and some of her people survived and learned how to get along."

"Some of this I've heard but not all of it. Where are you going with this?"

"Agnes knows more than she lets on, like maybe who the black market guys are. And if she doesn't, I'm sure Peter does."

"Why Peter? He's quiet and to himself, and old. He doesn't look like he would know much," I said.

"I agree except Peter is a real mystery. I checked on him, researched his background. There's a section of his early life missing. He went to school in Cut Off, the nephew of a local fisherman. Finished school there, inherited his uncle's place, got a social security card and a driver's license in the name of Pierre Thibodaux years ago but goes by the name Peter. Pays almost no income tax and stays real low under the radar. No hospital records except for once, about ten years ago, he went to the emergency room, got stitches in his hand, paid cash and left. But the real mystery is there are no birth records on him. He is supposed to be from around Crowley, but nothing exists on him. The computers are pretty sophisticated these days and you can find almost anyone but not Peter, least ways, not his early life."

My cell phone rang and I looked at the screen. Maggie was calling. "Hey, I'm talking with LeRoy Bertrand. I'll call you right back."

"Well I'm glad you're sounding better. OK, call me back. Charles and I have been worried about you."

I paused, digesting "Charles and I" then turned back toward LeRoy. "I get it. You want to arrest Agnes and Peter, then threaten them with jail unless they cooperate, be your informants. Is that it?"

"Yeah, that's about it," LeRoy said. "Travis, I want to help them and I will, but I've got a job to do. This black market is multi-faceted, bigger than I can tell you about, and too damn big to ignore. We have to shut it down, whatever it takes."

"It stinks, LeRoy. And I don't like it." I turned and walked back up the alley to the kitchen. I dialed Maggie's cell phone. It went to voice mail and I didn't leave a message.

An hour later I heard LeRoy use his radio to call for back up. Peter and Agnes were standing outside in the alley with Brother Lee when two, dark green, four-wheel drive pickup trucks with Louisiana Wildlife and Fisheries emblems on the doors pulled up, blocking the alley. It was sickening to watch the agents hand cuff Peter, then Agnes, and lead them to LeRoy's car and put them in the back seat.

Brother Lee was more upset than I. He paced around the kitchen, stopped and stirred the shrimp Creole while staring into space, oblivious as to what was going on around him. Scatback stayed out of the way and remained busy wiping the same counter over and over.

"I feel like a damn snitch," Brother Lee yelled. "I wouldna done this in a million years. No sir."

"This is gonna work out. LeRoy doesn't want to put them in jail, but I wish he wouldn't have used us to get what he wants." I looked at Scatback and said, "We should have a good crowd for lunch. Let's make sure we're ready so we can keep up."

By two o'clock the restaurant had settled down, the rush was over, and Becky came into the kitchen. "Maggie's at a table, says she wants to see you." I took my apron off, threw it on the counter and walked into the dining room. Maggie and Charles were seated together drinking coffee.

"We've been worried about you," she said. "You weren't answering your phone. I came by your apartment but it was dark. I assumed you wanted to be alone, but Travis, being alone isn't necessarily the best thing for you."

"I'm ok. It was tough for a few days but I'm better. How'd you know I was here? I haven't been in the last few days."

"Charles has been calling each day, asking if you had gotten back to work. Today Becky said you were here. He called me to meet him for lunch."

"What can I do to help?" Charles asked.

"Do you know a good lawyer? My friends are gonna need one."

I told Charles and Maggie the story of Agnes and Peter. It helped talking to them but for some reason I was bothered. They looked too comfortable together. It was then I realized I was threatened by Charles. Jealousy gnawed at me like a tooth ache and I questioned why I was feeling this way. I was relieved when Maggie asked me to stop by after work.

The Friday night crowd had been slow and I had more time than usual to help Scatback. I showed him the ratios for the different sauces typically used in a restaurant. The béchamel sauce was one part butter, one part flour for the roux and then eight parts warm milk.

"Sometimes we sweat some onions in the butter first," I told him, "sometimes we don't depending on what we're making. Add salt and white pepper and you've got it." He was mesmerized as it came together. "There are about thirty-one fundamental ratios for cooking all the basic things such as soup, bread, pasta, sauces and more. You'll learn. It's not difficult."

"It don't look near as hard as I been thinking it was."

"Yeah, well don't tell anyone our secrets and they'll think you're a great cook." I said. "Tomorrow we'll work on New Orleans style barbeque shrimp. And it doesn't have anything to do with regular barbeque sauce. Usually it's served in a big bowl of the sauce with lots of French bread. Instead, let's you and me come up with a different way to make it. How about Scatback's barbeque shrimp pizza? We'll serve it on flat bread, lots of thickened sauce, peeled shrimp, and cheese. Your first signature dish. Whadda ya say?" His face lit up and his gold tooth flashed as it reflected the harsh fluorescent light of the kitchen.

Maggie was waiting for me when I knocked on the door. It was practically written on her face and I could tell this was not good. She hugged me and kissed me on the cheek, took me by the hand and led me to the small sofa.

"I want you to be honest with me," she said.

"I think I always have been."

"Charles asked me to go to dinner with him. We had such a good talk at the restaurant. It was all so natural, like we'd been friends for years." Maggie paused, "I turned him down, but it made me think."

"Did he ask about us?"

"No, he had no idea about us. I told him we were good friends and had been for years, since your time at Hope Haven. And… we had an arrangement. I told him I couldn't go with him. He was such a gentleman. He apologized, can you believe that? He hadn't realized he was intruding."

"I guess this is where I'm supposed to be honest," I said.

"Travis, I care deeply for you, I think I even love you, but I've been lying to myself. I was sure nobody would want anything to do with an ex, almost nun. I had convinced myself of this. You're so much younger than I and you need to settle down, maybe have a family. You can't have that with me. When Charles asked me out it was different. He and I have many things in common besides our faith and the path we originally followed, although faith is a big part." She reached for my hand and I did not pull back. "I hate to admit it but the truth is…truth is I used you. Oh, I didn't realize it at the time but it's still the truth. I used you to feel young, to feel good about myself, and to feel like I was somebody. That was wrong, but it's the truth." She squeezed my hand tightly. "I'm sorry. I so desperately want you to understand, and for us to be friends."

"Is this what friends do, hurt each other, make excuses for what they've done, be *brutally* honest then ask to still be friends?" I watched her eyes water, her lips purse together but she didn't look away. I squeezed her hand, lifted it up and slammed it on the sofa. "What happens if it doesn't work with Charles? Are you going to come running back seeking comfort, wanting to *be* somebody?" I regretted my words instantly but didn't apologize. "Your timing stinks. First Andi is murdered and now you want to play house with someone else."

"You didn't let me answer," Maggie said. "I have no expectations of Charles except to be treated nicely. Travis, I'm drawn to him and I can't explain it. I also sense it is time to let you go. I was selfish and took advantage of a young man when all he was doing was trying to find his way. I became an obstacle in your path. I didn't realize all this, or maybe chose to ignore it. If it doesn't work with Charles then I will reenter the order, become a nun like I intended many years ago."

I stood up and paced back and forth in front of the sofa. "That would be a mistake. You do too much good work to give it up to become a nun. Besides, Charles *is* a good man. He'll be good to you. So… I'm leaving. I'll get over it and we'll be friends. But not at this moment. I've got some blood letting to do."

Maggie moved to get up as I walked to the door. "Don't. I'll let myself out. The night air is cool and I need a large dose of it."

I considered walking to the river, do some Tai Chi on the rocks, or maybe throw myself in. Instead I made my way to my apartment, showered, changed and walked back to Bourbon Street, drinking a large beer in less than two blocks as I made my way to Hard Times Gentleman's Club. I have almost never frequented the strip clubs. Living and working in the French Quarter changes your perspective. It's as if all of us working there are connected, but tonight was different. First Andi, then Agnes and Peter, now Maggie, but I pushed it all from my mind and thought of one thing. Myself.

"Hello Rufus, got a seat for me inside?" I said. Rufus, a large white man in his late thirties, wore his traditional tuxedo. He works the door of the club and has bounced more drunks than any ten bouncers on Bourbon Street. There is a strict hands off, do not touch the ladies policy and Rufus never compromised it.

"I told you before, I always got a table for you, Travis. But, I never expected you to take me up on it. Are you okay?" He extended his bear claw sized hand and I grasped it firmly, feeling like a small boy shaking hands with an adult. "Follow me." Rufus led me inside, passed in front of the bar, up two steps, and opened a gate ushering me through. He pulled a chair out at a small round table in the VIP section of the club. "Sit here, I'll have Darlene come take care of you."

I strained to hear him over the loud dance music, nodded and sat down, not sure of what he had said. He walked to the end of the bar where a lady in a tight and revealing uniform stood, a drink tray spinning on her index finger.

Rufus had eaten at Brother Lee's so often he was considered a regular. We had met one night several years ago as I walked home. He tossed a drunk out of the door of the club and knocked me to the street when doing so. I had taken the fall on purpose, going with the momentum of the reeling drunk, timing my fall rather than absorb the brunt force and risk injury. He apologized over and over but I had not been hurt. It had been comical and I laughed about it. I invited him to stop by the restaurant, told him I'd fix him a special plate, and the next day he took me up on my offer. He became a regular, usually dining early in the evening before the crowds, always coming alone, and always with a large book. His reading choices varied but he once told me Pat Conroy was his favorite author. One evening as he sat reading a book and sipping coffee, I approached his table.

He placed the book on the vacant seat to his left, did not look up but I noticed his eyes were misty. *The Lords of Discipline* was on the chair. He blinked several times, looked up at me and told me it was unconscionable what one man was capable of doing to another.

I had never visited Rufus at the club even though he had invited me many times. It was obvious he was pleased I had accepted his offer, but I think also slightly confused. I turned and less than ten feet away was the side of the stage exclusive for the VIP section. A young girl, barely eighteen, danced, gyrating to music of her choice. Her skin was porcelain doll white, she had short blonde hair, wore bright red lipstick, a sequined G string and nothing else. Two butterflies were tattooed on her lower back and she was oblivious to her surroundings except for the music. There were two other people in the VIP section. An elderly gentleman, at least sixty, sat at a table close to the stage, and with him was a woman dressed in a business suit which generously covered her knees. Her dark hair was pulled back, she wore small glasses, appeared to be late thirties, and was distinguished in her appearance.

The lady from the end of the bar approached, placed a drink on my table, bent over me and said, "My name's Darlene. That's a scotch and water made from Rufus's special stock. It's on him. He said to keep you happy, and I always do what Rufus tells me." She stood up and winked at me.

I handed her a twenty dollar bill and she tried to refuse it. "I insist you take this," I said. "I'll settle up with Rufus later."

She opened her mouth wide and said, "Ha!" I noticed the sparkle of a tongue ring as she exclaimed. I stared, transfixed on her tongue. The quizzical look on my face caused her to bend over again and place her mouth less than an inch from my ear. "It's a tongue ring," she said, hotly breathing the words across my ear and down my neck. "And it ain't to fix a lisp." The oral implications were evident in her tone.

The music was more than loud, a hard driving noise, reverberating against the walls of the club. It was obnoxious but it helped me forget Maggie, at least for the moment. But each young dancer sashaying across the stage reminded me of Andi. The next dancer was barely five feet tall, flat breasted and looked no more than twelve years old, though I was sure she had to be at least eighteen. A picture of Andi's stepfather flashed in my mind as I thought of her younger sister. Not anymore, not with him, I thought. Turning away, uncomfortable with the look of adolescence, my attention was drawn to the man and woman. A dancer with large breasts had been called to their table and was straddling the woman's legs. She reached for the lady's glasses, removed them and placed them on the table. Holding her breasts apart she leaned into the women and pressed them against the woman's cheeks. The older gentleman laughed loudly, took several bills off the table and placed them in the garter belt of the dancer. It was dark in the club but I was able to see the woman smile. Rufus approached my table and sat in the large, overstuffed chair to my left, not blocking my view of the dancer and the lady.

"You must have a good reason for being here tonight," he said, leaning close to me, talking loudly over the music. "And it's none of my business. But if you need anything speak up. How's the scotch?"

The music stopped and the juvenile looking dancer disappeared behind the curtain from which she had entered. Background music, playing at considerably lower decibels, started.

"Ten minute break," Rufus said. "So I came over to check on you. It's impossible to talk when the girls are dancing."

My eyes traveled to the man and woman. The dancer was seated with them, talking, her hand on the ladies knee. "They appear out of place," I said.

"Happens more than you'd think," Rufus said. "Tourists in town for some convention, I didn't ask which one. The guy came up to the door, asked if his lady could come in. I told him the dancers prefer her and he laughed. Pressed fifty bucks into my hand and asked for a table away from the crowd. Said he didn't want anyone bothering his lady friend." Rufus stared at the couple and the dancer removed her hand.

"The last dancer looked too young to be in here."

"Yeah, but she's twenty-two. I checked her closer than the others. Making money to pay for college, she graduates in May from Loyola with a degree in social work. Nothing like some first hand experience."

"It's creepy, she looks so young. I'm not comfortable looking at her," I said.

"She's good for business. Lots of these guys are reminded of their first sexual experience. It usually happens at a young age, playing doctor or whatever they call it. The boys are ten or twelve, the girls the same age, usually neighborhood kids playing together. She, her name is Abbey, reminds them of their first time. Big turn on. But you growing up in Hope Haven with no girls around, you wouldn't make the connection."

"How do you know this stuff?"

"That's the funny part. Abbey told me, said she got it from her psychology classes. It's largely a fantasy and your typical guy is basically harmless. I don't question it as long as there's no trouble. She makes more money some nights than the other girls, so it doesn't bother her. I've learned she has an open mind." Rufus looked around the club and said, "Break's almost over."

Looking at the couple again I saw the large breasted dancer sitting on the lap of the lady. "I thought there was a no touching rule in here."

"The ladies can touch, the men even like it when they play. But strictly hands off for the men. If they don't follow the rules they get bounced. I run it tight around here, less trouble that way."

Darlene brought my third drink and again refused to take any money. She stood by the table longer than necessary. Rufus gave her a look, and with a down turned mouth as if pouting she walked back to the bar. "Watch out for her, she likes you," Rufus said. "And she doesn't like many who come in here."

Rufus rose from his seat, looked around the club again and with his large outstretched arm made a motion for someone to come his way. "I got to get back to the front door." He stopped half way to the bar, looked down as if talking to someone, and without looking pointed in my direction. Abbey poked her head around Rufus's large frame and then disappeared again behind him. As he moved to the front door Abbey walked up to my table. She wore her hair in two pig tails, one on each side of her head, had big, dark, painted-on freckles, and wore a school girl uniform. She sat in the same chair Rufus had used and stared at me, expressionless.

The music blared before we had a chance to speak and a new dancer came out from behind the curtain and started her three-dance set. Abbey got up, moved closer to me and began dancing, seductively removing her school uniform. She mouthed words but the loud music made them unintelligible. She came closer and spoke directly into my ear, "This dance is on Rufus."

I'm sure I made a fool of myself. I lost track of the drinks after seven or eight. Darlene was bringing them faster than I could drink, but I tried. The last thing I remembered was Abbey on my lap and the large breasted dancer from the other table straddling Abbey, performing the same dance she had for the convention couple.

CHAPTER TWENTY-ONE

My mouth was dry and tasted like I had licked the gutters on Bourbon Street. Opening my eyes happened in slow motion while my pulse throbbed. It started at my feet and reverberated up my body culminating in an explosion inside my head with each beat. I was extremely warm, heat radiating onto my back. Movement in the bed caused my head to jerk up then fall back to the pillow with an explosion, my eyes closing as I moaned. I was afraid to try to turn over, and my body was refusing to cooperate. She cleared her throat.

"Are you awake," she asked, the soft sound of her voice familiar.

As I struggled to move onto my back I felt the waste basket, usually positioned by my bed, move and then heard it hit the floor. The mattress dipped as she shifted her weight. "Ugh," she said settling into her new position. She was not small. Abbey came to mind and I thankfully dismissed the thought sure it was not her. "You okay?"

I lay still, my head pounding and aching worse than a recently broken nose. I didn't nod but instead mumbled words even I couldn't understand. Fearing the worst, whatever it might be, I closed my eyes and rolled onto my back, waiting for the inevitable. My hand came to rest on a towel. Pulling hard I removed it from beneath me and covered my face with it. She sat up in the bed next to me and adjusted herself while a large mound of warm flesh pressed against my side. Slowly the towel was pulled from my face. Opening my eyes I stared into Alexis's face. "Good afternoon," she said.

Trying to scramble from the bed my foot caught in the sheet covering us. I tumbled to the floor grabbing my head, the pounding accelerating with the rush of adrenaline. The room spun around several times until I sat up. Holding my head to no avail, the ache increased as I moved. Alexis, the sheet around her waist, her large, round and tight breasts with dark areolas exposed, leaned toward the edge of the bed and said, "I'm proud of you. As drunk as you were I thought sure you'd be vomiting most of the night. I put the towel down because there was no way you wouldn't pee in the bed. But you surprised me, no vomit, and no pee."

"Alexis, why are you naked in my bed? What happened last night?"

"Well I tried to fight you off but you wouldn't take no for an answer. Kept calling me Maggie, except for the time you mumbled on about Abbey. I didn't give in, it was more like rape, yeah that's it, more like forced sex."

I grabbed the bucket, sure I was going to vomit. "I'm sorry...I...I don't remember..."

"Stop! Nothing happened last night. I was funnin with ya. You were so drunk that little soldier of yours couldn't have answered the call to duty anyway. You were so cute."

Alexis's confession did not make me feel any better but the nausea passed and I put the waste basket on the floor. My confused expression caused her to laugh.

"What happened was this brute of a man, wearing a tuxedo no less, carried you into the courtyard. It was four-thirty and I was up dealing with this," she said, pointing at her large stomach. "This child is *not* on my sleep schedule and moves around, a LOT. I was awake and heard the commotion so I looked out the back door. I saw him lay you down, take your keys and open the door. I tried to resist but being so damned nosy I asked him what he thought he was doing. Anyway, he explained the whole story to me, how it was his fault you got so drunk and all. Said he works at Hard Times Gentleman's Club." She paused, "Seriously Travis, Hard Times? It ought to be called Hard UP. A little pregnant humor." I gave her no reaction. "So, he puts you over his shoulder and walks up the stairs with you. I couldn't believe it, I mean what are you, six foot two or three, couple hundred pounds or more?"

"I'm six one and one eighty nine last time I checked."

"Hmm, I thought you were bigger," she said, eyeing my naked body and enjoying herself too much at my expense.

I put the waste basket between my folded legs in an attempt to cover myself. "Why are you in my bed, and naked, especially if nothing happened?"

"I told Rufus, that's what he said his name is, funny name, too." She stopped, obviously thinking of Rufus. "Anyway, I told him I'd take care of you. I had visions of you throwing up and choking to death. Not that I was able to do the Heimlich on your drunken self, but I was too scared to leave you alone." She waited as if expecting a thank you. "Humph, must have been maternal instinct kicking in. And you're naked because I undressed you not wanting you to pee in your clothes. *I'm* naked because between your body heat and this built in heater I'm carrying, well, I was burning up. Jesus, I thought I was on *fire*," she said, pausing to move closer to the edge of the bed and look down on me. "Don't flatter yourself, it was more me than you causing the heat."

"So nothing happened last night, I mean between us?"

"Look, I still have on my granny panties."

I looked without realizing it and then turned away. "Wait, you said good afternoon. What time is it?"

"It's almost three o'clock, in the afternoon. Don't worry, Uncle Terry called the restaurant, said you were not well and wouldn't be able to make it. Brother Lee was concerned so you need to call him later." Alexis moved her legs over the side of the bed and sat up. "We need to get you showered and cleaned up. Then you can tell me about Maggie and Abbey."

"I can shower by myself. Besides, it's barely big enough for me, much less you in your expanded condition."

"Come on, let's see what we can work out," she said while grabbing her nightgown and rising from the bed."

It was dizzying walking down the stairs, as if I had been turned around a dozen times before descending. Alexis walked behind me

123

holding my hand. The room stopped spinning by the last step and my balance was restored, the pounding ache gone. We stood in front of the shower. "There is no way we both fit," I said.

"Okay, then you first but I gotta tell you, I'm disappointed."

"Alexis, I think I can manage by myself. You don't have to take care of me anymore."

The look of rejection was evident on her face. "You're being selfish, Travis. What about me?" she asked.

"I…don't know about you. What do you mean?"

Alexis looked at me, her lower lipped quivered and she began to cry, silent tears ran down her cheeks like dew in the morning down a windshield. The silence was broken by guttural sobs which got louder the more she tried to stifle them. "I wanted my back washed, that's all. I can't do it myself anymore," she said between sobs. "And Uncle Terry is no help. I'm helpless…and I'm scared."

Without thinking, without remembering I was naked and she wore only panties, I reached out and hugged her tightly, bringing her close to me. Alexis tried to put her arms around me but her extended belly limited her reach to my back, her hands separated at least six inches and unable to touch. And then it happened. I looked down, my eyes wide and face turning red. "I…I…don't understand. I drank so much last night my blood should be too thin to clot much less…I'm sorry. God, I'm so embarrassed."

Alexis stopped crying and stared, then looked up into my eyes. "I'm not sure what to say. I think this is a compliment but…" She paused, and made the situation worse by laughing. She leaned against the shower stall to support herself, the laughter subsiding but producing new tears rolling down her face.

"Turn the cold water on," I said indignantly.

"Not a chance BIG boy. I want a shower and *you* are going to wash my back."

CHAPTER TWENTY-TWO

It was five o'clock in the evening; I had washed Alexis' back, rubbed her shoulders and promised to do so again, soon. She had gone back to Terry's and Jerry's place and I was hungry. Tater was waiting for me when I walked out of my apartment. His facial expression told me more than I wanted.

"Travis, I hate to do this but we need to go back to headquarters."

"Why? Why me? I answered all their questions too many times already. Nothing's changed since I was there last time. Tater, I didn't do anything. I'm upset Andi is dead and I don't want to discuss it anymore. Do I have a choice?"

"Technically, yes. You can refuse to come with me. They'll issue a warrant for your arrest on suspicion and pick you up. You'll get a lawyer and, well you get the point."

"Some choice," I said. "Stop at the restaurant first, I need to tell Brother Lee where I'm going and when I'll be back."

The ride to headquarters was quiet. Tater hadn't been told any-thing except to pick me up and bring me in. I was too angry to discuss it with him and he was conflicted with doing his job or helping a friend. Street lights were coming on as darkness descended on the city. Tater parked on the street and he and I walked up the stairs into police headquarters. This time Tater accompanied me into the interrogation room.

"You're not a suspect at this time," Detective Gravois said.

I looked at her with suspicion. Her name tag read Pam Gravois. She was tall, maybe five feet ten or so, thin but muscular in a wiry way, the type of person who is much stronger than they look. She appeared to be in her early forties, her skin a light chocolate color and hair cropped close to the scalp, neat like a mini afro from another era. I thought how tough it must have been on her going through the academy twenty years ago, female, black, and alone in a white man's world.

"Then why am I here?"

"Detective Conrad, I think you call him Tater," she said suppressing a smile, "thinks you can be of help. He said you lived on the streets for a short while after running away from Hope Haven."

"Yes, but a long time ago. That life's behind me," I said. "And for the record I didn't run away. They were shutting down the boy's orphanage so I left. I was almost eighteen."

"I understand, but you're still involved with "that life" to some extent. Is it true you've tried to help some of these kids?"

"A few over the last couple of years. I had hope for Andi, had a feeling she wanted help but was afraid to ask. But even worse, she had trouble taking the help. I was getting close, she was coming around more." I looked down at the table, "But it doesn't matter now."

"Travis, this is simple," Tater said, "we're trying to clean up the Quarter, get these kids off the street. As cold as it sounds, they're bad for the tourist trade. But more than that, the street is bad for them. You're the exception. Most of these kids don't make it. And we think this is more than an isolated incident. Whoever did this might do it again."

"You relate more to these kids than the average person," Detective Gravois said. "We need your help. Keep your eyes open, see what you can pick up and tell Tater whatever you find out. The department will determine if it's important. Can you do this?"

"So you think I'm innocent?"

Detective Gravois looked at Tater and said, "Yes, and Tater bet his detective's shield on it."

Tater and I got back in his car and headed up Tulane Avenue toward the river. "You okay with all this?" I asked.

"Yeah, I'm okay with it," he answered. "Travis, you had nothing to do with Andi's murder so betting my shield on it was nothing, no risk. I want to make sure we catch this person before it happens again."

My stomach was churning and my hunger from earlier had turned ravenous. I had not eaten since the day before and was feeling weak. "The alcohol from last night has worn off and I could eat a house," I said.

"I got the cure," Tater said. "Let's head up into the Irish Channel, stop at Parasols and get a couple of roast beef poor boys, dressed, with extra gravy."

Parasols Bar is legendary in the uptown area of New Orleans. It hosts the biggest St. Patrick's Day party in the city and has for years. We walked in and Tater was greeted like a lost son who had found his way back home. He shook hands and was repeatedly slapped on the back while we made our way to a table. I looked around noticing the place had not changed since my first visit over six years before; the same tables and chairs, same Irish flag, and the same décor. Some things are still right with the world I thought.

The next morning was Monday, November 1st, All Saint's Day. The hang over was long gone but I was not in the right frame of mind to go to the restaurant and work. It would take a few days but I was ready to start the cure. The weather was cooperating and the first day of November was mild. I dressed in gray slacks, black shoes in need of polishing, and a neatly pressed white shirt with button down collar. Leaving my apartment I knocked on Terry's door.

"Where's Alexis?" I asked when Terry answered the knock.

"I'm right behind him. Don't tell me you can't see this big belly."

"That'll do nicely," I said, admiring her long, red maternity dress. "You don't even need to change. It's a ten minute walk to the cathedral and mass starts in thirty. Let's go. It's going to be crowded but they make room for a pregnant woman."

"So you're using me to get a good seat?" she said. "Maybe I'm an atheist, maybe I don't want to go to church. And it's Monday. Church was yesterday. Guess you lost a day with your little drinking episode, huh?"

"I know it's Monday. Mass is in thirty minutes so let's go."

Alexis turned and walked away, then returned holding her purse. She waddled around Terry and through the door. "The things you do for a man you showered with."

"Stop!" Terry yelled. "I don't want to hear another word, you hear me, not another word." He glared at me and said, "And I'll talk to you later. Alone!"

Alexis and I walked up Governor Nicholls to Royal Street, turned left and headed toward the cathedral. The front entrance from Jackson Square would be crowded, and the side entrance would be used mostly by locals, the tourists not being familiar with the cathedral. It was quiet around Jackson Square except for the church goers. The previous night had been Halloween, and most tourists and some locals were recovering from the debauchery.

The French Quarter had become a bastion for festivities and Halloween was no exception. There was no doubt in my mind the night had been filled with costumed revelers drinking well into the morning hours. Thankfully, I had skipped the celebration, my intestinal fortitude not capable of withstanding another drunken onslaught such as the one I had waged two nights before.

Alexis placed her arm in mine, a signal to slow down. The few people we passed smiled and one elderly lady stopped us and in-quired as to the due date, telling us what a cute couple we were and wishing us well "with your baby". Alexis used the opportunity to hug me tightly and told the lady I would be a great father. I pulled at her and we hurried along.

"It's true, you'll make a great daddy someday. I hope you don't wait too long," she said. "As it is you're gonna be a fabulous uncle."

"What do you mean?"

"Well, isn't that the way it is down here? Everybody is an aunt or uncle, even if you aren't related. So you can be my baby's uncle."

Well, I thought, at least she didn't ask me to be the daddy. Walk-ing straight ahead I reconsidered my last thought. Maybe it would be a good thing. "Let's get to church," I said. "We can talk about the rest later." Alexis pulled on my arm slowing me down again.

We entered the cathedral through the side entrance from Pere Antoine Alley which put us close to the front. With most churches the front section is last to fill and so it was with the cathedral. I pulled Alexis along to the second pew on the right and we sat on the end. With hushed voice soft as a lake breeze I explained the catholic ritual of All Saint's Day mass. Alexis interrupted me and whispered, "Travis, I'm catholic. Just because I'm pregnant and not married doesn't mean I have no religion."

"I'm sorry," I whispered back. "I guess catholic people…"

"And quit blowing in my ear! It's driving me crazy," she said, nudging me with her elbow.

Carefully, I pulled out the kneeler and went down on my knees, bowed my head, and prayed. I prayed for Andi and my heart ached. I prayed for Maggie, and Charles, hoping it was best they had found each other. And I prayed for Alexis. The weight of being alone, pregnant, and far from home was heavy on her. She used humor and sexual innuendo to mask her burden, to disguise her fears, but behind her eyes was the truth and she couldn't conceal it completely. As I ended my prayer requests and slipped out of the zone I had entered, the presence of Alexis became evident. Sitting to my right she had also tried to kneel, but her butt remained on the pew while her knees barely touched the pad of the kneeler. Her belly rested on her thighs while nudging up against the back of the pew in front of her. A comfort came over me as I witnessed her put her trust in a higher power.

The mass was typically ritualistic and I recalled the times with Maggie as she helped me understand letting go of guilt, trusting in God, and how to achieve peace while in church. After leaving Hope Haven my attendance at church had stopped. Being homeless had caused me to become bitter and angry. I thanked God for Brother Lee. I did not ask for forgiveness for what I had done to Andi's stepfather.

Alexis and I left church after the mass, leaving by the front entrance and walking through Jackson Square. She wanted to walk telling me it was good exercise and it would help when it was time to deliver the baby. A sobering thought as the reality of a new baby coming into the world registered. Paternal thoughts swirled in my head and Brother Lee's words came back to me: "You can't save them all", but this was different and why did I feel responsible to try.

We headed down Decatur Street toward the French Market, passing Café du Monde but not stopping. "You never told me the story about Maggie, what happened, why you got so drunk, and Abbey?"

"I'm not sure you want all the details," I said, but then proceeded to tell her, even the discomfort of having watched Abbey dance naked, looking like a twelve year old. It bothered me again as if I had committed a wrongful act.

"Travis, you have much to learn about women," Alexis said. "Abbey wasn't twelve and she knows what she's doing. You have enough to deal with taking care of yourself. Abbey will be fine, she'll finish school, maybe become a therapist or even a doctor so let it go." Alexis stopped, pulled on my arm and said, "What's bothering you?"

A group of young homeless kids, all too young, had congregated at the plaza next to Margaritaville. They appeared more rag-tag than the Little Rascals; dirty, disheveled, and lost. It was unusual to see them huddled together as if projecting a solid front, secure in their group.

"I let Andi down. She could've been saved but I wasn't there for her, made it difficult trying the tough love thing. It all caught up with me so I binged. It wasn't my intent, maybe have a few drinks, but before I knew it I was passed out. Thank God for Rufus." I paused for a moment as we walked. "That's what's bothering me."

"What about Maggie?"

"I'm happy for her. It upset me at first but she and Charles look good together. She and I were using each other. Mostly it was good but it was never meant to be permanent."

"Ever make love to a pregnant woman?" she asked, as if it was a perfectly normal question.

"No. And it's not on the top of my list of things to do."

"Yeah, well why not?"

"Well, I imagined it would happen when I'm married." Her stare burned right through me. "Stop looking at me like that. Besides, we just left church."

"It wasn't an offer," Alexis said. "Yet. So tell me why not, what about it bothers you."

"I would be afraid of hurting someone if they're as pregnant as say, you, for instance."

Again Alexis stopped, an incredulous expression to her face. "I can't believe you graduated college. How old are you? I mean, really Travis?"

"What?" I stammered and paused, "I mean you for instance, almost seven months, it's fragile, right?"

"Didn't you take a human anatomy course?"

"Biology wasn't my strongest subject. English, remember?"

"Yes, and I was literature but I learned there's more than tab A goes into slot B. Jesus men are so thick some times."

Alexis and I turned left at Governor Nicholls Street. I gave up trying to use man logic and walked home in silence.

CHAPTER TWENTY-THREE

1960 near Empire, La.

Pierre had been spending more and more time at his fishing camp near Empire than at his house in Cut Off. It had been ten years since Minos had passed, he was thirty years old, and had become comfortable as a recluse. He had studied World War II in school and still read about it. The Nuremburg Trials were a favorite topic of his high school history teacher and the discussions of the atrocities had moved him to tears. He was ashamed of his heritage, but moreover was afraid of it, afraid of what people would think if they found out he was German.

Pierre often thought of his mother, young, unmarried, and eighteen when he was born. She would still be living in France if she had survived the war. An image of her face at the train station, eyes watery, lips tight, and her head held high as she handed him to the conductor. The train had not left on time and his mother waited for more than an hour, watching him through the window, not moving from where she stood. As the train pulled out of the station in Metz, she remained in the same spot, and Pierre wondered how long she had stayed, waving, fighting back tears, silently sobbing.

Perhaps his mother had survived, and Pierre reveled in believing she was still alive, but her Jewish heritage surely must have marked her for death like so many others in Europe. The sound of a boat motor broke his concentration and he moved to the door of his camp, opened it and looked out across the marsh. Two men dressed in uniforms approached in a boat with state markings on it. Pierre was unfamiliar with the men and the official looking boat. They waved as the boat nudged his dock. The one man cut the engine and the sound evaporated across the open marsh, replaced by the gentle lapping of water against the hull.

"Are you Pierre?" the agent who had been driving the boat yelled.

"Oui," Pierre answered.

"We're new to this part of the world. We transferred over from the Lafayette area. I was told you know the back waters from below Venice over to Grand Isle better than anyone."

"Who told you so?"

"Father Paul from Mount Carmel high school said he knows you from when he was a pastor in Cut Off. Said you was the guy to get to know about this area, even more than the other agents who've been here a while."

"How you find me?" Pierre asked.

"Back at the Empire marina, they told us how to find you." He looked at the other agent and said, "This here is Kenny, and my name is Lester. Our job is mostly to keep people out of trouble and make sure they don't kill themselves getting lost back here. The wildlife and fisheries agency is mostly political but it's gonna grow. One day we'll be a full force police agency, I can tell ya right now. Louisiana coast and marsh has some of the best fishing and duck hunting in the world." Lester watched Pierre, waiting for a reply but none came. He looked at Kenny then back at Pierre, "Father Paul said you're a loner but he also said you're a good man. I trust Father Paul."

Kenny got up from his seat, stretched, his arms rising high over his head, and looked at Pierre's Lafitte skiff. "Nice looking boat ya got there. My uncle in Lockport makes boats just like it. Pierre, if you need anything leave a message at the marina."

Pierre watched the agents settle into their seats, readying to shove off from the small dock. "Y'all want some café? I can make it real quick."

Lester and Kenny got back out of their boat and tied it off, walked up the ramp and into Pierre's camp. "I been back here a long time," Pierre said. "Don't want no trouble. I want to fish, make some money, leave people alone. That's all."

"Pierre, you won't get any trouble from us. Keep your license up to date and help us if we ask. We won't bother you none," Kenny said.

"A man could disappear out here for years and no one would ever know. We had a hard time finding you, that's for sure. Too many canals are dead ends. Them oil companies been tearing up the marsh, dredging, laying pipes, destroyin it. But I suppose you know more about it than us," Lester said.

Pierre nodded, took a sip of his café au lait and looked at the two agents. "I spends some of my time at my place in Cut Off. My uncle left it to me long time ago. Otherwise, I mostly be here."

The agents finished their café and walked down the ramp to their boat. "He's a good one to make friends with," Lester said. "I'd bet he knows more about these waters than God."

CHAPTER TWENTY-FOUR

November, 2004
The French Quarter, New Orleans

Brother Lee was busy in the kitchen when I walked in. Thursday, and it had been four days since my binge at Hard Times. The clock showed six-thirty, early in the morning even for Brother Lee. Scatback was busy at the sink, rinsing lettuce for salads. Neither said anything. I grabbed an apron off the shelf and tied it around my waist.

"So, what's new?"

"Boy, last one here is first to say good morning. You ferget everything I taught you?" Brother Lee said without looking away from the pot on the stove.

"Good Morning! And no, I didn't forget. Guess my mind's still on overload."

"You sure it ain't because of too much drinkin? I heard about the binge you went on the other night."

"Rufus has a big mouth," I said. "But he's right, I drank way too much. I don't remember much until late the next afternoon."

"Don't let the bottle get ya," Brother Lee said. "Ain't that right, Scatback"

His dark skin belied the blush of his face as he stood at the sink, looking down at the washed lettuce. "Too many of them project people gots that problem, for shore. But not me. No sir, one thing my momma told me too many times. Stay off them booze and drugs. I done pretty good most times." Scatback turned and looked at Brother Lee. "Most times I do good. I don't drink near as much as I use ta."

"I shared the pain," Brother Lee said. "I kicked it, but it weren't no easy thing to do."

"I haven't had a drink since that night," I said. Brother Lee threw some salt into the pot as he stirred. I stepped closer, recognizing the aroma hanging in the kitchen. "Butter beans? We haven't served those in a long time. Why the change?"

"Rufus axed for em. Said his momma made em the best. Must be true cause he's a big ole boy if I ever seen one. It's the special today, butter beans and pork chops with corn bread."

"You putting jalapenos in the corn bread?" I asked, knowing the answer.

"I ain't never seen no jalapeno growing on a ear of corn." Brother Lee dropped the spoon into the pot and wiped his hands on his apron. "Simple plain ole, down home, good cooking. That's all we need."

"You sure are easy to rile up old man," I said. "When you gonna take some time off, spend some of the money you've been making? Especially since I showed up, business has been real good the last few years."

"It been good before you got here and be good after you gone."

"Yeah, well I'm not going anywhere, understand?" I said.

"I know that's right," Scatback said. "I still got lots to learn from you."

"And you will. Did you ever go see Ms. Maggie?"

"Yep, shore did. She's helping out, too," Scatback said. "I axed her why an she just said 'cause.' She's real worried bout you," he said, stepping away from the sink toward me. "Ain't none of my bizness but she be worried for a reason."

"Okay you two. Here's the story, short and sweet. I introduced her to Charles, they hit it off right away, and I'm on the sidelines, benched permanently."

Brother Lee approached me and said, "And you okay with that?"

"I wasn't, but I am now."

The morning passed into afternoon. The more I taught Scatback the faster he learned. His knife skills had improved dramatically and it was fun to watch him work, chopping vegetables, paring fruit, and slicing bread. He could trim and prepare a roast leaving enough fat for flavor but not too much to be greasy. A stuffed pork loin was his favorite and he had learned to dress and tie it, put it in the oven and have it ready as fast as Brother Lee. De-boning a chicken would be a little more challenging, but he would soon have it mastered. If nothing else his attitude made him a natural for the kitchen.

By early afternoon we had sold out of the butter beans. I looked out on the dining room and noticed Rufus sitting at a table, reading, and drinking from a large glass of water with several lemon wedges floating in it. Scatback was moving around the dining room helping Becky clear tables and clean up for the evening. Removing my apron I walked to the stove and looked into the empty pot.

"What do we tell Rufus about his beans? The pot's empty."

"Tell him we got em if he wants em," he said. Brother Lee opened the oven door and took out a large bowl full with enough beans for two large men. Next he took out a plate with four thick pork chops and placed it on the counter. "Got them too."

Rufus placed his book on the chair as I approached. "Hemingway? I thought you had read all of his works?" I asked.

"I have but sometimes I'll read a book again," Rufus said. "Our lives change daily and sometimes our perspectives with it. What I read ten years ago would read differently today. But, sometimes not. Sometimes I simply like to read it again."

Becky approached the table and refilled the glass with water, placing a small plate with more lemon wedges next to it. "You ready to eat?" she asked, ignoring me.

"Brother Lee has his lunch already prepared and waiting," I said. "Bring half and keep the rest warm."

Becky looked at me, one hand on her hip while the other held the pitcher of water, droplets running down the side and falling noiselessly onto the floor. "And what may I bring my master?"

"Bring me a little less smart ass and a glass of water," I said as I sat across from Rufus. Becky turned and walked away before I finished speaking, her hips swayed with an intentionally exaggerated movement to defy my comment.

"That one likes you but take it from me, don't mess with the help," Rufus said.

"You took care of me last week. I owe you."

"You owe me nothing," Rufus said. "You've been taking care of me for months. Let me come in here, eat, read, take my time and never tell me anything. Most restaurants don't allow that."

"Well I never had to carry you up stairs and put you to bed because you ate too much. I couldn't do it anyway as big as you are."

"It wasn't like you, to get drunk and stupid. I figured you had a reason, the least I could do was watch out for you."

"Stupid? What do you mean by stupid?"

"Suffice it to say, men aren't allowed to dance on the stage."

It's an unnerving feeling when the mind is blank and it shouldn't be.

Brother Lee went home early at my insistence. He would be back first thing the next morning which suited my schedule. Scatback wanted to stay but I made him leave right after the dinner rush was over. As soon as Becky and Chris were finished cleaning the dining area they left and I closed the restaurant. It was good to be alone. Occasionally, late at night, I would play with changing recipes or developing new ones. Most people don't realize how many failures are incurred while creating a recipe worth keeping. In the pantry was a box I had received from a professor at the LSU agriculture center in Crowley. Inside was a variety of rice they had been working on for several years. It was jasmine rice blended with a type of long grain rice typical to those grown in Louisiana and Arkansas. There was a distinct aromatic presence to the rice, nutty but mildly so. The idea of stuffing a pork loin with the more fragrant rice came naturally to me as if I'd been doing it for years. The kitchen clock showed eleven-fifteen, too late to experiment so I removed my apron.

There was enough leftover cooked food in the cooler to make a generous portion of pork chops, Brabant potatoes and bread. The athletic club on North Rampart Street had closed at ten but I always got past the night watchmen if I approached baring gifts.

By midnight I had made my way to the club, bribed the guard, got dressed in sweat pants, and finished warming up with Tai Chi exercises meant to calm and enlighten. But this night I needed more. For an hour I abused the heavy bag with self defense techniques Mr. Chin had taught me away from the other boys at Hope Haven. Spinning back kicks, elbow lunges, open palm thrusts and various combinations delivered to the bag for an hour had exhausted me, and I crumbled to the floor, sweating but sated. The indoor saltwater pool was calling me and after a twenty minute swim I was revived.

Bourbon Street was still busy at two in the morning. My work out bag was slung over my shoulder. I made my way up the street and through the slow moving throngs of tourists who continually stopped to gawk before moving on again. The night air was cooler than usual for early November and reeked of the spilled beer, and I reveled in it.

Rufus filled the door way to Hard Times and did no more than nod as I walked by. Intimidating as he stood guard, no sane or sober trouble makers would dare entrance to his club, I was certain. I nodded back and walked on to my apartment. I might get three hours of sleep before my next task which had bothered me and lurked like a demon since Andi had been killed. The next morning I would slay the demon and start to rid myself of the guilt.

CHAPTER TWENTY-FIVE

The warehouse where Andi's body had been ravished by wharf rats was old, dirty, and as foreboding as a dark forest in the dead of winter. I had walked up Esplanade Avenue toward the river, crossed the track on the top of the levee and stood in front of the large rolling warehouse door. There were no ships docked at this wharf and no crews working inside. Though it appeared to be locked the large door was moveable and I squeezed through into the warehouse. It was more intimidating on the inside. The lights were off and hints of sunrise were evident through the ventilation spaces between the wall and roof, but almost no light entered. Standing still I inhaled the stuffiness of the quiet space. There was no need for a guard as the warehouse was empty, and no one should want to be here.

The inside of the warehouse was large and cavernous, so dark the far end was not discernable. Three hundred feet long, maybe more, impossible to tell in the darkness, and intimidating as hell for there was a presence about, maybe the rats, or maybe the homeless hiding and watching. A set of rails bisected the length of the space. I stumbled and fell, not seeing them in the darkness. A large rodent ran across my hand and I jumped up cursing. I didn't see it or hear it, but the thud against my head extinguished what little light existed and I fell again.

As if from far away I heard someone say, "Sit there and be still or you wind up like him." The voice was familiar but sounded distant. My face pressed hard against the dirt covered floor, oil stained sand caked on my lips, foul tasting and causing me to gasp for air. The voice sounded closer as the man spoke again. "You getting soft and careless, nothing like I taught you."

I rolled over onto my back, brushed the sand from my mouth, and looked at the silhouette standing over me. I barely noticed his outstretched hand offering me help up. I grasped it and he pulled, my head pounding and aching with my effort to rise. Releasing his hand I decided to sit before standing.

"I don't think you being here is a coincidence," I said.

Mr. Chin crossed his arms over his chest and said, "No coincidence. I've been following you for two days."

"Why?" I asked.

"Maybe better question is, why didn't you realize," he said.

"My head is killing me and I don't have time for games. And if you've been following me why did you let me get hit?"

"Too dark in here, didn't see him until after he hit you," Mr. Chin said. "He's right there, taking a nap."

"If he's taking a nap why were you talking to him?"

"Korean humor, so I don't feel so bad for putting him to sleep."

I got to my feet and stared down on the body lying motionless three feet from me. It was hard to tell in the darkness if the body was male or female, old or young. "How long was I out?"

"Less than a minute, but him a different story. Maybe five minutes, or more. Hard to say, I cut off his air supply with a choke hold. Sleep like a baby."

"Help me drag him outside," I said, grabbing a pants leg at the ankle. Mr. Chin took the other leg and we pulled the body to the warehouse door and maneuvered it outside. "He's young, maybe thirteen or fourteen," I said. "Hits hard for a young kid."

"Big board helped. Lucky for you he's not so strong."

I rubbed my hand over my head where the board had struck me and felt the lump. The ache was still there but less than before. The young boy opened his eyes and instantly panic stared up at us.

"Who are you and why'd you hit me?" I said.

No answer, the fear still prevalent as he tried to figure a way out of his predicament. Mr. Chin reached down and helped him to his feet, not letting go of the boy as he stood before us. "Answer him," Chin said.

"I was scared, there been bad people around here. I'm sorry, ok. Let me go and you won't see me no more, ever."

"How old are you and how long you been on the street," I said.

"Maybe sixteen, I ain't real sure. Been travelin for bout two years. Been here couple a weeks but seen enough. Got to move on, man. It ain't safe."

"You don't know how old you are," I said.

"I don't even know what month or year this is and don't care neither. Let me go. Don't want no trouble, no cops, nothin. C'mon man." He tried to pull away from Mr. Chin but to no avail. In a second he was on his knees as Chin put pressure on his shoulder, digging his thumb into the boy's flesh at the collar bone.

"Stop! Shit man, that hurts." The boy yelled.

"Why isn't it safe?" I asked.

"I been here a couple of weeks like I told you, but three girls are missing, up and disappeared. I seen em a couple of times but that's it. All the kids are scared, hiding, staying low. That's why I was in there," he said, motioning toward the warehouse. "I seen you and got spooked so I hit ya. I'm sorry so..."

"Get up," Mr. Chin told him.

As soon as Chin released him the boy ran. Chin moved to grab him but I stopped him. "Let him go. He's scared and can't be much help anyway." I watched the boy run up Esplanade Avenue and turn down Decatur Street. I recalled my meeting with Detective Gravois and her concern for the street kids. The boy said three were missing but I was only aware of Andi, and no others. I made a mental note to call Tater. I turned toward Mr. Chin. "As for you, why are you following me?"

"Maggie called Father Billy, said she was worried about you so he called me. Asked me to check on you. I watched you for a while. You got soft, and sloppy. Too easy to catch you off guard."

I thought about what he said and as usual, he was right. Getting drunk, Andi sneaking up on me, being spotted in Mississippi was all careless, and not what Chin had taught me. I had become comfortable with my life and slipped into a false sense of security when in fact, being aware had always worked better for me, helped me survive even when despondent and on the street.

"Close your eyes," Chin said. "Take a deep breath through your nose and hold it."

I closed my eyes and lifted my face upward. The warmth of the early sun cascaded over me. Exhaling, I opened my eyes to see Chin mimicking my actions.

"Come, we get café au lait and beignets," he said. "You buying."

Lacking conscious awareness is how Chin described me. Oblivious is more accurate, and rightfully so. Chin had trained me to always pay attention, always be aware to what was going on around me. It probably saved my life when I was on the street. Nobody got close if I didn't want them to. Even Brother Lee when he found me, I was aware he was there before he noticed me. It was time to become more spiritual, not religious for I am religious in my own way, but spiritual as in touch with myself, my spirit, and all that affects it.

"You're English is much better. So's your vocabulary," I said to Chin.

"Been here a while so it's best to learn the language and to speak it properly." Chin took a bite of his beignet, staring at me as he chewed, a small cloud of powdered sugar falling onto the table.

""You taught me better, but I haven't done better. Is that what you want to hear?"

"Don't want to hear nothing, want you to be safe. Don't waste your gifts. Skills deteriorate with time, you must work hard to keep them. You always worked hard."

"I'm listening, but only because you're right," I said. "Tell me, if Father Billy was so concerned why didn't he come see me? Why send you?"

"Father Billy is a busy man, lots of people need him. But since you ask, he wants to see you. You need to visit him at his church."

It was curious because Father Billy had never asked me to visit him. I had visited on many occasions, but always at my doing, often randomly, but never at his request. Chin and I finished the beignets and café au lait, talked of many things, his brother's restaurant, the family in Korea, the meaning of life which neither of us admittedly understood. The waiter, out of my view, quietly approached our table from behind me. Looking at Chin I held up a twenty dollar bill before the waiter moved around in front of me.

"You being a smart ass now," Chin said.

Chin and I walked back to my apartment, shuffling through the tourists on Decatur Street. I watched Chin move deftly, never allowing anyone to be within two feet of him, his movements oblivious to all but me. We stopped at the gate to the courtyard.

"Tell Father Billy I'll see him soon." Chin bowed and started walking down Governor Nicholls Street. "You and Mrs. Chin need to visit the restaurant, have dinner on me." Chin waved without looking back.

Leaning with my back against the courtyard wall I took out my cell phone and called Tater. "I'm not sure what's going on but Detective Gravois might be right. These street kids are spooked. Stop by the restaurant later this afternoon and we'll discuss it." At times Tater is short on words. Ok is all I got.

The gate opened easily, unlocked from when I had left. I moved through it and into my apartment. I was being watched but had no idea by whom. It was good to again be aware.

CHAPTER TWENTY-SIX

March, 1975
Empire, Louisiana

Pierre offloaded the last hamper of crabs from his boat, placing it next to the others on the dock. Two Vietnamese women tried to help him but he waved them off, shooing them away with his hands. They scurried to the end of the dock and squatted, speaking softly to each other. He watched them for a few seconds then made his way into the office to receive payment for the crabs.

"What we gonna do with them people?" Johnny, the owner of the marina said as Pierre entered. "Always hanging around, trying to get into our business. Nothing good gonna come from this."

"Five hampers of crabs," Pierre said. "All number ones, mostly males, six dozen a hamper." He looked through the window at the two women. "I don't think they mean no harm, they tryin to survive is all."

"Yeah, well I think the gover-ment should a left em in Viet-Nam, ya ask me. We already had some fights. Gonna get worse, too. Ya seen them two on the dock?" Johnny asked. "Trying to hustle tips for helping when nobody don't need no help. Can't none of em hardly speak no English either. Lots of gibberish and hand waving."

Pierre held his hand out and Johnny paid him for the crabs. "Ok, that's six dollars a basket. I'll be back with more crabs," he said, and moved toward the door.

"Keep your eyes open," Johnny shouted. "Some old lady, one of them people," he said, motioning at the two women still squatting on the dock, "done got lost or somethin. She went out in a flat boat she bought from Degas, used some of that gover-ment money they all got, and took off looking to catch some fish. Ain't nobody seen her in two days. No way she can find her way around in the marsh. Last anyone seen she was moving across the bay on the west side."

Pierre stepped outside and walked toward the two Vietnamese women. He motioned for them to follow him as he walked and stopped when he reached the hampers where he had left them. It took several tries using his arms and hands but he managed to convey to the women he wanted them to move the hampers inside with Johnny. He handed each of the women a dollar and stepped down into his skiff.

There was a slight chop on the water as Pierre sped across the bay headed back to his camp. It would take him thirty minutes to reach his dock if he went straight there, but the missing woman bothered him. After more than thirty years Pierre still perceived himself as a foreigner, an outsider. Maybe, he thought, if Minos had lived longer he would feel differently.

Pierre throttled back the engine and idled while considering where a woman in a flat boat, strange to this inland marsh, might try to catch fish. The main channel from Barataria Bay to Empire was wide and deep enough for some of the larger boats. The marsh grass was high, typically a foot to three feet tall, and thick. From a distance it was impossible to see the many small canals cut through it. Pierre had learned the canals, largely from trial and error, after years of traveling the back waters. For over an hour he navigated the canals, his skiff often hitting bottom. It was low tide and the canals had maybe twelve inches of water, sometimes less.

Pierre stood on the transom of the skiff and scanned the marsh. The sun was high and visibility was excellent, five miles or more. As the skiff rocked gently Pierre caught a quick flash of light reflected off of something that should not have been there. He started the skiff and nosed it into a small cut excavated off the canal. The skiff hit bottom and stopped. The cut was ten feet wide, too small for his skiff even at high tide, but easily large enough for a flat boat. Pierre walked to the bow of the boat and jumped down into the six inches of water, his white rubber boots sinking several inches into the thick mud. Ten yards into the cut, and nestled behind a large bush and marsh grass, Pierre saw a flat boat but no sign of the owner.

The small aluminum hull was twelve feet long and had a twenty-five horsepower motor. A lone, red, five-gallon gas can was attached and, Pierre assumed, empty. He grabbed the rope tied to the front and pulled the boat toward him.

"Hi! Hi! Hi!"

Pierre jumped back, startled by the high pitched yell coming from the small woman who had been crouched down, hiding behind the boat. He stared at her, not letting go of the rope.

"No," she yelled pulling on the back of the boat.

Pierre dropped the rope and stepped back. "Out of gas?" he asked.

A cacophony of Vietnamese, meaning nothing to him, spewed forth as the lady waved her arms. For ten minutes they stared at each other, Pierre speaking English and the lady yelling Vietnamese at him in a high pitched voice. Shaking his head he moved to the back of the flat boat and lifted the gas can. "Empty," he said. "Get in." Backing up away from her he pointed to the inside of the smaller boat. Grabbing a rope dangling into the water he started backwards toward his skiff, pulling the flat boat, and hoping she would get in. Either not understanding or simply refusing him she instead placed her hand on the side of the boat and sloshed through the water with him, taking two steps to his one. She reached with her other hand and pulled her large-brimmed, conical shaped hat, hanging from a string around her neck, over her head.

Pierre backed his skiff out of the cut, turned it around and reversed back into the small, dead end channel. Before he had a chance to secure his skiff the small Vietnamese lady had tied her flat boat to the skiff's transom and crawled aboard. It was apparent to Pierre she could handle herself around boats. A jug of water, secured to the center console of the skiff with a bungee chord, caught her attention. Pierre released the chord and handed the jug to her. She tilted the jug up knocking her hat back, and drank. Water overflowed from her mouth soaking her thin blouse as she struggled to swallow more quickly. The blouse, when wet, revealed she did not wear a bra. Pierre averted his stare.

The skiff rode well in the open water as Pierre headed for his camp. The flat boat bounced behind but the knot the woman had tied held strong and secure. There was extra gas stored under his raised camp. He would fill her tank and send her on her way. It would be faster than taking her back to the Empire marina. The March weather was warmer than usual and Pierre basked in the sun as he drove the skiff, pleased he had found her, and equally pleased to be getting rid of her. Twenty minutes later he tied up to his dock and retrieved a five gallon gas can from under his camp. Pierre stopped when he realized she was not in his boat. He looked up at the top of the stairs and watched her open the door.

"Hey," he yelled. The diminutive woman ignored him and entered his camp. Pierre untied her boat from his skiff and secured it to a cleat on his dock. He lifted the gas can from her boat and filled it with his gas. Although he was almost too big for the flat boat he knelt down by the motor, adjusted the choke and pulled the starting chord two times. On the third pull the motor started, coughing and sputtering, but started. After idling for a minute the motor smoothed out and Pierre was sure it was safe for her to return to the marina. He shut off the motor, stood and wiped his hands on his pants then turned toward his elevated camp.

Pierre made his way up the stairs and went inside. "What you doing?" he said as he watched her use an old broom, sweep dirt and dust into a small mound in the middle of the room. "Mon dieu," he said in French, meaning 'my God', a phrase his mother had used often, and one he still used all these years later.

The Vietnamese lady stopped when he spoke, looked closely at him and said, "Mon non est Agnes." Her accent was not right, but her French was correct.

Pierre responded, "Mon non est Pierre." She moved closer to him and waited. They had exchanged names. Hers was Agnes, which Pierre found strange. Tentatively he spoke in French and a line of communication was opened.

"Why do you speak French?" he asked.

"The French occupied Vietnam for many years before the war. They had a huge influence on our culture with their food, music, dancing, even their language. Many of the older people speak French. It is almost a second language to many Vietnamese."

"Why do you speak French? Real French, not the bastardized form the crazy people here speak," she said.

"My mother was French, born in Metz many years ago," he said, intentionally not mentioning he, too, had been born in Metz.

For several hours they spoke, telling each other much of their life stories. She was a widow of a fisherman, for a little more than four years, bore three children but had become separated from them with the fall of South Vietnam and the mass exodus. She did not know if they were alive, and if so where they might be. Pain was etched on her face as she spoke of her family.

Pierre said, "How did you come to have the name of Agnes?"

"Agnes good American name," she said. "I'm American now. I'll never go back to Vietnam." She looked at him and said, "Why Pierre? I think maybe's not your real name."

"It's the name I use, given to me by the man who raised me since I was twelve. He was a real Cajun."

"You look like Peter to me. I'll call you Peter, good American name, good biblical name," she said.

Pierre considered the name for a moment. He gazed out the open door and concentrated on the marsh stretching for miles. The horizon formed where the sky met the marsh and he nodded. Peter, he thought, Peter who denied Christ three times before the cock crowed twice. And he, Pierre, who denied his heritage, denied who he was, perhaps Peter is fitting he thought. She'll be gone soon, and if calling him Peter made her leave sooner then so much the better.

They spoke until dark which was too late, and unsafe, for Agnes to return to the marina. Pierre cooked fresh fish for their supper and served it with plain rice. Agnes cleaned up, a respite for Pierre since he was used to doing for himself without help since Minos had died. Agnes spent the night with Pierre but did not share his bed. The next day they returned to the marina in his skiff, sold another five baskets of crabs Agnes had helped him catch, and together returned to his camp. That night she shared his bed and never left him.

CHAPTER TWENTY-SEVEN

November, 2004
New Orleans, La.

Detective Gravois had asked me to keep my eyes open, pay attention and contact her if I noticed anything suspicious with the street kids. The suspicious part, I thought as I walked to the French Market after closing the restaurant, is it all looks normal. There were new kids in the Quarter, ones I had never seen before, which in itself was not unusual. I was used to them coming and going. The street was hard for the younger ones and offered no easy or fast solution to their problems so they moved on, still searching, and still coming up empty handed. Andi and a few others had been the exception, staying around, not leaving, defiant but desperate.

One o'clock in the morning, and except for Bourbon Street, the Quarter was quiet. The park next to Margaritaville had half a dozen homeless kids hanging around, hitting on tourists for spare change. They were more spread out than before, not huddled together as I had seen them right after Andi's death. As a group they were more intimidating to the tourists and locals, and less likely to get the money they were shamelessly after. Individually they were pathetic, lost and afraid, not to be feared in the least but pitied, and hopefully enough to get the handout desperately sought. One kid, dressed in black which belied the dirt from weeks unwashed, held a guitar with four strings. He strummed it trying to get dollars thrown into a worn leather cap lying on the sidewalk. I crumpled up a dollar bill to keep it from blowing in the wind and dropped it into the cap. A terrible rendition of a Jimmy Buffet song warbled from his mouth and I held up my hand, motioning him to stop.

"You sing worse than you play guitar," I said. "Keep singing and I'll take back the dollar." I sensed he wanted to flip me off, or worse, but I turned and walked away before he recovered from my insult. I don't have much sympathy when it comes to these kids. Maybe it's because I was on the streets, but the truth is sympathy perpetuates their situation, prolonging it. Andi was the exception and it pissed me off to see the kids who had it better wallow in their self pity. I need to work on being more sympathetic I thought.

The gate to the courtyard of my apartment creaked as I pushed it open. It should have been locked but wasn't and I attributed this to Alexis. I locked it, turned and noticed a light on in an upstairs room of the main house. A silhouette appeared in the window, unmistakably Alexis, and opened the lace curtains. Waving I started toward the door of my place when I heard her tap on the window. When I looked up she raised her hand, motioning me to stop. Five minutes later Alexis emerged from the kitchen door wearing a thin, purple satin nightgown. Her swollen breasts strained at the material as much as her extended belly.

"I know we're like old friends, but isn't that a little too immodest, even for us?"

"It's not about modesty," she said. "I needed to feel like a woman and not like a big cow. And since we showered together…oh never mind. Open your door, I need some masculine company. I love my uncle and I'm grateful for his help but jeez, those two are more woman than I am sometimes."

"It's one-thirty in the morning. Sleep is a good idea right about now. Maybe you should try it."

"Until baby settles down I'm not sleeping. He, or she, is running a marathon on my bladder and I can't sit, stand, lie down, or get comfortable. Plus I feel like I constantly have to pee."

"Thirty minutes is all you get, then I'm going to bed," I said as I pushed the door open. Alexis stepped inside taking my hand and pulling me with her. I grabbed her shoulder and froze where we stood. "Were you or Terry in here today?"

"No, we never come into your apartment, well except that one time but not since then. Why…"

"Shsss." I waited, listening.

"Travis, what are you…"

I placed my hand over Alexis's mouth and pulled her back to me, hugging her close to my chest. "Someone was in here today," I whispered, "and they're still here."

Alexis pulled my hand away and through clenched teeth said, "You're scaring the shit out of me, and I don't have much control as it is."

I eased us back out the door and released Alexis. "Stay here," I said. The apartment was too small to have many places to hide. The loft or the bathroom. Taking a deep breath I readied myself, focused, and let the tension drain from my body. The door crept open as I pushed and a moment later I reentered, leaving the door open. Two steps to the left and I pushed open the bathroom door, flipped the light switch on and pulled back the shower curtain. Crouched down in a ball, head drooped and face hidden, dressed in black, was a small person, hiding and non-threatening. My heart pounded and my adrenaline rushed through me even more. This makes no sense I thought. "Andi?"

She knocked me back, albeit only a foot, into the bathroom wall, hugging my neck and sobbing. Andi squeezed so tightly I struggled to talk. "Easy," I managed to say.

Releasing me she wiped her eyes with both hands at the same time. "Where the fuck you been? I been waitin for hours, cramped up in your stupid bathroom."

"Where the fuck have *I* been?" I yelled. "Where have *you* been. You're supposed to be dead. I saw the body." My eyes watered and my heart was ready to explode.

Andi stepped back into the shower stall. "Dead? DEAD! What you talking about?"

"I saw the body. It had the chef's shirt from Brother Lee's, the one I gave you." Fighting the tension and taking a deep breath, I regained control.

"Well it weren't me," she said. "I gave the shirt to another girl. She and two of her friends was meetin up with some guys, she wanted somethin cleaner than what she had on so I swapped with her. The guys showed up before I got outta there so I hid. We was all in the big warehouse and these two guys came walkin in from the other side. It was too dark to see their faces but I heard them. One sounded kinda funny, like a foreigner, and the other sounded Chinese or somethin."

"Stop right there," I said. "Get out of the shower and come in here." I moved into the main room. Alexis had walked in and turned the light on. She stood with her feet spread wide for balance, holding her belly. "You," I said to Alexis, "sit on the couch. And you sit on the other end." I grabbed a chair, turned it around and straddled it backwards, resting my arms across the back.

"Hey, the baby stopped," Alexis said.

"Put your legs up on the couch. Come on, I'll make room," Andi said.

Alexis swung her legs up and placed her feet within inches of Andy. Without asking Andi removed Alexis's slippers and began massaging her feet. "I used to do this for my momma," Andi said. "After she worked all day and her feet hurt her so bad I'd rub em."

Alexis's feet were swollen and must have ached. She didn't try to stop Andi and relaxed as Andi worked. "Andi, where have you been? I thought sure you were dead. Why didn't you come to me? Do you have any idea how upset I've been?" I asked.

"What? You care, man? I was scared shitless and had to take care of myself."

"Look, start over and tell me what happened."

"Like I told you before, these three girls was gonna meet some guys but I didn't want no part of it. They was doin it for money but I said no. Ain't no man ever doin nothing to me again less I want him to. That son of a bitch my momma married done enough for free, the bastard. I'm sure he's after my little sister and ain't nothing I can do."

"You don't have to worry about him anymore," I said. "The authorities have him. Tell us what happened."

"What authorities?"

"I'll tell you later, now what happened?"

"We all was in the warehouse, me and the other girls. I was leavin but then Missy, this girl from Arkansas, got real nervous, said she needed a cleaner shirt. The one you gave me was still clean enough so I swapped with her. As I was leavin I heard them men coming so I ran to the corner where it was real dark. I was scared they would see me but they didn't. Then they started arguing over money. Missy got real mad and started walking off. It was hard to see but I could tell it was the big guy with the funny accent that grabbed her and pulled her back. She slapped at him and he took her by the neck and shook her real hard. I heard a snap, so loud it echoed in throughout the big building, but he didn't quit, he kept squeezin and shakin. He dragged her over by the side close to the river where they come through the door, and he throwed her on the ground. Then him and the Chinese guy took the other two girls that was crying, gagged em and took em off. I was so frightened I stayed there for hours, afraid to move, afraid they was still around, maybe outside by the river. Even when them big rats ran across my feet I didn't move or say nothin I was so scared."

"So what happened, after they left? Where'd you go?" I asked.

"I had to get outta there so I ran, ran down Esplanade till I couldn't run no more. Then I walked until I got to the big park. I been hidin there ever since. Cept it got so cold at night I had to leave. I was sleepin in the bushes at night and during the day I'd beg money and drinks off the guys playing golf. But I think some of em must of complained cause I started seein a few cops nosin around. So after dark today I come here. Weren't hard to get in, easy like before."

"We have to tell the police. What can you tell them about Missy?"

"Don't know nothin. Said she was from Arkansas but don't mean it was true. And might not a been her real name neither. Most of the streeters don't want to be found so they use fake names and stuff. Hell, most of em been on a milk carton or flyers posted on walls and all. For most of us...goin back is worse than almost any-thing. Cept now Missy is dead, but maybe even that's better than goin home. Woulda been for me."

I wanted to tell her dead was not better, but I thought about it and said nothing. Alexis moved her legs and sat up, her feet back on the ground and in her slippers.

"Well it's time to get some sleep," Alexis said. "But first, you stay put while I get you some clean clothes. I'm sure I'll find you something that'll fit. And while I'm gone get in the shower, use LOTS of soap, and wait for me."

It was three o'clock when Alexis had finished helping Andi dress and comb out her hair. The many knots in her hair continually stopped the comb, causing Andi to yelp. I was sure it was the first time in over a year someone had cared for her.

"Why are you fidgeting and pulling at your pants?" I asked.

"I got a string up my butt!" Andi said.

"It's a thong and the only panties I had," said Alexis. "One size fits all, well, almost all," she said rubbing her belly. "She's coming with me. There's room in the main house and those two queens will make a fuss over her when they see how pretty she is."

"Until she opens her mouth," I said glaring at Andi.

Undeterred she stared back at me, a slight grin forming and said, "How's you and your fuck buddy getting along?"

Alexis leaned in close to Andi and whispered in her ear. "What! She dumped him! After all you done for her," Andi said looking at me. "What a dumb bitch." She moved toward me and hugged me around the waist. "I'm sorry," she said, her head against my chest.

"We have to call Tater in the morning so get out of here and let me get some sleep." I wasn't sure who was helping who as I watched them leave.

I tossed and turned, the image of the girl in the coroner's office haunting me. I tried to let it go, but even with Andi being back it remained, vivid and clear. The other two girls came to mind. Who were they, where were they, and what happened to them? I needed to turn this over to Tater and let it go, but I had no confidence I'd be able to.

CHAPTER TWENTY-EIGHT

Tater showed up at the restaurant at nine o'clock. Detective Gravois was with him. We sat at a table in the dining room drinking coffee and I told them the story Andi had told me. Scatback brought us a plate of biscuits but had his head down, not looking at us.

"Do I know you?" Detective Gravois asked, directing her question toward Scatback.

"Yes'm," he said, looking up at her. "You rested me one night couple years ago."

"What for?" she asked.

"Caught me with some dope on me. But it weren't mine. One of the guys I was hangin with had it, slipped it in my pocket and made me carry it cause he been busted plenty. But I couldn't say nothin. You don't snitch on them nig…boys from the projects and live. It was my first offense, and bein underage I got off with a warnin."

"And now you're working here?" she asked.

"Yes ma'am. Cleanin and doin dishes, but Chef T is learnin me to cook."

"Then hold your head up and be proud, dammit. Nothing's worse than an honest black man sulking like he's been beat down."

Scatback walked back to the kitchen standing straight and tall.

"You gonna save him, too?" she asked.

I shook my head and started to speak but Tater interrupted me. "Let me tell ya somethin bout ole Travis here. Don't go too hard on him because mostly he can't help himself." Tater paused and I waited to see where he was going with this. "When we were about fifteen and still in Hope Haven we got this new kid come in. His name was Andrew but went by the name Slim because he was so skinny. A meek and quiet type, no trouble at all. The first night we're all in our beds and Travis looks at Slim across the room and sees him sittin up in the bed, knees drawn up to his chest. Travis tells him it's time to get some sleep and Slim, he sits there and continues rockin back and forth. Travis asks him what's wrong and Slim says "nothin's wrong," but he don't lay down, keeps rockin back and forth. So Travis gets up and goes over to Slim and sits on the side of the bed. I can't hear but..."

"I asked him what was bothering him," I said, interrupting to finish the story. "Slim told me it was always at night when they would come. I didn't have a clue so I asked him what he meant. Slim looked at me with vacuum eyes, as if remembering the terrible things that had happened. Then he said he had come from an orphanage outside of Dallas. At night one of the attendants would come take him to a small room and abuse him, sometimes more than one attendant. He said he was raped too many times to count, and when he told someone they beat him for lying. And later the same night the abuse was even worse. Slim told me things I'm embarrassed to repeat," I said. "But one night a new attendant caught two of them with Slim, and that's when he was moved to Louisiana. They didn't want a scandal so they moved him out."

"So Travis tells Slim ain't nobody gonna come take him away, ain't nobody gonna hurt him this night or any night," Tater said. "Travis tells Slim to get some sleep, said he'd stay awake and make sure. And he did. Travis sat up all night watchin over Slim. Each time Slim woke up Travis would be looking at him. He sat up the first night and each night for almost a whole week."

"I had to. Can you imagine what it must have taken for him to tell me what was done to him? A man, even a boy doesn't want to talk about that kind of stuff. Come on, Pam surely you've seen things like this."

"It's not the worst thing I've heard of with young people but it's pretty bad. What happened?" she asked.

"Travis got in trouble for falling asleep in class, but after the first week Slim settled down and started sleeping. So, there ya go, the first one Travis saved," Tater said.

"I guess I understand," Detective Gravois said.

"There was big trouble when Sister Marie found out the real reason they sent Slim to Hope Haven. The orphanage misled, no, they lied to the archdiocese of Dallas, told them Slim was Catholic and didn't want to be in a state orphanage any more. If Hope Haven had known the truth all hell would have broken loose."

"But that's not why we're here, Travis," Detective Gravois said.

"We need to talk to Andi," Tater said. "The sooner the better."

"She likes you," I said. "Calls you Tater cop. She'll talk, but give her a day to get settled."

"A day, but no more. Don't forget, we've got a dead teenage girl in the morgue, no name, no address. Laying in an ice box and *no one* to claim her."

"I haven't forgotten," I said. "I CAN'T forget."

"Calm down you two," Detective Gravois said. "Travis, I think she might be able to help. Even if she didn't see their faces she still might know more than she realizes. Standard police procedure, the right questions asked the right way, sometimes we get people to remember things they haven't recalled or been able to tell us. We'll go easy on her to a point, but we need as much as we can get. Besides, she sounds pretty tough for a young girl."

Brother Lee and Scatback were busy preparing for lunch. There was little for me to do until Becky and Chris started hanging the lunch orders in the small kitchen window that offered a view into the dining room. So I watched them work. At two o'clock the rush was over and clean up was finished.

"I've been out of sorts lately, not pulling my weight around here," I said to Brother Lee. He sat on an old wooden stool, his favorite spot, leaning against the wall next to the rear door to the alley. "It's not my style to leave you hanging but things have been difficult lately."

"Sometimes a man gets too much on his plate, not his doin, just happens. How he handles it what's important. Some run away but that ain't you. Do what ya gotta do. It gonna settle down soon. Now, we got dinner to get ready for."

I threw myself into my work and the harder I worked the better it was for me. By ten o'clock the restaurant was closed, cleaned up and ready for the next day. Becky and I were the last ones to leave and I watched as she bagged her dinner to go, grabbed her purse, and walked through the kitchen to leave by the back door.

"Your nieces have been asking when Uncle Travis is coming to see them."

"I've had my hands full, lately," I said.

"Is it true, you and Maggie, are you a free agent?" Becky asked.

I stiffened a little, uncomfortable, remembering what Rufus had told me. "Yep, on my own, plan on staying that way for a while."

Becky moved closer and placed her hand on my shoulder. "Seeing the girls might be good for you. Therapy of sorts. Up to you, but I'll bring them around soon anyway. They love to come here. Brother Lee spoils them too much, but that's a good thing." She moved toward the door after kissing me on the cheek.

"Visit the girls, nothing else?" I asked

Becky stopped at the door and turned around, shifted the bag of food to her other hand and said, "What? You thought there was more?" She tilted her head and stifled a smile, thinking before speaking. "Look, I got rid of one man...well he got rid of me, but the point is he had *way* too much baggage. You on the other hand have no baggage at all. You're free, no family, no obligations, a lone wolf if ever there was one. No thanks. I need more middle of the road and you ain't it. Sorry, I love ya Tee, but not a good idea."

Becky blew me a kiss and walked out the door. Embarrassed by my presumptuousness and humbled by Becky's straight forward honesty I made a mental note to talk with Rufus. He's in the wrong business to be misjudging women so badly, I thought.

People-watching on Bourbon Street is almost always entertaining which translates to drunks can be amusing, and there is always a lady or two willing to flash her breasts, and more, for a cheap pair of beads. After my binge I had avoided taking Bourbon Street on the way home, but feeling recovered and in control I was comfortable with the crowds, even looking forward to them. I turned and headed up Bourbon Street on the way to my apartment.

When I reached Hard Times I stopped and observed a small crowd watching three guys arguing with Rufus as he stood in the doorway. They had obviously had too much to drink, and knowing Rufus, I was sure he had not so politely asked them to leave.

It's a feeling I get once in a while, as if a demon is pent up inside me and needs to be released. I watched the three guys wave their hands at Rufus and threaten him from a distance, and my demon began to rise. They wanted him in the street where they would surround him. I found this amusing. Rufus moved down the three steps from the club onto the sidewalk, but I moved into position between him and the three drunks and held my hand up to him, stopping him from coming closer. The move confused the three as I intended. With my back to them I was sure at least one would grab me for interfering. The guy in the middle didn't disappoint me.

"Hey, what the fuck you think you doin, asshole?"

As soon as he grabbed my shoulder and yelled at me I spun, and with a slicing chop delivered a blow to the side of his neck so hard it paralyzed him where he stood, rendering him unable to move or react. With a sweeping right leg I sent him to the pavement while delivering a thrusting fist to his nose, flattening it and causing blood to flow freely. I moved my right foot back one step and assumed a ready position.

"Take your friend and leave," I said. "He needs your help. There's first aid available one block over on Royal Street inside the police station." Rufus stood behind me, towering over me but not interfering. The other two drunks grabbed their friend and lifted him to his feet, draped his arms over their shoulders and walked down Bourbon Street.

"What do you think you're doing?" Rufus asked.

"Good timing I'd say." I spoke without turning around, still watching the drunks stumble away from us.

"I had it under control. I didn't need your help."

"I wasn't helping you, I was helping them," I said, turning around to face Rufus.

"Right about now the guy with the busted nose doesn't feel like you helped him."

"They had way too much "courage from the bottle." They wanted you and weren't gonna be happy until you stepped out into the street with them. At which point you'd have hurt all three of them. This way, the one guy paid for all three's stupidity. Like I said, I did them a favor."

Rufus laughed and said, "Your reasoning defies logic, my friend. The truth is you enjoyed it. I think you like to fight. Sure didn't look like Tai Chi."

"Tai Chi with a twist," I said. "Hey, sounds like a new drink. Maybe I'll work on a recipe for you. A smooth and relaxing drink but one that will kick your ass if you're not careful."

He took a step back onto the sidewalk shaking his head. I looked beyond him. Abby was standing in the doorway of the club, diminutive and innocent looking. A knowing, wicked smile appeared and she winked at me.

"She likes you, been asking about you, wants to be your friend." Rufus turned back to me and added, "She never makes friends here."

"Can't have too many friends," I said, "but women confuse me and Abbey scares me. By the way, your assessment of women needs a little work."

Most people would feel guilty. The three guys were outmatched sober, but even more so intoxicated. Regardless, I would sleep well and never once think of them.

CHAPTER TWENTY-NINE

Tater was waiting outside my apartment the next morning at eight o'clock. Andi and I got in the back seat and he drove us to headquarters, a place I was too familiar with. Detective Gravois met us and then asked me to wait outside while they talked with Andi. It wasn't my place to disagree but I didn't like it. I paced the hall, visited the men's room, drank water from the cooler with the rusty spout, and decided I had had enough.

Opening the door and entering without knocking I said, "I thought you guys promised to take it easy? It's been two hours."

Andi turned toward me and said, "They been fine. We was talking is all. She got family in Mississippi close to where I'm from. She been there a few times so we was talking about it, girl talk, sort of."

"Sorry Travis," Detective Gravois said, "I should have invited you in. Like she said, we got carried away."

"I was telling em how it was before I left. It's better but they still got problems with the blacks and the whites. But I told em no black man ever treated me bad as that son of a bitchin stepfather of mine." She looked at Tater and said, "Then Tater cop tells me someone whooped him up somethin fierce, said he won't be hurtin nobody like that no more cause the authorities got him." She stared at me but I didn't say anything. "But I still ain't goin back."

"We have an issue here," Detective Gravois said. "Andi is a minor, and because we've established who she is and where she's from, we're obligated to tell the authorities in Mississippi."

HOUSTON NEAL GRAY

"Why?" I said. "Is she listed as a missing person? Do you have an Amber alert in her name?"

"What's an Amber alert?' Andi interrupted.

"Don't bother answering," I said, ignoring Andi's interruption. "Andi's staying with her cousin, Alexis, helping her with her pregnancy, right, Andi?"

"Stop right there," Tater said. "We get it so knock off the bullshit. Andi can stay with her *cousin*. But if we get a report then we have to act. Damn it, Travis, we are the police."

"There won't be a report. The mom's an alcoholic, and with a little luck the step dad goes to jail. You want to help? Have child services pick up Andi's sister and get her to a safe place." My anger was rising the more I spoke. "Are we done here?" I asked. "I've got to get to the restaurant."

"Almost. We have to show Andi the pictures of the body, the girl wearing the chef shirt."

"Is that necessary? Andi's sixteen and I don't think it's a good idea. Besides, the girl doesn't have a face, not much of her body either."

"It's ok, I told em I'd look. Don't think it'll help much. All I know is Missy from Arkansas."

Tater opened a file and slid an eight by ten glossy colored photo across the table at Andi. It upset me and I watched Andi closely. Her eyes opened wide and she covered her mouth, her body convulsing. I grabbed for the photo, sliding it back toward Tater. "It must be her," Andi said. "That's the shirt I give her." She turned toward me. "Let's go, please."

Tater drove us back to the Quarter and waited for me as I walked Andi through the courtyard and knocked on Terry's door. Andi rushed at Alexis as soon as the door opened, burying her face in Alexis's chest and wrapping her arms around her.

Tater insisted on bringing me to the restaurant even though I wanted to walk, needed to walk. The car came to a stop at the end of the alley. He wasn't finished with me. "I'm not as seasoned as some of the other detectives but I got a gut feeling Andi might be able to identify these guys. Keep her close and watch out for her. You

163

have any trouble, or if you even think it might be trouble call me right away."

"There's already trouble. You still have two missing girls if that boy was telling me and Mr. Chin the truth. And Andi's story verifies it. In fact, the boy was one girl short."

The restaurant was busy. Brother Lee had led me to believe all was well but they were frantic when I walked into the kitchen. It was almost eleven and they needed help. I hustled Scatback to the dining room to help Becky and Chris while I took over with Brother Lee.

The guilt of being less involved in the restaurant rightfully consumed me, so for three days straight I opened up the kitchen at six, started cooking and didn't stop until closing. I stayed off Bourbon Street on the way home and was in bed each night by eleven. I was back on track but three things still bothered me, the dead girl, the two missing girls, and Peter and Agnes getting arrested. I didn't expect to see them again.

CHAPTER THIRTY

Reluctantly LeRoy Bertrand agreed to meet me at the restaurant. The ruse with Peter and Agnes gnawed at me, but Brother Lee was as mad as I'd ever seen him. Nobody likes to be used but when it happens you at least want to feel like some good came from it. Brother Lee didn't want anything to do with LeRoy, and Peter and Agnes were not likely to ever come back.

"Travis, Peter and Agnes are fine. I arrested them, they told me next to nothing, and I let em go with a warning. But they know more, I still think they can help," Leroy Bertrand said. "It's getting them to talk that's the challenge. I did some more checking. Years ago Peter used to have a commercial fishing license, but in the mid seventies he stopped renewing it. Coincidentally about the time he met up with Agnes."

"Why would he give up fishing?"

"He didn't give it up. Peter still fishes but Agnes handles the business end. She never believed in licenses or limits. She and her husband fished wherever and whenever and as much as they wanted. It's still that way in Asia. The people there have over fished their waters and it gets harder for them to make a living. They have to go farther and farther out to catch fish. Agnes, as well as most of the others, came here and worked the same way. Agnes is one of the few hold outs. Most of the Vietnamese play by the rules and do it right. Agnes is happy staying small time, and Peter follows Agnes. Does what she wants and so far has gotten away with it."

"Ok, LeRoy. I'm much younger than you, maybe a little naïve, but it's obvious there's more to this than you're telling me. You used

165

Brother Lee to set up Peter and Agnes so how about a little more of the truth. How desperate are you guys?"

"I tried to tell you before this is bigger than you can imagine. Illegal selling of fish to restaurants is nothing compared to what's going on."

I was getting nowhere with LeRoy and it frustrated me. His vagueness was insulting. Worse was how badly betraying Peter and Agnes weighed on me. It was unlikely I would ever see them at the restaurant again considering how they had been treated."

"Ok, LeRoy." I paused while staring at him. "This is what I think. You've been taking but you haven't been giving. You've taken Peter away from me and its time for you to give him back. I won't see him again and I can't blame him. I've got questions about Uncle Tony and maybe he can answer them. So, take me to him. You and me, together, we go visit Peter and Agnes. And don't give me any bullshit about agency protocol. You can make it happen."

LeRoy's face flushed red with being challenged. "Don't push it Travis. I'll make it happen but because Tony was a friend of mine and a good man. The agency has a ride along program, usually for people involved with promoting the agency or other police departments, sometimes the feds. Not for John Q. Citizen, but I'll see what I can do."

"One other thing," I said.

"Are you shitting me?"

"I want a commercial fishing license for Peter and Agnes. I'll pay for it, but I want you to work it out. You have all the information on Peter, you said so yourself you checked him out. Do the paper work, I'll pay, and we deliver it to him on your boat. No more harassing them for your benefit at their expense."

"Give me a couple of days. Gonna take that long for the paperwork and clearance for the ride along. I'll contact you when it's all ready."

LeRoy walked up the alley and got into his illegally parked agency truck, driving off faster than normal, his anger evident.

CHAPTER THIRTY-ONE

July, 2000
Cut Off, La.

Peter looked at Agnes and said, "I've got something I want to do. It will take all day. I'll have to stay at the fishing camp overnight then come back here."

Agnes stopped sweeping and looked at Peter. "I can go with you. I no like being here alone. I can stay at camp."

"It will be a long boat ride, no fishing, and boring," he said.

"Is ok, I rather be with you."

Peter loaded up the skiff with food, water, and other supplies including a shovel. The next morning he and Agnes left at six o'clock and made their way across Little Lake into Barataria Bay and headed east. Peter had filled up the gas tank and brought two extra five-gallon cans. They would make it back to Empire with a little fuel to spare, but the extra gas was in case they used more than he remembered needing.

By noon they were several miles east beyond the mouth of the Mississippi River. The summer air was still and hot, the sun intense as it hovered above, and the cloudless sky offered no reprieve from the heat. It had been years since Peter ventured this far to the east. The fish, shrimp, and crabs were still plentiful on the west side, and he seldom had the urge to travel the waters south of Delacroix even though they were known to have abundant amounts of all he fished for. Minos had taught him to navigate all the waters, but he, too, had spent little time on the east side of the river after finding Pierre.

Peter throttled back and the skiff came off plane, slowing to a crawl, the wake sloshing forward and rocking the boat. They idled as Peter scanned the island, looking for a familiar landmark. Years of storms, tide changes, and coastal erosion had devoured the island, and what was once a playground for weekend fisherman and campers had been reduced to little more than a large sandbar. It was not surprising to Peter. The entire coast of Louisiana had changed drastically through the years and the gulf, on a daily basis consumed more and more of the marsh and wetlands.

Peter accelerated modestly toward the island until he reached the remains of the old lighthouse. The gulf had encroached upon the island and the lighthouse stood several feet deep in water. The tender's house was gone, and the rusted skeleton stood alone, abandoned and in disrepair. There was nothing left to see so Peter reversed course and idled east, parallel to the shore, hoping to find a specific tree within a mile of the lighthouse.

There was no way to be sure. So much had changed but one lone tree offered the best opportunity so he beached the skiff, killed the engine and grabbed the shovel and a plastic bag. Jumping down onto the sand Peter turned and helped Agnes out of the skiff. Shoeless, she pulled her pants legs up to her knees and waded in the water. Small in stature and wearing her large-brimmed, conical hat she looked child like, belying her fifty-five years.

"Wait here," Peter said. "I think this is it but it's closer to the water than I remember."

Peter walked ten feet to the dead tree which resembled little more than a large branch sticking out from the island. The shovel made for quick and easy work in the fine, sugar like sand. He dug two feet deep, more than he expected he would have to, and almost gave up. Time and the elements had taken a toll on the island. Maybe I'm in the wrong spot he thought when his next shovel full of sand turned up a piece of cloth barely recognizable. In five minutes he had found the remains of the items he had buried almost sixty years ago. The remnants were no more than small pieces but it was what Peter had come for. He spread the plastic bag open near the hole and placed several scraps of material, pieces of the jacket he had worn, into the

bag. The boots were more easily identified. The shoelaces had deteri-
orated but the heavy leather and rigid soles had held up much better.
Picking up the boots carefully, sure they were about to fall apart,
he examined them. The German Swastika was still visible and Peter
burned with shame as he placed them in the bag.

Agnes watched Peter as he rose, turned toward her, and walked
back to the skiff, throwing the bag into his boat. "We can eat here,"
he said. He reached into the skiff, lifted the ice chest and placed it
several feet from the water. The gulf was calm, the water smooth as
glass, so smooth it was hard to distinguish the horizon in the glaring
sun. They ate of hogshead cheese sandwiches Agnes had made and
drank sweet tea with mint leaves she had grown in a flower box
hanging on the side of the house in Cut Off.

"The bag?" Agnes asked.

Peter met her eyes then turned his toward the gulf, mesmerized
by the water and deep in thought. "A boy who should not have gone
to war," he said without looking at her.

Agnes placed her hand on his shoulder and said, "I understand
about war. I lose a husband, my children, and the greater the loss,
the more it stay with you."

Peter had been with Agnes twenty-five years and had never told
her the whole story. Minos was the only person who knew about
Peter, his early life, where he had come from, his real name, and why
he was abandoned. Minos had made Peter promise to never tell anyone and Peter had never broken his promise. Peter was seventy years
old and tired of running. He silently begged Minos for forgiveness,
and told Agnes his story.

The skiff rode fast and high in the smooth water. Peter pushed
the skiff's limits, exalting with the relief of having shared his burden
with Agnes. An uncharacteristic smile appeared as the wind buffet-
ed his face. It was almost like the freedom of confession. Agnes held
tight to her hat and marveled at Peter standing tall and straight, still
strong even at his age, and kind.

Peter navigated the Lafitte skiff into Barataria Bay but instead
of taking the canal to his camp he steered toward Empire. It was six
o'clock and they would be at the marina in forty minutes. Agnes

deserved a dinner prepared by someone else for a change, an indulgence they seldom allowed themselves, and then only in Cut Off. Agnes protested but Peter insisted.

Johnny watched Peter enter the marina and met him and Agnes at the dock, helping to tie up the skiff. "This is late for you, Peter," Johnny said to his old friend. "What brings y'all over here this time a day?"

"Agnes and I come to eat," he said. "Have a nice dinner here." Peter stepped out of the skiff on to the dock, turned and helped Agnes up, and they stood together next to Johnny.

"Over there," Johnny said, pointing across the parking lot. "That restaurant got the best food. Degas owns it. Gonna own this marina soon, too."

Agnes looked at Peter but remained quiet. Peter said, "Why you sellin to him?"

"Time for me ta go. Don't like what been happenin round here the last few years, and you know what I'm talking about, too," he said nodding at Peter. "Besides, if'n I don't sell to him he gonna build one right next to me, run me outta bizness. So, I'm sellin and getting while the gettin's good. Now, y'all go on over there and have a good dinner. I'll watch your boat. Be dark bout nine but guess that don't matter none to you. You'd find your way if ya was blind and in a hurricane."

They ate their dinner quietly as was typical for them, finished all the food, wasting nothing, ever, and were back in the skiff by eight o'clock. At nine o'clock Peter tied up the skiff to his dock and helped Agnes up the stairs to the small porch where they stood and looked out over the marsh. The sun was half set and splashed it's reflection in the still, calm waters, burned the sky a bright orange and was gone in ten minutes.

Darkness surrounded them. Peter returned to the skiff, lifted the bag from the storage compartment in the center console, and carried it to the fifty five gallon drum he used to incinerate trash. His mother surely has died he thought, and his evil father had been dead for years. Dropping the bag into the barrel he then doused it with the charcoal lighter fluid he used to start the fire in the half drum he had converted to a barbeque pit for grilling fish and oysters. There would be no flash or explosion as with gasoline. The match flared brightly as it struck, hypnotizing him for a few seconds, causing him to contemplate what he was doing. Nodding his head he tossed the match into the barrel of trash and refuse, returned to Agnes, and together, his arm around Agnes's shoulder, they watched the flames stretch from the barrel, but then diminish and disappear. The fire smoldered and would burn for at least an hour. They stood by the door, the darkness of early night and a moonless sky embracing them, and listened to the marsh come alive with the sound of the nocturnal insects and animals, announcing their presence while scavenging to eat.

CHAPTER THIRTY-TWO

November 16, 2004
The French Quarter

It had been fourteen years since my Uncle Tony had been killed in the boating accident, and not once had I returned to the waters he had patrolled. My anger at his loss had long subsided, but with still unanswered questions, and the unfairness of it all, the dormant anger awakened and rose up in me again.

LeRoy Bertrand was parked outside my apartment at five a.m. as promised. A bag of beignets rested in the middle of the seat and two large coffees had been placed in the cup holders. "Not exactly chef food but it makes the drive to Empire more interesting, especially since the sun hasn't got up yet," he said.

Empire marina in lower Plaquemines Parish was at least a two hour drive down highway 23. Looking straight ahead and sipping the café au lait I asked, "Do you have the license?"

"It's handled," LeRoy answered. "But keep it quiet. I've skirted the law making this happen. I wouldn't have done this but I'm feeling a little guilty for using you guys. Sometimes we get carried away tryin to do our job, angry with the politics and roadblocks we shouldn't have to deal with. So I've made an exception, pulled a few strings. Plus I got a *special* friend who helped me out…"

"Stop right there. You're telling me too much and more than I want to think about." The anger had subsided and excitement grabbed me as we drove across the Mississippi River Bridge and headed toward Plaquemines Parish. Why had it been so long I wondered? Two hours but over a decade away. Crossing my legs Indian style and placing my hands on my knees I sat quietly, meditating, remembering, and coming to peace.

Breaking the silence LeRoy said, "I don't get you Travis. Going off like that, not a peep. How do you do it?"

We had been driving for an hour. The sun was cresting the levee of the river to our left, washing the road and bathing the sprawling marsh with first light. "The deeper you can go inside yourself the more you can see on the outside." LeRoy didn't look at me nor respond. "I'll teach you one day, like I was taught. It'll change your perspective, even on a trip like this." LeRoy nodded as if seriously considering what I had said so I asked, "I want to hear what you haven't been telling me."

"I guess that's fair. But let me explain about the agency, and your Uncle Tony was like this to his core," he said, turning toward me then looking straight ahead. "Most of the wild life agents, not all, but the biggest majority get hooked on what we do. Louisiana has been called "the sportsman's paradise" and it's true. We all take it for granted but once you start working in it ya get caught up. The quiet beauty, the abundance of fish and game, it's almost too much to absorb. Why you think the Cajuns settled here? They could hunt, fish, and trap year round, never running out of food for their families. I love it, Travis, and I don't want nobody fuckin it up."

LeRoy's passion flowed and I listened intently, not interrupting, remembering the same passion Uncle Tony had. But I had not realized it when I was young. Traveling with him had been fun, exciting, but I was never as captured as LeRoy had become.

"You'll always have people breaking the law, going over the limit of fish or ducks, even deer. It's a problem, but a manageable one." He glanced at me again for a second. "Life here is a delicate balance of nature and the elements, and we've allowed them to get screwed up for years. The government selling oil leases, the big companies cutting up the marsh, laying pipelines from here all the way up north. And on the other side of the river, too," he said motioning with his head. "The corps of engineers dug the Mississippi River Gulf Outlet, the Mr. Go they call it, back in the sixties. It was supposed to be for big ships to have easier and faster access to New Orleans. It keeps getting wider and wider and the marsh is disappearing. One day it's gonna be a problem. More tax money, that's what this is all about, as long as we have more tax money. But we're fighting back and hoping it's not too late."

"What has this got to do with Peter and Agnes?" I asked.

"I was getting to that. Most of the agents would do anything to keep the balance of the wild life and ecosystem preserved. All of it, not just some of it."

"LeRoy, get to the point because I can tell you I ain't buying it. Peter and Agnes are not destroying the marsh."

"Let me finish. Fishing without a license is important to us. We manage it as seriously as anything else and Peter, as well as too many others, is a minor problem. But it's not the big problem. Travis, the black market is huge. We've takin to calling it the black gulf because of what's happened in the last few years." He paused to let it sink in. "We have tons of mullet in our waters. Most people consider it a trash fish and don't eat em. But the other fish, and the birds, too, eat em. Louisiana has thousands and thousands of migratory birds that fly through twice a year. They'll stop, rest and eat, then take off to Mexico and South America. When the season changes they'll migrate back north and do it all over, year after year. It turns out mullet roe, fish eggs, are a delicacy in other parts of the world. The mullet are being fished illegally, in massive quantities for the roe, and we need to stop it and fast."

"How does all this happen and nobody does anything?"

"Do you have any idea how big the Gulf of Mexico is, and how small boats are, even the big boats?"

"Needle in a hay stack I take it."

"We use informants, people who see what's going on and will help us."

"Peter and Agnes," I said.

"Well no, not yet anyway. But nobody can survive back here as long as Peter and not see and hear things."

"So you arrested him and Agnes to put pressure on them to help you. That's pretty shitty, LeRoy?"

"Not as shitty as massive fish kills and the greed that drives the black marketers," he said. "And we got a new twist to all this." He again looked at me. "Shark fin soup."

"What the hell has this got to do with Louisiana?" I asked.

"Nothing, directly, so to speak. But it's huge in the Asian market, from Vietnam to Korea, they pay big money for it, especially China. Another delicacy that's been around for years and makes big money. It's jokingly called Chinese Viagra. The Asian waters have been over fished, almost to extinction in some parts."

"And we have tons of sharks. Most people hate them and want them dead," I said.

"True, but we can't allow that to happen. Sharks are part of the balance. The slaughter is the sickening part. They don't want the shark, only the fins. They catch the sharks, cut the fins off, and throw the shark back in the water. They can't swim without the fins and they sink to the bottom and die. You have any idea how many fins you can store on a large boat? Thousands," he said answering his own question. "Thousands and thousands."

"Hard to comprehend," I said. "How much money are you talking about?"

"Not sure, but the going rate on fins is about ten dollars a pound wet, and thirty dollars a pound dry. Ten thousand pounds of dry fins is a lot of money. And ten thousand pounds is not hard to hide. No taxes or fees, big money straight into the black market guy's pocket."

"Why Louisiana? Why here and not down in Mexico or Central America where the rules are not as strict?"

"Several reasons, and simple. More sharks here because we have more fish, the big fish eats the little fish, etc. And, too much corruption down there. The government looks the other way but somebody has to pay. And it's easier to ship out of the U.S. The entire operation is pretty sophisticated."

"It stinks," I said. "How long has this been going on?"

"We're not sure but probably longer than we think. One day we get a tip and start investigating. One thing leads to another and we start putting the pieces together. It's bigger today than ever, but then that's the nature of greed. I'd guess it goes as far back as maybe the eighties."

LeRoy pulled his state truck into the lot of the marina. It was six forty five and the sports fishermen were scrambling to get their boats in the water and head out before the sun got too high. The state boat used by the agents was already in the water and tied to the dock. A man wearing white, rubber shrimp boots watched as we drove up.

"That's us," LeRoy said, pointing at the boat with the Wild Life and Fisheries decal. "And there's Degas waving at us. I called him and he had the boat put in the water for us. It beats having to wait, especially with all these guys in line scrambling, and in a hurry to launch. We keep one here and one down at the mouth of the river in Venice."

"So maybe my Uncle Tony started seeing what was going on when he was working back here."

LeRoy opened the door and waited to get out, turning toward me. "Don't go making this into a dragon to be slain. Tony died in an accident, bad luck, nothing else. I hope this isn't a witch hunt. Come on, get out and let's go. It's a good day, little windy so the water will be choppy, but it'll calm down by mid morning."

We approached the dock. LeRoy shook hands with Degas and then introduced us.

"I imagine I look like a local yokel to you, but I grew up in New Orleans," Degas said, shaking my hand. "My momma was from New Orleans and I was born there. I'm named after the French painter, Degas. Spelled the same, d-e-g-a-s but pronounced day-gah. We lived in a house a block away from the Degas house, the one he lived in when he moved to New Orleans. My momma loved his paintings so she named me after him."

"So you been back here a while I guess."

"Long time, know most of the people round here, and knew your Uncle Tony real good," he said. "LeRoy told me you was comin and said Tony was your uncle."

"I don't remember Uncle Tony mentioning you."

"Well, I keep to myself most of the time. I remember seein ya when Tony would take ya out on his boat. But I never got the chance to meet you. Anyway, y'all have a good day and be careful out there."

LeRoy said, "Wait here a minute." I watched LeRoy hurry to catch up with Degas. They stopped, talked for a minute, and LeRoy gestured at Degas as he turned and walked back toward me.

Degas turned and walked toward the restaurant behind the marina. "Come on, let's get the boat started and head out," Le Roy said.

LeRoy idled the boat away from the marina, respecting the no wake zone, but once clear he started showing off his boat handling skills. I had donned the orange life vest, mandatory state regulation, and held on as he sped across the bay, the chop hammering the boat as we cut through it making our way to the open water. Many times I had ridden with my uncle, carefree, basking in the sun, dreaming of being an agent like him. I thought maybe I should be bitter, but as LeRoy piloted us toward the gulf I was surprised with the calm feeling engulfing me.

Memories of days like this flooded me, riding the front of the boat, rocketing through the open water, headed to Uncle Tony's special place, special to a twelve year old anyway. He taught me about the marsh, the canals, the off-shoots twenty or thirty feet long, where some of the biggest redfish and speckled trout would hide. He had also taught me how to tie fishing knots, bait hooks, cast where I was aiming, and bump along the bottom teasing the bigger fish into taking a bite. And in the winter time I learned how to build a duck blind, put out decoys, stay warm and dry, and shoot at precisely the correct time to bring the larger ducks down close to the blind. Fourteen years after Uncle Tony's death I was remembering it all. I was confident I could still do it, and it was a testament to him who had taught me so well. Soon, I thought, I'll be back soon.

LeRoy throttled back the engines and the boat slowed to a crawl, rocking with the swells lapping across the bow. "I thought you might like to see the gulf before we visit Peter. But we can't go out any farther. It's too rough offshore today, five to six feet seas out there. The boat can handle it but I'm not sure you can," he said.

"Maybe another time," I said while thinking I should have done this long ago.

LeRoy reached into the console and grabbed a pair of high power-er binoculars. He said nothing while he scanned the gulf back and forth several times before placing the glasses back in the console. "It's good to check," he said. "Sometimes you see things you don't expect. The bad guys are out there and they don't advertise. Dark hulls and most times running with the lights off. Hang on," he said, and swung the boat around accelerating as he completed the one-eighty degree turn.

By ten o'clock we were in the canal to Peter's camp. It was a man-made canal and had been used by the oil companies years ago to lay their intricate network of oil and gas lines. We had motored at low speed about six hundred yards when the raised camp came into view. A Lafitte skiff was tied to the dock and LeRoy maneuvered his boat along side it. Peter was working under the camp and walked toward us. He wore dark brown shorts, and a white undershirt exposing his arms and shoulders. The muscles were still firm but his skin bore the tell tale sign of years in the sun. I looked up and saw Agnes walk out onto the small porch.

"This is a friendly visit," LeRoy said. He swung his boat around and placed it along side the dock nose to nose with the skiff. "Travis and I want to visit for a spell, nothing official."

Peter looked up at Agnes, their eyes met and she retreated into the camp. "Come, Agnes will make coffee," he said.

LeRoy and I stepped onto the dock and followed Peter up the stairs. He held the door for us and I noticed a crude, homemade tattoo on his right deltoid muscle. The numbers 0188 had faded but were still recognizable. I had seen many similar tattoos in Hope Haven and thought nothing of it.

I didn't expect much as I entered. Though it had been many years ago I still had visions and memories of visiting some of the old fishing camps with my uncle. None of them were well maintained and most were not livable on a daily basis. Agnes was busy making the coffee and ignored us as we entered. Their camp was more than livable. It was one large room about twenty feet by thirty feet, compact and efficient. A small, gas-burning stove next to a sink with cabinets above was in the far left corner, and a round dining table and chairs, enough for four people, was close to the wall several feet from the stove. In the other far corner was their bed, neatly made and appearing much more comfortable than the bunks I had seen in the other camps. A lone couch was against the wall to the right, placed between two windows through which ample light entered the room. The ceiling fan in the middle of the room was not moving and I realized the generator was off, no electricity, but not necessary either.

"Sit here," Agnes said, pointing at the table and chairs. It was more a command than a request. She poured the coffee, Peter's first, then us, her own last.

"Why the visit?" Peter asked.

""It was my idea," I said, looking at LeRoy then back at Peter. "Brother Lee and I would never have used you and Agnes. It was not our idea and ...

"Knock it off Travis," LeRoy said. "I already told them you guys had nothing to do with it." He opened his satchel and pulled out the papers and commercial fishing license. LeRoy placed them on the table and said, "Here, all legal. You can fish as much as you want and sell to anybody, for the next year anyway. Travis insisted after what happened with you getting arrested."

Peter looked at Agnes and did not pick up the papers. Reaching her small, weathered hand across the table she picked up the license, rose from her chair and placed it in a cabinet above the stove. Agnes picked up the coffee pot and poured more into our cups.

"This is more like a home than a fishing camp," I said.

"Agnes and I had to rebuild it after Hurricane Bob in 1979. We decided to make it much stronger, used good materials, new generator." Peter looked at Agnes and said, "She made the curtains, sanded and painted the floor. It's very strong," he said. "Your Uncle Tony helped us. He got galvanized steel for the frame. Much stronger, and last forever. One of the oil companies owed him a favor."

I was caught off guard with the mention of my uncle. "How did he help? Are you saying my Uncle Tony did something illegal?" I asked.

"Never," Peter said. "Tony stopped them from making a big mistake cutting a canal through an area with an old gas line. The land wasn't marked and the charts were wrong, but Tony knew it was there. The oil company insisted it was okay but Tony wouldn't budge. They found the gas line. Lucky for them, too, because if they had cut the line it would have cost millions; some in repairs but mostly being shut down and unable to work while the government investigated. They helped us as a favor to Tony.

"He made sure I was building it strong, and even helped on his days off. You wasn't with him yet so he had more time. But after his brother died, and you came to him, Tony was concerned with taking care of you. We didn't see him as much but the camp was long finished by then."

"His brother was my father," I said, even though I was sure Peter had known this for a while.

"Yes, and we didn't see Tony much after that. Too busy raising you. But when he would come, even for a short visit, he always talked about you."

"I never understood how Uncle Tony could get killed back here. This area was second nature to him, it was like his home."

"It was a bad accident," Peter said looking at Agnes instead of me.

Either he didn't believe it, or he was lying. I wasn't sure which, but when he averted his eyes from mine it was obvious. Changing the subject I asked Agnes about growing up in Vietnam. We spoke for almost an hour and Peter and Agnes started to accept me. They were still guarded and deliberate in choosing their words, but we were moving closer.

"Travis, we need to get moving. I've got real work to do."

We all stood and I said, "One more thing. Thanksgiving is on the twenty-fourth, eight days from now. Brother Lee always closes the restaurant and has a big dinner there. He cooks for family and friends, makes lots of food. Peter, I'd like you and Agnes to come celebrate with us."

Peter looked at Agnes, reluctant to answer but when she nodded he turned toward me and said, "Maybe so. We usually eat alone at home in Cut Off. We will drive up from there."

180

LeRoy and I drove up highway 23 to New Orleans. After all these years the uncertainty of Uncle Tony's death haunted me, even more so with Peter's deliberate evasiveness. What was he not telling me, and did Agnes know, too? The way he looked at her and the quick exchange with their eyes when he said it was an "accident". LeRoy and I hadn't spoken much on the drive back. I was deep in thought, remembering Uncle Tony, concentrating on the good times, and how he would have wanted it. The calm was gone and my anger again welled up. Still, even after all these years. Would it ever go away I wondered.

It was eight o'clock when LeRoy dropped me off at the restaurant. I walked up the alley and entered through the back door to the kitchen. Middle of the week and it was normal, not too busy and under control. "Whatcha doin here?" Brother Lee shouted as I entered.

"Got back earlier than expected so I wanted to help."

"Nope, Scatback and I got it. You taught him too good. Hell, might not even need you no more," he said without looking at me.

My silence drew his attention and he turned toward me. "Boy, you better learn to joke a little. Life is too short to be too serious. I never mean what I just said."

Brother Lee, the sage, was right as usual. "Hell, I'm wonderin if you still gonna pay me when I retire next week," I said.

"That's more like it. Now, since you here go take care of yo guests, boy."

"What guests?"

"Some doctor lady called for you. I told her you probly won't be here but she showed up anyway. In the dining room, with a friend eatin."

"What doctor lady?" I said, moving toward the door to the dining area and looking out. The room was almost full, with one table not occupied. Most of the guests were eating, but a few had finished, the reason the kitchen had not appeared too busy. I didn't recognize her at first without her white lab coat. Seated close to the door with another lady was Doctor Cousins. I pushed through the door avoiding Becky as she balanced a tray of dirty dishes trying to get into the kitchen.

"Watch it, bub," she growled. It's good to be missed I thought.

"I'm sorry I wasn't here when you called," I said, approaching the table.

"Well, you said to call so I did. We came anyway even though you weren't here. This is Doctor Babs, a friend from medical school."

Her friend reached over and slapped her on the arm. "My name is Michelle and this one is being a smart ass. I chose obstetrics and gynecology, so a baby doctor. I *detested* her and the others calling me Doctor Baby, so it got shortened to Babs and stuck." She offered her hand and said, "And you are Chef T, I presume?"

I shook her hand when offered and sat at their table. "Travis, but most people around here call me Chef T. How was your dinner?" I asked.

"Excellent," Babs said.

"We had the soft shell crabs," added Doctor Cousins. "You'd think I would never eat fried food as many autopsies as I've done. Clogged arteries, layers of fat, and the things you find in someone's bowels."

"Take it easy, Gwen," Babs said. "She's trying to make you squeamish."

"It's almost working," I said, realizing I had not picked up on her name other than Doctor Cousins.

"The young man with the gold tooth almost insisted. He was clearing the table next to us, heard me mention your name to our waiter, and then offered his opinion on what we should eat. And, said he'd cook them for us."

"That was Scatback, he's turning out to be a good cook."

"What a cast of names y'all have here," Babs said. "Hell, I'd fit right in."

"What about dessert, ladies?" I asked.

Babs looked at Gwen, hesitated, then turned her attention to me and said, "Got any Bananas Foster?"

"No, afraid not, a little fancier than we want to be. It's usually prepared fresh at the table and, well, you can see we aren't set up for that. But, how about a chocolate banana torte? Brother Lee's specialty."

"Sounds decadent," Gwen said. "So, yes we'd love some."

"It's rich. Want to share?" I asked.

Babs looked at Gwen. "We share some things," she said. Then looking back at me added, "But not dessert."

This time Gwen reached over and slapped Babs on the arm. "Don't scare him off you big tramp."

"Free spirit, I prefer the term free spirit," Babs said.

"I'll be right back." I was trying to be cool but they had unnerved me and, as it turned out, was what I needed after spending the day in the marsh.

I returned with two plates of the dessert and placed them on the table. "Dessert's on me," I said.

"Sounds delicious," Babs responded, an intentional huskiness to her voice.

"What is this, mating season and no one told me," I said.

"No, it's not mating season," Gwen said.

"*Practice* mating season," Babs added.

"You're too vulnerable, Travis, most gentlemen are. When Babs gets the best of someone she seldom lets up. Sorry, she's more bark than bite."

"Damn, I think I'm disappointed," I said, turning and walking back to the kitchen.

Chris came into the kitchen and said," Those two ladies want to talk with you again."

One of the perils of the restaurant business is when a patron wants to talk it is hard to dismiss. Thinking I'd been jousted with enough I reluctantly returned to Gwen and Babs. "What did I forget?" I asked.

"Nothing," Gwen said. "The real reason I came here tonight was not the food but to tell you I finished the autopsy on the young girl, Andi, I think you called her."

"Oh, I forgot you haven't been told. It wasn't Andi. The young girl was someone else. Andi showed up, she's with a friend, helping out with a pregnancy." Then it hit me. "Hey, Babs, maybe you can help. My friend's pregnant, been here a couple of weeks and I'm sure she doesn't have a doctor. She needs someone like you, about the same age, single, understanding. Can you do me a favor?"

"Well it depends. Can you do *me* a favor."

"Wait a minute," Gwen said. "What about the young girl?"

"Sorry, I got distracted. We don't know anything about her except her name might be Missy and she might be from Arkansas." It struck me as I spoke how insensitive I had become about the dead girl. "Give me your phone number. I want to discuss it more with you but not right now, not here. I'm on overload today."

"So, about my favor," Babs said. "Yes, I'll help her." She reached into a small clutch and pulled out a business card. "Have her call the office and set up an appointment. Tell her to use your name and I'll work it out." She held the card, holding on firmly as I grasped it. "The favor?" she said before letting go.

I was feeling like a piece of meat for sale and needed to change my attitude. "Ok, name it Miss Free Spirit."

"Ha, you wish. Gwen and I are going over to the Karaoke bar on Bourbon Street for a few drinks. Meet us there after you finish here." She directed a wicked smile at Gwen. "Men are so freakin predictable." Turning toward me she said, "Bring your singing voice, one song, my choice, and you get your favor."

A rendition of "Fever" by Patti Page came to mind. I was out of my league without a prayer. Babs looked the type. But worse than the song choice, the Karaoke bar was next door to Hard Times. Would I be able to sneak in without Rufus seeing me, or Abbey?

CHAPTER THIRTY-THREE

I stayed sober refusing to over indulge again. But Gwen and Babs had much too much to drink and wound up at my place, too tired and too drunk to make it home. My double bed turned into a triple and there was no arguing. They were sober enough to not take no for an answer, but so drunk as to be harmless. Sleep came quickly for all of us.

"Travis!" It was a whisper but I heard tension in the voice. "Travis, wake up!"

Face down with my head between the two pillows, I opened my eyes. Gwen was on my left and Babs was on my right. If I moved Babs would hit the floor. Turning my head I stared up at Alexis. Behind her, grinning and practically salivating, stood Andi. "Don't locks on doors mean anything?" I said in a soft voice, still not moving.

"Yes, when you use them. The door was unlocked, and after all the noise y'all made last night, and I have a problem sleeping as it is, I couldn't help but look out the window. What a site, these two hanging on you, and you wrestling with them while trying to open the door. You looked like a regular man whore."

"Free spirit," I said.

"Quit yelling," Gwen moaned.

Andi laughed and Alexis said, "No one is yelling sweetie pie. BUT WE CAN!" she blurted. Babs tried to get up and Andi's quick movement prevented her from rolling off the bed.

"Ok, you two," I said to Alexis. "Downstairs before this loft collapses. "And you two, get up and let's go."

185

"Coffee," Gwen said into the pillow.

"I'll make some downstairs, Come on, let's get moving."

Alexis looked bigger by the day, her pregnancy in full bloom. I went down the spiral stairs first, in case gravity and momentum got the better of her. Somehow she managed and Andi followed. I made a move toward the small stove and Alexis said, "Don't bother. I've got a full pot already made. Andi and I will be right back with the coffee and cups. Bachelor pads are ill equipped for company."

Gwen and Babs had come down from the loft and were sitting on the couch, their heads back and eyes struggling to stay open by the time Alexis and Andi returned with the coffee. I made the introductions while Alexis poured the coffee.

"God, why did we drink so much?" Gwen rasped.

"Because we always forget about the morning after, especially when we're with a cutie like Travis. Thank God he was there."

Gwen sipped her coffee and said, "This got us through med school. I can't tell you how many all nighters we pulled, double shifts, you name it. Babs and I lived on coffee and now we can't live without it. They better never find out this stuff causes cancer."

Babs sat up, concern on her face when she realized Alexis was the friend I needed the favor for. "I'd say you're about seven months, right?" Babs asked.

"Yes. The original due date was January tenth. I haven't seen a doctor in a couple of months."

"We'll change that tomorrow," Babs said. "I'll work you in at the end of the day. Travis has my card. He did me a favor and I owe him one."

Babs looked at me when she said it and I thought back to the Karaoke bar. I had been wrong, it wasn't "Fever" she wanted to hear. "Seventh Son" by Johnny Rivers, who got his start in Baton Rouge, was her request. I grimaced as I thought how badly I must have sounded.

"You didn't sound bad, but stick to cooking." Babs said.

Andi sat quietly on the floor, legs crossed. I watched her for a minute not realizing I was staring. She looked different, almost happy. She interrupted my stare. "Whatcha lookin at?"

"You," I said. "You're…different. Certainly quiet and that's a big change. "What are you thinking about?"

"I was just wonderin, being a doctor is a big deal, right? Why would you two get so fucked up?"

Alexis, standing next to Andi, nudged her. "Sorry," Andi said. "I mean drunk."

"We're both pushing thirty, single, and consumed with work," Gwen said. "And maybe for me one too many autopsies on a person too young, like your friend, well you thought was your friend. Guess maybe we'll never know who she was."

"I do volunteer work at the free clinic, also Charity Hospital," Babs added. "I've delivered more crack babies than I care to remember. And heroin is making a come back. Black tar they call it. The babies are born addicted, shaking and crying, and there's nothing we can do. We save a good many of them but not all, and sometimes it gets to you. So on occasion Gwen and I let loose."

The silence after their explanations was uncomfortable and Babs changed the mood. "So," she said rising from the couch, looking at me, and patting Alexis's belly, "I take it this isn't yours."

"NO! It isn't his," Alexis said.

Babs nodded. "So there's hope for you and me yet."

"You tramp," Gwen barked.

"I ain't never met no doctors like y'all before," Andi said.

"How old are you, sweetie?" Babs asked.

"Sixteen. Made sixteen a couple months back."

Babs looked at Alexis. "Bring her with you. She needs to be checked out. You've been living on the street, right?"

"Yes'm. Almost a year."

"It's almost eight o'clock. I've got to get to the restaurant and I'm sure you two have to get to work. It's Thursday and I doubt you're off," I said.

"We're working but not until ten. We plan ahead," Gwen said. "What, no fancy chef breakfast?"

"Next time."

CHAPTER THIRTY-FOUR

I was feeling rejected. By Sunday afternoon I was finished at the restaurant and trying to decide what I wanted to do. I had not heard from or seen Alexis since the morning with Babs and Gwen. She had not even bothered to tell me how the visit to Babs went or how she and Andi had made out.

The Athletic club on North Rampart was deserted, not so unusual for a Sunday, and I made my way to a locker, changed into my work out clothes and started a rigorous routine of Tai Chi followed by a long stint on the heavy bag. After a swim in the salt water pool I showered and dressed.

I stepped down onto the sidewalk and my still overheated body shivered with the chill of the evening air. Darkness was minutes away from enveloping the French Quarter and even on a Sunday night it would come alive more than most cities on a Saturday night. Feeling exhilarated from the work out and the fresh air I reached into my bag and pulled out my cell phone. Tater answered on the first ring.

"I'm starving," I said. "Come pick me up outside the club on North Rampart Street. Hurry up." Tater seldom missed a meal and would arrive in ten minutes or less.

The unmarked police car pulled up, the window went down and Tater said, "Get in."

"What took so long? Especially since you didn't dress up." Tater wore blue jeans, tennis shoes without socks and a baggy Tulane sweatshirt. No fancy dining for us tonight which was fine with me.

188

"Football, normal guys watch football on Sunday. Now, what's up with you?"

"Nothing, I didn't want to eat alone."

"You pull me away from a football game because you're lonely? Are you kidding? I thought maybe you had a lead, or something about the dead girl."

"Sorry to disappoint you but no, just hungry. Come on, drive over to Dave's and let's get something to eat."

The dining room at Dave's was mostly empty, partly because it was six o'clock, early by New Orleans standards, and partly because it was Sunday. I waved at the hostess as Tater and I walked in and headed to the kitchen. Dave was busy prepping plates, clearly expecting a dinner rush. Hilda, his wife, was making small salad plates. They had met on Bourbon Street, a one night stand so hot and steamy, according to Dave, they never separated. They fought with the same intensity as they loved.

"Your dining room would be full if you'd ever stop serving mediocre food."

Dave didn't look up from his task but said, "The only thing mediocre around here was the swill you made when you covered for me after my appendix busted."

Tater spoke up, "I always liked your food, Dave."

"You kiss-ass," I said to Tater. "Come on Dave, surely you have real food that's edible." Hilda came up to me, hugged me tight and ground her hips into mine.

"That's what I thought," Dave said. "Was that how it was when I was laid up in the hospital, you two grinding away. No wonder your food sucked."

Hilda slapped me on the butt and said, "How you keep such a tight ass working around food all day?"

"Because I'm still single. I don't spend all my off time in bed trying to set a record marathon love making session like you two. You gonna feed us or what?" Inwardly, I was jealous of their relationship, one of the few in the food industry I was sure would last forever.

"Yep, like I figured, you won't eat your own cooking but you'll come *here* for a good meal," Dave said. "How about a grilled cheese, or maybe step it up a notch and get a BLT?"

"Food, in a bowl," I said. "Real cooking, you still do that, right?"

"Grab two stools, sit there at the end of the counter and stay out of the way."

Hilda stepped out of the kitchen and returned with two ice-cold St. Arnold's Weedwacker beers, in the bottle, no glass. Dave moved about the stove, two pans sizzling as flames danced around them, flaring up and over the edges as he shuffled them back and forth, grease spilling out onto the burners. Ten minutes later Dave placed two large, shallow bowls in front of Tater and me. "Grillades and grits, tonight's special. Free for you Tater, Travis has to wash dishes."

"I'll be glad to wash dishes. There aren't going to be any customers anyway."

The competition among restaurants in New Orleans is fierce, producing an abundance of quality food to rival any city in the world, and Dave's was no exception. The grillades, tender marinated medallions of prime beef, sautéed in a rich gravy and served over creamy grits was a comfort food as good as any dished up anywhere in the city.

"How about I get the recipe for this, so I know what NOT to serve my customers?"

"I'll stop by one day so you can return the favor. Maybe some shrimp Creole, but only if Brother Lee makes it. Not the crap you stir up, canned tomato soup is better than your stuff," Dave said. He turned toward us and asked, "What's this about Travis? You didn't come here for the food."

"You still donating meals to the Ozanam Inn for the homeless?"

"Yeah, as much as I can afford. Why?"

"Homeless people see things," Tater said. "But they don't talk much, stay to themselves. We got a dead girl. Young, maybe fifteen, no real name, no idea where she's from. Maybe one of them saw or heard something. They won't talk to the police, but maybe if you snoop a little, they might talk."

"I heard about the body, but don't remember anything about it being a young girl," Dave said. "But that was over a week ago. There was a buzz at the inn but I didn't think anything of it. I'll ask the director if he's heard anything."

Dave became somber, deep in thought. He had lost a sister to drugs and it still bothered him he hadn't been able to save her. The thought of the young girl reminded him. I kicked myself for bringing back his pain.

The hostess crashed through the door from the dining room yelling, "Damn it Dave, I told you not to hire that busboy. He called in sick and the dining room is filling up. And we're short a server, Maggie's it and she can't handle it all."

I stood up and said, "We're finished eating. Hilda, you be the other server, Tater will handle bussing the tables and I'll help Dave."

"How the fuck I go from police detective to busboy?" Tater growled. "Hey Dave, I'm kiddin, give me an apron."

Three hours later, nine o'clock, Tater and I walked out of Dave's and back to his car. "You got a parking ticket? You've got your police placard sitting on the dashboard."

"Yeah, well parking enforcement's a different division. They hate cops. Fuck em. I'll get it fixed, but it's a pain in the ass to deal with."

"Drop me off at my place, I got an early morning at the restaurant."

Tater stopped in front of Terry's and Jerry's house and left the engine running. "I can still get home and catch some football," he said, then paused. "Travis, this girl's a police matter. Let us handle it. Tell Dave to call me if he hears anything and don't be tryin to get too involved."

Alexis was standing next to the concrete bench where Andi sat, arms crossed over her chest and head down when I walked into the small courtyard. Neither acknowledged me as I approached. "I think maybe I should go inside," I said.

"She's pissed off at me cause I been gone for a while," Andi said.

"Not a while…almost all day. I've been worried sick. My heartburn is killing me as it is and this doesn't help."

"Where've you been all day?" I asked.

"I went lookin for a couple of the kids I would sometime hang with, maybe see what's up. I didn't mean nothin by bein gone. I got antsy, that's what my momma used to call it, needed to move around."

"Nothing else?" Alexis said.

"Well, I had a few dollars and I knowed some of em could a used it. I didn't want you bein mad at me for givin my money away."

"You should have told me," Alexis said. "A lie by omission is still a lie."

"That's a little harsh, Alexis." I watched Andi as she looked down. She had been on her own for well over a year. Sleepless nights in the cold and restless days in a stifling heat mixed with unbearable humidity had been her life. She was desperate to survive but afraid to reach out, and had no one to reach out to. She didn't understand being loved and cared for. I had been the victim of her ire, lashing out at me when a thank you would do. "What about it, Andi?"

"Wait," Alexis said. "I was afraid for you, worried, that's all." She tried to bend over, stopped and said, "Shit, if I bend over I'll fall."

Andi stood, wrapped her arms around Alexis and hugged her. "I'll do better. I guess I got a lot to learn."

"It's time for me to get some sleep, I said."

"Travis?" Andi said. "I think there's another girl missin."

I had started walking toward the door to my apartment but stopped short when Andi spoke. Turning toward her I said, "Are you sure? Maybe she moved on, decided to leave."

"Maybe, but I don't think so. She ran away from a foster home in Baton Rouge. Her and me hung out for a while. The foster parents used to make her do all the work and then beat her with a big phone book when she refused. Said the book didn't show when they hit her with it like a belt or their fists."

"Why couldn't she have moved on?"

"Cause, she ain't from another state, ain't used to crossing state lines. She don't *know* how to move on, plus she always looked scared. She was real weak, not like me. And she told me she weren't never goin back so I think she would a stayed here."

"I'll call Tater and see how he wants to handle it. It's not his division but he'll know what to do."

"Cat, short for Kathleen. That's her name."

"Hey, you two never told me how you made out with Doctor Babs."

"Oh, shoot," Alexis said. "I was supposed to give you a message. She wants you to call her, gave me her cell phone number to give you. I'll be right back." She waddled away with one hand on her lower back.

"We done ok. She said I had a vitamin deteriary I think, needed to eat better. I cleaned up real good but she made me feel like I was dirty, poking, taking swabs which is disgustin ya ask me. Gave me free vitamins though. Thinks I'll be ok."

"Deficiency, a vitamin deficiency," I said as Alexis returned and handed me a piece of paper with a phone number scribbled on it. "What about you?"

"Prenatal vitamins, more rest, etc. Did an ultrasound and asked if I wanted to know the sex of the baby. I said not yet, maybe next time. I should get the blood results soon but she was happy with the baby's heartbeat, so she's not worried."

It was quiet inside my apartment, bringing to mind the chaos surrounding my life. I called Tater, told him about the girl and what Andi had said.

"I don't deal in runaways much unless they're connected to a homicide. If the foster parents are as bad as Andi says, they probably didn't report her gone. They'll wait until the social worker shows up, make an excuse for her not being home, then arrange for another meeting."

"Why is that?" I asked.

"Cause they want the money. They get paid by the state and if the girl's gone the money stops. They'll milk it for a while hoping she comes back. Eventually they'll report her missing, but maybe not for several months. I'll have someone from juvenile check into it but don't get your hopes up.

"Thanks, and don't forget Thanksgiving dinner at Brother Lee's," I said.

"I'm working," Tater said. "But I'll see what I can do."

"You're homicide and it's a holiday."

"Yeah, and a prime time for families to get together. We have the most trouble with domestic problems during holidays. I'll try, maybe a quick plate to go."

I thought about Tater's comments and realized my ideas about families, and especially at times like the holidays, was Pollyannaish at best. I looked at the piece of paper and dialed Babs' number. She insisted on stopping by my place to discuss Alexis, and though I was concerned, she didn't want to talk about it over the phone. Lying on my couch I worried about what she would tell me. Twenty minutes later a tap on my door roused me from a soft sleep.

"Come on in and cut to the chase. Is Alexis ok?"

"Alexis is fine, the baby's healthy, blood work's good, and she's doing great. Andi, too, considering all she's been through. She has some internal vaginal and rectal scarring, caused by the monster of a stepfather who abused her. Those wounds heal, but usually not the emotional ones. Not for a long time, anyway."

"Well if they're ok why didn't you tell me on the phone? What's the bad news?"

"I came for the rest of the favor you owe me. And I'm tired of waiting." Babs moved into me and kissed me deep before I could resist. "This is your lucky night, Chef T. Let's go cook up something spicy," Babs said.

Free spirit I thought to myself, a free spirit. "You didn't really just say that. Stick to doctoring, you'll never be a poet." I'd been numb since Maggie and I had parted and sex had been absent from my conscious thoughts, even when I involuntarily reacted with Alexis in the shower. But the idea of it took over and the result of my abstinence was showing.

"I like a pushover," Babs said eying my aroused state. "I know the way."

Babs was loud, very loud, and aggressive for over an hour. I lay exhausted, questioning if I was in good shape or not. A mental picture of Terry and Jerry standing in the courtyard applauding came to me and I half expected it to happen in the morning.

The alarm went off at five a.m. and Babs rolled over placing her arm across my chest. "Either a quickie now or an all nighter later. What's it gonna be?"

"I've got a big pot of red beans waiting for me to cook them so later is better. Besides, three times you abused me last night. You give wounded warrior a new meaning."

"Well if I had it more regular I wouldn't be so sexually gluttonous," Babs said, nudging me. "That was an invitation."

"Got to open the restaurant, remember?"

"I'll call a cab. You can ride with me and I'll drop you off."

"Shower first so let's step on it," I said.

Babs and I walked through the courtyard to the waiting taxi. Fortunately, I thought, Terry and Jerry must be sound sleepers. The light in the window upstairs was off and I did not notice Alexis watching as we left.

CHAPTER THIRTY-FIVE

November, 2004
Cut Off, La.

Peter and Agnes had been early risers for so many years they weren't able to sleep late even on Thanksgiving Day. By seven o'clock in the morning they sat at the kitchen table drinking coffee, discussing if they should go to New Orleans as Travis had requested. The drive from Cut Off would take two hours and would make for a long day with the same amount of time driving back.

"Peter, you seventy-four years old, time to stop working so much. We should go," Agnes said, placing her hand on his.

"I like my quiet, private life. But for you I will go."

"Vous m'avez ete bon," Agnes said, speaking in French which was still easier for her than English, even after thirty years.

"You have been good to me, too," Peter said. "My life got better, and easier after you came to me."

"Then we go. Brother Lee is a good man. He will be happy to see us."

They both turned when Tran, Agnes's nephew entered the room. "Where you goin?" he asked.

"To New Orleans for Thanksgiving Dinner," Peter said.

Tran had stayed with Peter and Agnes off and on for the last two years, usually two or three days at a time. He was forty years old, never married, and had been arrested several times, usually for public drunkenness and fighting. He worked around the marina when he wasn't fishing. Agnes had been kind to Tran, a family obligation she carried from her Vietnamese heritage, and because her natural maternal instinct compelled her. But Tran was always difficult, often in trouble. Peter was tolerant for Agnes, but he did not trust Tran and worried about what he was involved in when he was not fishing.

"You can come with us. I'm sure Brother Lee not mind," Agnes said.

Peter had seldom seen Agnes wear anything other than the traditional pajama style garments typical of the women who worked in the fields and on the waters in Vietnam. This day Agnes wore a dark green dress, embroidered with gold flowers on each sleeve. Her long, black hair had been brushed until it hung straight and shined with a luster like highly polished ebony. A large comb, molded in the image of a peacock, held her hair back and away from her face. She was as lovely as he had ever seen her and a smile came to him while he admired her beauty. Peter did not own a suit but had one sports jacket he had not worn in several years. He donned the jacket hoping he was suitable to Agnes, hoping she was pleased with him.

By ten o'clock Peter was driving to New Orleans, Agnes next to him and Tran leaning against the door, giving Agnes more room. The truck was old but rode smoothly as they traveled north on highway one.

CHAPTER THIRTY-SIX

November 24, 2004
Thanksgiving Day
French Quarter

Brother Lee was ahead of schedule which was typical for him on Thanksgiving Day. I was doing less than I would have liked but because he had gotten to his restaurant at four in the morning much of the cooking was well underway when I arrived at seven.

Becky and Chris had their own families and would not join us for Thanksgiving so they had set tables together the night before, arranging them in long, family style settings capable of seating groups of sixteen at two locations. With several random tables set up against the walls there was room enough to accommodate fifty people, and with Brother Lee's family it was hard to estimate how many would show. As always, there would be enough food for at least that many and still have leftovers to take home, one of Brother Lee's requirements. If you came to eat you had to take food home. Brother Lee lived for this day more than Christmas. When I asked him why he favored Thanksgiving he had said, "Christmas is the Lord's day and is about celebratin Him, but Thanksgivin be about getting together with family". Brother Lee was my family and it made sense to me.

"Hey boy, you gonna fry them turkeys?" he yelled at me.

"I injected three of them yesterday and placed them in the cooler. They've been sitting out for over an hour. So yeah, old man, I'm gonna fry em up soon as Scatback gives me a hand. He's helping his mom in the dining room. She insists on arranging the food and putting ice in cups."

I figured it out soon after Brother Lee saved me. One of my biggest pleasures is eating great food someone else had prepared. But better still is seeing the appreciation and contentment of people after eating food I had prepared. Thanksgiving at Brother Lee's was a day I was able to revel in both joys.

By noon the food was cooked and we were ready to eat. Brother Lee, Scatback and I had prepared fried turkeys, roast turkeys, hams, stuffed pork loins, mashed potatoes, candied yams, oyster dressing, collard greens, cornbread, seafood mirliton dressing, and more pies than fifty people could eat in three days. The food had been spread out buffet style on three tables, each six feet in length, and there was no room to spare.

Peter and Agnes were the last to arrive, showing up at twelve-fifteen. They introduced Tran and then sat quietly at the end of a row of tables while everyone else helped themselves. It had taken convincing, but Maggie and Charles had reluctantly agreed to attend. My confidence had returned after Babs had soothed my ego, and I was happy for Maggie as well as content she and Charles were good for each other. Maggie, recognizing the shyness of Agnes, grabbed Charles and with plates of food sat at the table with Peter, Agnes, and Tran. She insisted they share food, pushed the plates toward them and returned to the buffet. Maggie dished two more plates of food piled as high as possible.

Alexis and Andi had been reluctant to accept the invitation. All I got out of them was a maybe, even though Terry and Jerry had always celebrated Thanksgiving with a select group of similarly minded friends at a mansion on St. Charles Ave. I was hopeful they would change their minds and show up, but it was a long walk for Alexis and cabs are scarce on Thanksgiving Day.

Thirty-five people, black, white, Asian, young, old, even one transgender "person", in a small restaurant make almost more noise than a Saint's football game in the Superdome. By two o'clock the melee had subsided. A formidable dent had been made in the buffet offering of food but there was still enough for one more round. The drawback for me in fixing large amounts of food over the time span of a long morning is I'm often not able to indulge as I would want. Later, after all had cleared, my appetite would rise up and I would eat.

I was seated across from Peter and noticed when he looked past me, his attention drawn away from the conversation. Turning around I watched Tater enter from the kitchen and behind him was Andi. As I got up to greet them Alexis entered, moving in short steps while holding her belly and breathing hard.

"I found these two walking down Toulouse. This one wasn't gonna make it," Tater said, gesturing toward Alexis. "So I picked em up. I figured we were headed to the same place."

"Dammit, where's the bathroom? Sometimes I can't go ten minutes without having to pee," Alexis said.

Andi grabbed her hand and led Alexis down a short hall past the kitchen to the small restroom. Peter, Agnes, and Tran had risen and approached me.

"We must go. Long drive back to Cut Off," Peter said.

"All the food very good," Agnes added.

"The rule is you have to take some with you. There's a stack of food containers at the end of the table," I said, pointing where Scatback had placed the standard Styrofoam boxes used by restaurants for take out orders.

Tran approached me as Agnes took several containers and started selecting food from the buffet. Behind him Andi walked back toward us. "So kind of you to invite us and to let me come, too," Tran said.

"There is always room for one more. Brother Lee loves for people to come and…" I paused. Andi stood behind Tran, her face ashen and her lip quivering. She seemed glued to where she was standing. "Excuse me, Tran. I think Andi's not feeling well."

"Yes, please take care of her," he said turning around.

Andi didn't speak as I took her arm and helped her to a seat. Her eyes stared into space, not blinking, and had a glazed-over look. As I tugged on her arm she stumbled but then walked with me to a chair next to Maggie and Charles.

"Here, this might help," Tran said, offering a glass of water. Andi sat motionless, not accepting the glass, so I took the water from Tran and placed it on the table in front of her. "Agnes is ready so we go now."

I walked Peter and Agnes through the kitchen and into the alley. Tran followed. "I hope to see you soon, with *legal* seafood to sell. You get first basket of crabs free," Agnes said. She bowed to me and I did likewise as Mr. Chin had taught me years ago.

Andi was standing in the kitchen when I walked back inside, almost hyperventilating as she struggled to compose herself. "What is wrong with you?"

"His voice," she said pointing in the direction of the alley. "The night Missy was killed, I think his was the voice of one of them two guys. I told you I couldn't see them but Tran sounded like the one who took the other two girls away. He weren't the one killed Missy, it was the other guy, but he was there."

Her voice cracked and Andi crossed her arms low under her chest, her body trembling. "It's possible it wasn't him, maybe someone who sounded like him," I said, not believing it as I spoke. Andi followed me back into the dining room. "Where's Tater?" I asked Brother Lee.

"I let him out the front door. He was parked right up the street. He took his food and was gone."

Looking out the window I thought about all Andi had seen and been through. "I'll call Tater. You've got nothing to be afraid of, I promise." Then for the first time I put my arm around Andi's shoulders. "Come on, let's get some pie. And get a big piece for Alexis. She's looking a little malnourished."

It was four o'clock and most of the guests had gone home. I insisted Brother Lee go home as well and he reluctantly made his way out lamenting constant protests. Brother Lee walked to North Rampart Street and caught the bus. It was a straight route to the lower ninth ward where he had lived since birth. He was proud of his neighborhood and never failed to mention he "lived a couple blocks from the Fat Man", his reference to Fats Domino. Brother Lee owned a new car but never used it to get to work. The buses ran on a regular schedule and he had used them to get to the French Quarter long before he opened his restaurant. One day, after repeatedly asking him why he took the bus, he explained it to me. "The busses keep me from being in too big a hurry. I get to relax, do some thinkin, some prayin, gives me time to figure out what I'm gonna cook. Plus some of my ole friends ride them busses. We catch up from time to time. Can't do that driving a car. I saves the car for takin my lady friends around. And I got *lots* of lady friends." I never doubted his prowess with the ladies.

By six o'clock the restaurant was cleaned up and ready to open for lunch the next day. Andi had started cleaning before anyone else, throwing away the disposable plates and plastic cups while Scatback and I washed up.

As expected, the cab I called to bring Alexis and Andi home took longer than usual. An hour had passed and I was about to call again when the cab pulled up, honking as if in a hurry.

"Aren't you coming with us?" Alexis asked.

"No, I'll be home later. I'm bringing some food to Rufus. I didn't expect him to come even though he was invited. He's a quiet, loner type person, enjoys his reading and stays to himself. The club is open tonight so I'm dropping off some food and walking home."

"Well, don't come home like the last time after visiting Rufus," Alexis said.

"Yes, mom," I said. "But don't wait up."

I packed two containers full of food, placed them in a bag with a whole, uncut apple pie and walked to Bourbon Street. The weather had warmed up over the last few days and it was more like late summer than the middle of fall.

CHAPTER THIRTY-SEVEN

Rufus was standing inside the foyer of Hard Times checking out the few patrons as they paid at the counter before moving inside the club. The music was already so loud it was hard to hear. I waited until Rufus noticed and motioned me over to where he stood. I reached out, handing him the bag of food. It must have weighed five pounds.

"Thanks for the lunch. What about supper later?" he asked.

"There's enough food in there for two of you," I said.

"Or six strippers," he shot back, enjoying his own humor. "You want to come in?"

"NO! I learned my lesson the last time. Besides, I'm beat. Had a long day of cooking so I'm ready to take it easy. Tell Abbey hello for me."

"She doesn't work here anymore."

"What happened, did she go to another club?"

"No, she's finishing school and will graduate next summer, then on to grad school. She earned enough here to make it work. One of the few. Here," he said handing me a card. "She said to give you this, wants you to call. I was gonna give it to you at the restaurant but since you're here..."

I took the card, looked at the name and number, and put it in my pocket. "I'd feel like a pervert if I called her."

"Abbey is worldly, more than you would think." Rufus paused then said, "She's grounded. She does what she does without guilt, lives in the moment and it doesn't bother her what other people think."

"I'll think about it but I'm not comfortable. Enjoy the food and come by for an early supper tomorrow."

I turned and walked out onto Bourbon Street. As I headed toward my apartment it came over me, the feeling of intrusion. I picked up the pace as I walked to Governor Nicholls Street. When I turned the corner I stopped, my back to a wall, and waited.

He turned the corner in a wide arc and stopped several feet from me. "You've been following me for several blocks, why?" I asked with my fists clenched and my left foot forward, ready to react if necessary.

The man was average looking, about five feet ten inches tall, brown hair, lean but not skinny, maybe one seventy five in weight. And dark eyes. A smile appeared revealing teeth whiter than usual. He lifted his hands, palms showing, and then slid his hands into his front pockets, a gesture of disarming a threat. "I've been following you for three days," he said. "I decided to be more obvious for the last few blocks. All in all, not bad on your part. Most people would not have picked up on it, but still a little disappointing."

My face flushed red but I did not anger. "Keep talking."

"You were asked to visit Father Billy, and yet you haven't. Any reason?"

"Mr. Chin suggested it," I said. "It was a casual request so I thought I'd get to it in good time. Father Billy's a patient man, his calling."

"Well I'd suggest sooner is better than later."

I eyed him closely. The extreme confidence in his voice conflicted with his average demeanor. "Who are you?"

"Oh you mean like friend or foe?" he said with a chuckle.

"If you were a foe one of us would be lying in the gutter." I was calm but serious, and I exuded it as I spoke.

"Travis, if I were foe we would not have made it this far." He removed his hands from his pocket and held them up again, his open palms turned toward me. "You can relax. Come on, let's walk to your place. It's right down the street." It wasn't a question. He knew where I was headed.

"You haven't answered my question."

"Friend, and let's leave it there for now."

I started walking toward my apartment; sure he would be right beside me. "You give invasion of privacy a new meaning," I said.

"This is two thousand and four, the new millennium, our lives are not private anymore. Cameras are watching us right now even if it's a simple home security system. Surely you're smart enough to realize this. I'd be disappointed if you didn't."

"Back to Father Billy, what's this about? Why does he want to see me? And how does Mr. Chin play into this?"

"You'll need to ask Father Billy. As for Chin, he was merely a messenger. He hasn't been told anything."

"This is a little too cloak and dagger for me, like a big joke."

"Don't insult me, Travis. You're instincts are too good. It's not a joke." His tone was very matter of fact and he wasn't threatened or intimidated by my words.

"You're right, I know it's not a joke, but that's about all I know. What's your name? You've obviously been told mine."

He stopped by the gate to the courtyard of my apartment. "This is where we part. There is no need for names at this time. But I'd strongly suggest you contact Father Billy.

"No name? Ok, how about a business card that shows who you work for."

"We don't operate that way. No card, no paper, nothing. Ever," he said, staring at me. "You'll understand soon. And if you don't, then we've never met. Simple as that."

I watched him walk away. Several people were crossing the street at the corner and he blended in with them and was gone. "This is ridiculous," I said as I opened the gate and entered the courtyard. It was ten o'clock and Alexis sat on the bench, a blanket draped over her shoulders.

"You're home earlier than I expected," she said.

"Why are you sitting out here? And why the blanket? It's not even cold."

"I'm waiting for you. And one minute I'm burning up, the next I'm cold. I'm almost eight months pregnant and my body is out of whack. I'm going crazy."

"Where's Andi?"

"Upstairs sleeping. I could tell she's upset but she didn't want to talk about it so I didn't push." Removing the blanket she said, "Christ, now I'm burning up. Ok, let's go inside." Alexis rose, balancing herself, careful not to fall, and moved toward my apartment.

"Why inside? Can't we talk out here?"

"Don't you know it's dangerous to insult a pregnant woman? I'm apt to go crazy right now and no telling what might happen." Alexis glared at me and added, "Besides, I saw Babs leaving the other morning. You're nothing but a big man whore and I don't want your skinny-ass body anyway."

Glancing up at the window of Alexis's bedroom I nodded and then opened my door. "After you," I said, and watched her enter my apartment.

"Travis, will you sleep with me? I think I need that."

"You called me a man whore and..."

"No, I mean sleep, not sex. The baby is due in seven or eight weeks. Babs doesn't think it'll come early but it might. And," she paused, a tear formed in her eye and rolled down her cheek. "All this time I've been pregnant I've never slept with a man, never had him cuddle up to me, his chest against my back, arm draped over my stomach, my oversized ass pressed against his legs. I'd like to experience what that feels like before the baby comes, what it feels like with someone who cares. And I've got no one to ask but you." Alexis took my hand in hers. "I don't care that you slept, I mean had sex with Babs. God, she's loud. I mean, it doesn't matter."

"I guess the night I was drunk doesn't count," I said.

"No, it doesn't."

"I'll help you up the stairs. You first and I'll..."

"Push? You can be so debonair."

"No, I meant I'll help so you don't...never mind. For someone who's getting her way you might try being a little nicer. Did you bring a nightgown?"

"NO! I'll sleep in my granny panties. The whole point is to feel you, your skin against mine. Quit being so damn cautious and go with it."

I helped Alexis up the spiral staircase, stopping several times to push but keeping my comments to myself. She was all over the place emotionally and I didn't have words of wisdom to share. She sat on the side of the bed, breathing heavily, holding her stomach. "I'll be right back," I said.

Alexis had removed her oversized dress and thrown it on the floor. She lay on her back, her breasts swollen, the areolas even darker than before, and the nipples extended. She rubbed her belly and I noticed her navel was stretched tight and no more than a slight indentation. I placed a warm towel over her eyes and forehead and moved to the foot of the bed. Gently working the heated massage oil I had brought with me between my hands I began to rub her feet with purpose, caressing and squeezing, moving up to the calves, repeating the process. For thirty minutes I worked her legs and feet, tired from the effort. I wiped my hands clean of the oil and stripped down to my boxers. Alexis rolled to her side and I did as she wanted, moving next to her and hugging tightly, my arm across her belly. Still awake, her breathing not yet rhythmic with sleep, I caressed her cheek and wiped her tears.

Andi was outside when we walked out of my apartment the next morning. Alexis looked at her and said, "It's not what you think. It's better."

Walking back inside I called Tater. "I think I might have some information to help with the murdered girl," I said.

"Well, this is timely," he said. "Go ahead and talk."

"Andi got real upset when she walked up behind Tran, Agnes's nephew, and heard him talking to me. His voice sounded like one of the guys in the warehouse who killed Missy."

"That's not much to go on, a voice? But it's a start."

"Why did you say timely?"

"It means Dave called. He was helping out feeding the men at the shelter. Dave asked if any of them hung around the warehouses on the river. This one old man got roughed up, pushed in the river by a couple of guys getting into a boat. Said they had a couple of girls with em. He asked for a dollar and they pushed him. He fell into the river. Lucky for him he didn't drown. The river swirls around the docks and has a strong current."

"What do we do now?"

"*WE* don't do anything. You stay out of this. I'll call you after I check out Tran, assuming I can find any records on him. If he's ever been arrested I might be able to get a picture, show it to the old man at the shelter. If not, then I might need your help."

"Stay out of it, you said. And next you say you might need my help. Which is it, Tater? Sounds a little hypocritical to me."

"People are getting killed and I don't need you being one of them. Do what I tell you and don't push it." Tater paused to gather his thoughts. "I never thought about a boat. We don't watch the river. We leave it for the harbor police. The boat could come in, dock, and those guys could easily walk around then leave the same way, especially at night. No one would see or suspect anything."

"Don't leave me hanging, Tater," I said. "I've got some business with Father Billy. I'm going to try to see him on Monday, but I'll be around."

"I'll let you know what I find, but remember, this is a murder investigation so stay out of the way."

The walk to Brother Lee's was quiet. A cool front had moved over the city during the early morning hours and the humidity was lower than normal. It was an exceptional day. At eight in the morning, the day after Thanksgiving, the streets were almost empty. We didn't expect much business at the restaurant and had decided to go with menu items and no specials. Even after the hectic day before of cooking and celebrating we would have the kitchen ready in less than an hour.

It had been days since I had passed by Charles's house. Today I was not intimidated or uncomfortable and followed the familiar path. As I approached his house he was standing outside. Next to him was a workman dressed in all white, nodding as Charles spoke to him.

"Good morning, Travis. Thanks again for the lovely dinner yesterday. Maggie and I had a great time, much different than what I'm used to for Thanksgiving, but much better, too."

"What are you doing Charles? It looks like you're getting ready to change the door."

"Yes, well it's time I quit wearing my heart on my sleeve so to speak. The door has served its purpose. Besides, why would a man who wants to help people scare them off with this macabre presentation? Time for a change, and Abe hear is going to fix it, aren't you Abe?"

"Yep, it all goes except the eyes. You want to keep them so I'll fix it. Gonna take all day, maybe tomorrow too."

"Abe is going to remove all the distasteful carvings, fix the door, change the color to a light blue, but keep the eyes."

"Good decision." I moved on, certain Maggie was inside, but it truly didn't bother me. Thinking of Babs I recalled the song line "whatever gets you through the night".

Standing in the alley outside the restaurant I used my cell phone to call Father Billy. "Who is he and why was he following me?"

"I presume you are ready to come see me?" he said, avoiding my questions.

"Monday, like always."

"Yes, Monday. Can I expect the usual?"

"Irish stew, with lamb, not beef, as usual."

"Excellent. I'll be waiting," he said.

There was no sense in pushing the issue of who my follower was. Father Billy was rigid in almost all he did, but his voice was different. My curiosity was piqued. He had made his point.

CHAPTER THIRTY-EIGHT

The weekend at the restaurant was busier than expected. Perhaps it was because so many people had cooked such a feast for Thanksgiving no one wanted to cook for a while. I concentrated all my efforts on the restaurant giving Brother Lee a break and taking the time to teach Scatback more techniques as well as basic recipes. I worked late Sunday preparing the Irish stew for Father Billy. It would taste better the next day, much the same as gumbo and other large pot dishes. I fixed a container of the Irish stew for the guard at the athletic club and went for a strenuous workout. I had eaten more than usual and needed to burn off the extra I had consumed, and I needed to get myself ready for my meeting. Surely, I thought, Father Billy did not want me to consider being a priest.

The next morning Sal picked me up in his black Explorer. "I ain't gonna have no cops come snooping around again, am I?" he asked as we pulled away from my apartment and headed to his office.

"No, this is a friendly visit to see an old friend. I should be back at the restaurant in a few hours, in time for the evening crowd."

"When you gonna spend some of the money you been makin? You can afford a car if ya want one."

"Don't need a car very often, and there's no place to park in the French Quarter. Even Brother Lee takes a bus to work. Why, is this a problem?"

"Don't be an ass. I owe ya. Anytime you need it you call me, no questions asked."

Sal was a few years older than I and used to deliver produce to Hope Haven with his father who was an alcoholic, as was his mother. Sal did the driving because his father was almost always close to drunk by noon. A year after Brother Lee took me off the streets Sal's younger sister, Amanda, ran away, refusing to suffer the abuse of the mother's drunken rage ever again. Sal had delivered the produce Brother Lee had ordered and told me his sister was missing, asked me to keep an eye out for her. He was so worried and upset he wasn't aware of what he was delivering, and was almost to the point of tears.

The French Quarter was the easiest place to run to. Having run there myself it wasn't hard to find Amanda. Several days later she was behind Café du Monde close to the river. Two runaway boys, dirty and mean looking were set on taking advantage of her. She turned and ran to me when I called to her. The boys decided to close in on me from opposite sides. I didn't negotiate, didn't want to talk. The first one went down with a single kick to the face, a cut above his left eye bleeding freely. The second one moved to back away and maybe I should have let him go, but I didn't. I was too quick and he didn't see my clenched fist thrusting at him as I punched through his face. They were both on the ground and I left them there. I might have done more if Sal's sister hadn't been there. I had looked at her and for the first time considered my enjoyment in what I had done. It didn't bother me.

Sal pulled up in front of his office and Amanda came out, leaned into the car and kissed me on the cheek. "How's my knight today?" she asked.

"Knight?" I said. "Let's see, last time I was your savior, the time before I was your hero. How about I be Travis?"

"Naw, I like Chef T if I have to be normal. When ya gonna take me out?

"I want to stay friends with Sal. He already told me hands off, so?"

She glared at her brother then leaned in closer, kissed me on the lips and said, "Soon, mister."

Before I pulled away my cell phone rang. Tater showed up in the display and I answered.

"I done some checking and so far can't find much of anything on this guy, Tran. But what I did find makes me sure it's him because he lives in Plaquemines Parish and uses the marina in Empire as his address. It's all bullshit stuff, nothing major, but I'm still waiting for more results. I got a mug shot of him and it looks like the guy at the restaurant but I'm not sure. I only saw him for a minute."

"I'm on my way to see Father Billy but I should be back in a few hours. Anything on the missing girls?"

"Nothing I've heard, but I'm working the homicide. Detective Gravois is always overworked so the missing kids don't get much attention."

I sat outside the church in Sal's car for five minutes, collecting my thoughts and wondering why this was different than other times I had visited Father Billy. Though Monday was typically his day off he had asked me to meet him in the church rectory. Anxiety had replaced the usual anxiousness to see him but I calmed myself, grabbed the Irish stew I had warmed before leaving the restaurant and made my way to the rectory. I got no clue from his new secretary who politely asked me to follow her into his office. She dismissed herself and left me alone with Father Billy. Sitting at his desk he wore a Hawaiian shirt with khaki shorts. Charles was right, I thought, it was a lousy disguise. Father Billy still looked like a priest.

"I brought the stew but you expected I would."

Father Billy approached me, took my hand and without releasing it hugged me tightly. Stepping back he said, "Yes, you seldom disappoint. It's good to see you Travis."

"Sorry I didn't come sooner but there's been too much happening, much of which I don't understand and can't explain."

"Such as?" Father Billy asked.

"Black market seafood resulting in massive fish kills, missing street kids, a murdered girl, and somehow all this affecting my life."

"The world can have evil elements beyond our control," he said. In the corner of the room were a table and two chairs he sometimes

212

used as the confessional for the younger parishioners. Father Billy took a seat and motioned for me to sit. "You look well."

"Two questions, why was Mr. Chin following me, and who's the guy from the other night?"

"Chin was for your well being. You had not been here in a while, and when he asked about you he was concerned because you had been out of touch. It was mostly his idea, and it was timely."

"And the other guy?"

"I'm going to share some things with you. Let me finish before you say anything." Father Billy looked at me and when I nodded he continued. "You know I'm from Ireland, was born and reared there. What you haven't been told, what almost no one has been told is as a young man I was active in the IRA. I had no intentions of becoming a priest. In fact, by eighteen I had a girlfriend I was sure I would marry. In the mid-seventies things in Ireland were unstable at best. Our small group was sure we were doing the right thing, protecting Ireland for the better of the church and the people. Four of us, my two best friends and my soon to be fiancé were assembling a bomb in an old barn. It was not meant to kill anyone. We wanted to make a statement to the British, show them we were serious and capable of doing more damage than they feared. During the assembly process we ran short of wire so I went outside to get more from the car. The next thing I remember was waking up in the hospital. The bomb had prematurely exploded, largely because we didn't understand the first thing about what we were doing. The others all died, including my girlfriend."

"You said you never intended to become a priest…"

"Yes, and that was true. But after the explosion, and being in the hospital, I had a difficult time dealing with what I had done, especially the death of my friends. And I'm sure you can imagine the pain and guilt of my girlfriend's death. The pain and the guilt do not go away."

"That was thirty years ago, a long time to carry so much guilt."

"There were several Catholic priests involved in the IRA even though they, by calling, should not have been. One in particular, whom shall remain nameless, helped me get to America, made arrangements for a place to stay, a work visa, well, you get the point. So I ran much like you did. But as you also found out, you can't run from the pain."

"I don't understand why you're telling me this. Surely you've been forgiven. It was an accident, you didn't mean for anyone to get hurt."

"Most of the time I'm ok. And yes, God has forgiven me, but the hardest part for any of us is to forgive ourselves." Silence followed for a minute as Father Billy looked at The Sacred Heart of Jesus picture on the wall behind me. "I came to America hoping to leave my misdeeds behind in Ireland. For two years I worked in various odd jobs, mostly restaurants, until I decided to enter the seminary. It was ten years before I returned to Ireland to make peace with my past." His eyes glistened as he sat with hands folded and resting on the table, deep in thought for a moment. "My mother is still alive. I was with her two years ago, and it is time for me to visit again."

"My life is pretty good so I don't understand why..."

"Yes, none of this makes sense. Let me continue. The man who followed you the other night is an old friend. He was an orphan, much like you, who needed direction. I've worked with young people since being ordained, even some not much younger than I. They have been my focus. One young man, a particularly bright boy who did not harbor nearly as much anger as you, but just as alone, stood out. I met him while visiting the archdiocese in Virginia. It was a short stay, about a month, but he and I connected. This was twenty-five years ago. Through the years we've stayed in touch. He left the orphanage, went through college, and became very successful. I'm not sure what he does but it involves the government."

"But why was he following me and why are you involved?" I asked. None of this made sense to me and I was becoming uncomfortable.

"A few months ago he called me. Robert, the man who followed you, has done so periodically. I thought it was for old time's sake, but it was more than to simply find out how I had been feeling. The purpose of the call was certainly to catch up, but also because he was on a recruiting mission. The requirements were limited, but specific; a young man, mid to late twenties, a college degree, established profession, single, and no family. I told him about you. Then, unannounced, he shows up in New Orleans. We had lunch, but didn't discuss specifics of what he does or wants. He'll contact me shortly to find out if you're interested in talking with him."

"Recruiting for what, talk about what? I'm pretty happy with my life."

"It's up to you but I'd suggest you meet and talk."

"How do you fit into all this?" I asked, somewhat afraid of the answer.

"As I told you I had a visa to come to America. I didn't realize what was happening but I was visited several times by FBI agents. It was all to find out what I could tell them about the IRA, and why I was here, things like that. I was threatened with deportation. Long story short, my guilt and fear caused me to talk. I became a name and number to them. The fear and guilt were the reasons I went into the seminary, but not why I stayed. It was a blessing in disguise. This is my life's work. The young man I met while visiting the orphanage is Robert. He was almost eighteen and I was a young priest. We became close and he went on to work for the government. Like I said, this was almost twenty-five years ago. I'm not sure what he does, but it's important. My role is strictly a messenger."

"Give him my phone number and tell him to contact me. We'll talk, but only because you suggested it."

"Come, share the stew with me. I usually eat alone and today I'd like the company."

The drive back to Sal's took thirty minutes. I went over in my mind all Father Billy had told me several times. No scenario appealed to me, not working for the government, not even cooking for the president, which was a ridiculous thought, had any interest to me. At least Father Billy had not tried to talk me into becoming a priest.

Sal drove me to Brother Lee's and I finished the day cooking and then closing the restaurant. My cell phone rang and I expected it to be Robert. Instead I heard Alexis when I answered.

"I'm starving but too fat to go out and get some food," she said. "It's eleven-thirty at night."

"Tell that to the baby. I'm hungry. Please?" Alexis said. "And don't forget dessert."

"The kitchen is shut down but I'll do my best." Baby sitting before the baby was born did not appeal to me and I was feeling cramped. "Where's Andi?"

"Downstairs, I think. Haven't seen her in a couple of hours. I've been stuck in my room."

"I think you're stuck feeling sorry for yourself. Get up and go downstairs, I'll be there shortly." The flattop was the easiest and quickest to heat up so I turned it on high, grabbed the softest French bread I could find and rolled it out thin. I sliced up some chicken and made a variation of quesadillas with lots of cheese, tomatoes, onions, and peppers. In fifteen minutes I was out the back door and headed home. When I turned up Governor Nicholls Street I stopped, leaned against the wall of a vacant residence, and waited.

"I thought you were supposed to call," I said as Robert turned the corner.

"We don't like phones. They're necessary enough but too easily traced." Reaching into his pocket Robert pulled out a small cell phone. "But just in case," he said, palming it for me to see. "I prefer the personal touch. When did you realize I was following you?"

"Soon as I walked out of the alley behind the restaurant. But you wanted me to know. I'm sure you're better than this."

"Are you willing to talk…and to listen?" Robert asked.

"If you had called me I would have said no, but you've piqued my interest. Why would you go to the trouble of following me?"

"To make sure you fit the mold," he said, still vague with his answers.

"I'm busy," I said, holding up the bag of food for Alexis. "But I'm willing to talk."

"I'm going to take a couple of days, enjoy your city, the food, the women, relax and play tourist. I'll find you later. Tonight was simply to confirm my hunch."

Robert walked away. He had been intentionally mysterious and evasive but he had kindled a spark, which I was sure was his intent. The rest of the walk home was filled with question after question but I had no answers. Alexis was waiting by the door when I entered the courtyard.

"It's a little cool out here," I said, handing her the bag of food.

"One minute it is and the next minute it isn't. Come on, open your door. I want to eat with you."

"I'm not hungry. I ate at the restaurant," I said, opening the door. "But I guess you can come in and eat." I moved out of Alexis's way and she squeezed through the door. "Where's Andi?"

"She went for a walk. She does that from time to time but not usually this late. Don't worry. She's remarkably savvy for a young girl. I think she's drawn to the kids on the street, wants to find out what they're up to. We talk about it often." Alexis sat at my small table and opened the bag. "Think I'll start with dessert. My God, Tee, what is this?"

"Seven layer cake. Brother Lee's version of the mile high pie served at another restaurant. There's enough for three people but I can tell you'll manage." Alexis had already started eating before I finished describing what I had brought for her. Although she had told me not to worry I was concerned about Andi. I stared passed Alexis, lost in my thoughts. She had finished the cake and half the quesadillas and glared at me.

"What the hell are you thinking about?"

"Worried about Andi, it's almost one o'clock in the morning. I don't like this," I said.

"Relax, she's more than capable of taking care of herself. But we can wait up until she returns if you want. I'm sure we can find a way to amuse ourselves."

Her voice was wicked. "Your smile is making me nervous."

"I thought all young men your age wanted to get laid, had to have sex," Alexis said.

"Who told you that?"

"All the young men I ever dated, which is why I went for an older man. There was more in his repertoire. But look where it got me."

"It's a few weeks until Christmas and your due date is next month. Aren't you getting too close to have sex?" I asked.

"Babs said as long as my water hadn't broken, and there was no bleeding or other issues I was still good to have sex."

The knock on the door interrupted our conversation. Andi walked in, not waiting for me to get up and open the door. "I figured you'd be here," she said, looking at Alexis. "Are you ok?"

"Yes, and I was worried about you, leaving without telling me where you were going."

"I've got work in the morning ladies," I said, grateful Andi was back, safe, and getting me out of the conversation with Alexis. "Take the rest of the food and let me get some sleep."

"Saved by the knock on the door," Alexis said as she picked up the food and handed it to Andi.

"We'll finish our talk tomorrow." Following behind I asked Andi, "What's the word on the street?"

"Nothin new far as I can tell. Some of the kids are still around and maybe some moved on. But it ain't the same, I can feel it. I'm scared to go back out there but somethin keeps pullin at me."

"You don't have to go back out there," Alexis said. "Come on, let's go and let Chef T get some sleep."

CHAPTER THIRTY-NINE

Early December in New Orleans can be warm, or cold, and it is unpredictable. This morning was cool and the walk to the restaurant in the fresh air was enough to stimulate me, and by the time I entered the kitchen I was deep in thought. I couldn't shake the idea of Robert watching me. Even though he said he was taking a few days to relax and enjoy New Orleans I was sure he was out there, observing. It was a feeling I had and it challenged me. It was better to be the stalker than the stalkee. I decided to find him. Brother Lee and Scatback were preparing lunch so I moved to the phone in the dining room and called Father Billy.

"What can you tell me about Robert?" I asked.

"Robert is a private man and even if he wasn't it takes more than a two minute phone conversation to explain."

"Twice he's followed me and both times I knew he was there, but he wanted me to know. Tell me about him, anything will help. I don't think it's too much to ask."

Father Billy paused, and I waited. "Robert is a unique person. You and he have more in common than you would suspect. He is a connoisseur of food and drink, likes the ladies, is loyal to a fault, and private."

"I wasn't trying to get you to breach the confidentiality of the confessional," I said.

"Robert isn't Catholic so confession is not an issue. My respect for him prevents me from telling you any more. But there is more, and he will have to tell you when he deems the time right, or necessary."

"Can I trust him?" I asked.

"More than you can comprehend at this time."

There must have been a couple of conventions in town because the restaurant was much busier than usual for a Wednesday. Both lunch and dinner had lines out the door waiting for tables and we all worked feverishly to keep up. Scatback had adapted so well he managed to keep pace with the dirty dishes and still help me and Brother Lee in the kitchen. Giving him a chance was proving to be one of my better decisions.

By nine o'clock we were down to a few tables with people eating. "I want out of here by eleven o'clock. Can you make that happen?" I asked Scatback.

"Brother Lee done left at seven, before we got slammed," he said. "You can be leavin, too, if you trusts me to lock up."

It wasn't a matter of trust but Scatback wanted the assurance so I nodded. "Tell ya what," I said. "I'm out of here at ten. You finish and lock up. Becky and Chris will be gone, too, so you have it all on your own. Make the restaurant ready for the morning deliveries and I'll handle opening up. You come in late but in time for lunch."

Scatback tried hard not to smile but his mouth turned up ever so slightly as he cleaned. I changed from my chef's jacket into a long sleeve shirt I intentionally did not tuck into my check pants, hoping to cover them enough to not appear as work clothes.

Bourbon Street had become so popular there was never a slow night anymore. If people were visiting then it was busy and this Wednesday was no exception. I made my way to Hard Times and approached Rufus as he stood in the doorway inviting the tourists inside. His large presence made them feel safe instead of intimidating them.

"I need a favor," I said as we shook hands, his dwarfing mine. "The room upstairs with the balcony, anybody using it?"

"No, it's open. But I can't imagine you want a private lap dance upstairs. And, I don't allow it anyway."

"Even for me and Abbey? No exceptions?" I said jokingly.

"I told you Abbey doesn't work here anymore, but I can call her if you like. She'd love to see you again."

I ignored Rufus' remark and said, "I'm looking for someone and thought I might be able to see him from the balcony room."

"Take the stairs over there and you can avoid the dancers. You want me to send up a drink?"

"Yeah, have them mix this up," I said, handing him a piece of paper.

"Tai Chi with a twist?"

"I told you the other night it sounded like it'd be a good drink. I came up with a recipe for it. Try it and tell me what you think." I took the stairs and made my way to the balcony room. It was dark and I left the lights off. In the darkness I had a clearer view of Bourbon Street. But more importantly, I wouldn't be seen.

The drink was relaxing but after an hour of watching people move up and down Bourbon Street I had decided I'd had enough. Rufus was still at the door when I came down the stairs. "Thanks, guess it wasn't my night," I told him.

"Maybe not, but there's a guy inside who wants to buy you a drink. Gave me a fifty dollar tip to tell you he's waiting for you."

"Shit!" I said it spontaneously, frustration evident in my voice.

"He's in the VIP section, far corner with his back to the wall, tipping big and barely drinking."

There was no arrogance in Robert's demeanor as I approached the small table but confidence was more than evident. He motioned for me to sit and then beckoned the waitress. She approached with two drinks on her tray, placed them in front of us and took a twenty dollar bill from the stack of money Robert had placed on the table.

"I believe you call this a Tai Chi with a twist. It's good," he said. "It shows creativity and imagination, two vital elements in our business."

"What kind of game are we playing here?" I asked, speaking loudly against the noise of the pounding music. A dancer approached and though I waved her off she removed her top and was straddling my legs as Robert handed her two twenty dollar bills. There was no use in fighting it so I leaned back and relaxed. The dancer was attractive, large bosomed and obviously prearranged by Robert. She leaned closer into me and kissed my cheek as the song ended, picked up her top and sashayed off, smiling at Robert as she left.

"It's not a game, Travis. When it matters we are more than serious."

"Your attitude makes me uncomfortable, puts me at a disadvantage. And you're pretty free with the money. How do you do it all?"

"The money is a perk of the job, he said. "How do I do it? Well, another aspect of the job is that we almost never relax."

"Which one of us is wasting his time here?" I asked. Completely serious, I was aggravated with his matter of fact attitude.

"If my hunch is right then neither of us is wasting time. But tonight you need to relax as am I. It doesn't happen often so sit back, enjoy the drink and understand I'll get to the point later. You won't be in the dark for long." Robert held up more money and two dancers came scurrying to our table and started grinding.

Looking beyond the dancers I saw Rufus watching us, and by the look on his face he was concerned about me. I waved him over and he immediately walked toward us as if waiting to be called. The two dancers took the money and slinked away, intimidated by Rufus's presence. At the moment I made the introductions and they shook hands I realized there was no figuring out Robert or what he was up to.

An hour later I had finished the one drink while Robert had barely touched his. The stack of money, several hundred dollars at least, was almost gone and the dancers waited close by to see if Robert would replenish the stack of bills.

"That's enough for me. I've got the early shift in the morning. You should come by and try the food," I said.

"I already have. You're an excellent chef. I'm particularly fond of the fried seafood platter. It goes well with the local beer, Abita Amber I think it was. Not the healthiest but one must indulge from time to time," he said.

"I'm not going to try to figure this out anymore. I concede the upper hand to you."

Robert rose from his chair and I did likewise as he headed toward the door leaving at least eighty dollars in twenties on the table. The dancers scrambled for it before I was out of the VIP section. Rufus opened the door for us and I watched Robert walk away without a goodbye or wave.

It was a little after midnight when I approached my apartment. A police car was parked close to the gate and Detective Gravois was sitting inside filling out a report, the dome light making her recognizable. She looked up as I approached and then opened her door.

"You work late," she said as she got out of her car.

"Most nights I do but tonight was a little …" I paused searching for the right word. "I guess a little relaxation, a little pleasure laced with frustration." The curious look on her face didn't surprise me. "What are you doing around here and why this late?"

"I needed to talk with Andi and she wasn't here so I waited. She strolled in about an hour ago."

"What's up with Andi? Is anything wrong?"

"Not sure, but I had some questions about the young girl missing from the foster home in Baton Rouge. She's the second girl these people have lost, or driven away depending on what you want to believe. The other two children have been removed from their house and a possible criminal investigation is pending. Turns out Andi recognized the picture of the other girl, too, but never knew her so there was no connection. Abuse in foster homes is rare but it does happen."

"What about the murdered girl, the one found in the wharf warehouse? Anything on her?" I asked.

"You'll have to talk to Tater if you want to find out anything more. He'll talk to you, off the record. I'm pretty sure he went looking for the oriental guy, Tran I think his name is. But my hands are full with my cases so I don't have time for any of his." She looked at me as I pushed open the gate and said, "Stay out of trouble chef, and no more vigilante stuff. We'll handle it from here."

"A man's got to do what a man has got to do," I said, more in jest than serious.

"Uh huh, just what I thought." She slammed the car door, waving as she drove away. My apartment was empty and I was grateful there were no late night visitors waiting up for me.

Tater was sitting in his car waiting for me at the restaurant, parked by the front door. "I thought I told you to stay out of this," he said as I got in his car.

"I am staying out of it, but I'm curious. What did you find out about Tran? You said you were going to pay him a visit, snoop around down in Empire."

"I went down there but it was a bust. I asked around but nobody was talking. First they acted like he didn't exist but when I pushed it they told me to talk to this guy Degas who runs the marina and, as it turns out, a bunch of other stuff down there. Degas said he knows Tran, helps him out once in a while but nothing else. Doesn't see him too often."

"So no leads on the dead girl, nothing new?" I asked.

"The thing is, I don't believe the guy. One of those feelings I get when I think someone is covering for himself." Tater thought for a moment and said, "Maybe I'm wrong but I don't think so. Problem is, I need an angle to go on and I haven't found it yet."

"LeRoy, the wildlife and fisheries agent might have one. He certainly keeps up with Peter and Agnes. I'll see what I can find out. Maybe you two can meet up and exchange notes. LeRoy is working a case down in Plaquemines."

After the lunch crowd ended and there was a break in the activity I called LeRoy. The reluctance in his voice confused me but I pressed the issue. "I think you can get Peter and Agnes to talk with Tater. I'm not sure Tran has anything to do with the dead girl I told you about but Andi was pretty shaken up when she heard his voice. I think it's worth looking into."

"Travis, I have my own investigation going on and I'm trying to keep it low profile. I'll see what I can do. Meantime keep this to yourself and don't spread it around, ok?"

What LeRoy had said gnawed at me. There was too much going on and not enough answers, but I had agreed to mind my own business.

CHAPTER FORTY

"Where's Andi?" I asked.

"She's upstairs ready for bed. It's eleven o'clock, Travis. Why are you knocking on the door this late?" Alexis said.

"Tell her to get dressed and come down. I want to take a walk and need her to go with me."

Ten minutes later Andi was downstairs. "You ain't never wanted to hang out with me. What you up to, Tee?"

"We'll be back in about an hour," I said to Alexis. I waited until we were out on the street before speaking to Andi.

"Where'd you used to go to meet men, the ones who'd pay you to look?"

"Down at the end of the French Market and over the tracks, close to the warehouse where Missy got killed. I don't go back there no more."

Andi's attitude and demeanor had softened. Living with Alexis had been good for her and I was feeling guilty dragging her out this late even though she had lived on the streets for months. "I'm with you and nothing is going to happen. Come on, show me where."

We walked six blocks to the end of the market, Andi so close to me at times she pressed hard against me. She waved at several of the street kids we passed but she didn't try to stop even when they yelled out her name. We crossed the tracks close to Esplanade Avenue and found an area in darkness close to a wharf warehouse. We would be out of the light, but could still see someone if they crossed the tracks. The winds off the river whipped between the buildings and sent a chill through both of us. I put my arm around Andi's shoulders and hugged her close trying to keep her warm. After standing there for twenty minutes movement by the tracks caught my attention. Someone was coming from the area behind the market. Long shadows started creeping toward us as three bodies walked in front of the flood lights and entered the area. The shadows stretched out and disappeared quickly when the three bodies left the coverage of the lights.

It was hard to tell until they were about thirty feet away, but then I realized one was male and two were females. Andi was crouched down beside me trying to minimize her presence. When I looked at Andi she shook her head indicating she did not recognize the girls or the man. One girl lifted her shirt up and then quickly put it back down when the man slapped at her hands. "Not here" I heard him say, and then he moved along the loading dock of the warehouse to a door left unlocked, or previously broken into by him.

After the three of them were inside I said to Andi, "Come on, I got what I came for."

"What about them two girls. They might be in trouble."

"Someone once told me 'you can't save em all'. I'm starting to think he might be right."

We took the long way home down Decatur Street to Café du Monde where I bought Andi coffee and beignets. By two o'clock we were back at my place and found Alexis waiting up for us, stretched out on my couch, legs bent at the knees and her nightgown bunched at her waist.

"Don't say nothing. It took me an hour to get comfortable and I don't want to move."

"Lock the door on your way out. Andi will help you," I said as I made my way up the stairs to the loft bedroom.

CHAPTER FORTY-ONE

"You sure keeping funny hours for a chef. Want to tell me what ya been up to so much," Brother Lee said.

"Am I causing a problem?"

"Ain't no problem cept'n I'm worried about you. I'd do anything for you, includin mindin my own bizness." Brother Lee stirred the large pot of shrimp stew as he spoke, not looking at me, trying to be less intrusive with his concern. "A man goes through a lot in his life but don't need to do it alone if he don't want to."

"I've been confused lately," I said. "But one thing clear is how much I owe you, and what you've done for me. So ask me anything, hell, tell me to do anything, and I will."

"Nope, don't need nothing but for you to be okay," he said, still not looking at me.

The pot of shrimp stew was boiling but Brother Lee continued stirring it. I moved next to him, placed my arm around his shoulders and with my other hand turned the burner down to a simmer. "I *hate* to peel and devein shrimp, but I'll do six pounds for your stew."

"Don't need to. Scatback done peeled em already. They's in the cooler." His words bothered me as if I was letting him down. Brother Lee stepped back from the stove and studied my reaction. "You done a good thing with Scatback, teachin him about cookin and makin hisself better. That's the way it's supposed to be. The student supposed to get better than the teacher. You gonna be better than me, hell ya already is. If in ya don't make Scatback better, well then you ain't doin a good job."

"Ole man, some times you make too much sense," I said, grabbing the large spoon from his hand and stirring the pot.

"Scatback done moved out of the projects, him and his momma. They got a old shotgun house to rent on St. Roch Avenue close to the Marigny district. I think Ms. Maggie helped em."

Scatback was in the dining room sweeping the floor and needlessly arranging tables and fixing chairs already placed in the right locations. It was ten o'clock and the sun streaked through the windows like light sabers piercing the room. Pride coursed through me as I watched him work, recalling Brother Lee's words, and feeling I had made a difference in his life."

"Good morning Chef T," he said, slowly and deliberately. "How are you?"

"I'm fine Scatback," I answered. "Why are you speaking so slowly?"

"I been workin on my English. Ms. Maggie been helping me with my dictation too.'

"I think you mean your diction," I corrected.

"Yeah, that too, but I needs lots more work. Most times I don't think about it cause I'm too busy."

"I heard you and your mom moved out of the projects, got a new place to live."

"Yep, Ms. Maggie helped us with that, too. I'd a told you but you been too busy," he said. He looked at the floor as his right foot moved in a small circular pattern. "She's a good white lady. She ain't like some of em what does stuff for poor people cause it makes em look good but they really don't mean it. Ms. Maggie does it cause she loves all people. She gonna help me with my gold teeth. I don't think I want em anymore."

"Scatback, I kind of like the teeth. Don't change them unless it's what you want to do. Don't do anything to impress people or because someone else thinks you should. You're eighteen and you're a good man, don't ever forget it." We stood looking at each other for a few seconds, awkward in the moment, then I added, "Come on, let's see if we can make up some New Orleans style barbecue shrimp pizzas for the special tonight. We can serve em with the stew Brother Lee is cooking. I hate it, but I'll peel the shrimp."

"I got left over shrimps I already peeled. I done ten pounds early this morning before you got here." Scatback was already doing better than I, and it pleased me.

Tater and Detective Gravois showed up for a late lunch at two o'clock as I had requested. They sat at the table in the corner farthest from the kitchen and front door, close to the window. Tater wanted to keep an eye on his illegally parked, unmarked police car. Becky was placing water and a small basket of warm bread on the table when I approached them.

"Don't eat too much bread. The stew and pizza are better," I said, taking a seat next to Tater.

"This isn't about the food so why'd you invite us?" Detective Gravois asked.

"I'd like an update on the cases, the murdered girl and the missing girls."

"Travis, I told you to stay out of it," Tater said.

"I am, mostly, but I've gotten too close to ignore it completely. And since you're both here this might help." Tater put a piece of bread he had buttered onto the small plate to his left. "I was at the warehouses on the river with Andi the other night. I watched a couple of the homeless girls come over the tracks with a guy. The girls are hooking up with men over there late at night. I'm not sure how far it goes but those kids are desperate for money. I thought you might be able to use this to find some girls, or whatever."

"I'll look into it," Pam said. "Meanwhile, you stay out of the way. Stick to cooking. I can get an undercover cop to watch the area and see what's going on."

Detective Gravois and Tater were close friends but I was concerned I might have compromised his position by inviting them both for lunch and discussing his case in front of her.

Later the same evening I called Tater. "Tell me, did you show the picture of Tran to the homeless man at the shelter?"

Tater paused and the phone went silent. Then he said, "Travis, I think we're close to a break in this, but we can't afford any leaks." Tater paused again. "Yes, I showed the picture and yes, he identified Tran. Keep this to yourself and DON'T disappoint me. Me and another detective went back to Empire to arrest Tran on suspicion but he wasn't anywhere to be found. This guy Degas, the one who runs the show down there, said he hadn't seen him in a few days so we're still looking for him." As is typical for Tater he hung up the phone without saying goodbye.

LeRoy hadn't been around for a while nor had he called. I thought about phoning him next but instead made my way back into the kitchen from the dining room to help Brother Lee. "Smells like collard greens in here," I said.

"Yep, smothered and cooked with fatback, onions and the secret ingredient. Got lots of customers that like this. It's a side dish for any menu item during lunch. Lagniappe, no charge."

"What we gonna do for Christmas this year?" I asked.

"Same as last year. We gonna have a party the afternoon of Christmas day, close the restaurant cept'n for friends, serve gumbo, appetizers, you remember. I suppose you be goin to midnight mass at the cathedral like usual, right?"

"Maggie and I used to go to midnight mass together, but not gonna happen this year. I'm solo and might stay that way, at least for a while. But yeah, maybe mass and then be here early to get ready for the party."

CHAPTER FORTY-TWO

The last four days had been a blur. Nothing new had come up, Alexis was well but leaving me alone, Tater was busy with police work, and Robert had not shown up. I assumed he was not interested in me anymore which was a let down because I was curious as to what he wanted. And maybe because it was as if I had been rejected, wasn't good enough, and the thought of rejection conjured up old feelings I had hoped were buried for good.

Scatback was busy preparing chicken for the fried chicken lunch special so I grabbed the bag of garbage and stepped outside into the alley, placing it in one of the large trash cans. At ten o'clock in the morning the alley is usually quiet, deliveries have been made, people are working, and tourists roam the streets avoiding alleys even in daylight. Tater and LeRoy turned the corner and were walking toward me.

"Since when do you guys work together," I asked. Their manner as they walked was business and not social.

"Never," Tater said. "Let's go into the dining room and talk."

We entered the kitchen and I stopped at the counter with the stacks of coffee cups. "Fix yourself a cup of coffee," I said as I poured one for myself and then moved into the dining room and took a seat at the table closest to the front door.

"Anything unusual happen around here the last day or so?" LeRoy asked.

"No, it's been routine," I said. "A nice change."

"Travis, we have a situation," Tater said. "Agnes and Peter were shot two days ago. Tran, her nephew, is dead. And Agnes, too. It looks like murder-suicide."

Unexpected death is chilling and even more so when you know the person. When it is multiple deaths the world around you stops. I was numb from Tater's words and then my mind started rewinding, playing my latest encounter with them at Thanksgiving, back to when I first met Agnes and Peter in the alley trying to sell Brother Lee seafood. For five minutes I sat motionless and speechless. Tater brought me out of my trance.

"I'm sorry, Travis. I know you liked them and tried to help."

"Why are you two together? This is a police matter, not wildlife and fisheries."

"There's a cross over element," LeRoy said. "Tran was a suspect in the black market, shark fin case, and Tater has been investigating the murder of the girl. We both got the call on Tran's status since he was a person of interest in both cases. We hooked up yesterday to compare notes then decided to tell you together. It'll hit the news today. The jurisdiction is the city of Cut Off, so we're on the outside."

"Why two days to hit the news? These things usually get reported right away," I said.

"Peter is still alive but not expected to live. He was shot twice, lost a lot of blood, and is in the hospital. The locals wanted to investigate before making the announcement. They're satisfied it was murder/suicide so they released the report." Tater stopped, looked at LeRoy and then added, "My gut tells me there's more to this but my hands are tied."

"Tell me what happened."

"Turns out Tran had a drinking and drug problem. He did a stint in rehab but when he came out he started right back where he left off. This was a couple of years ago. Lately he was staying with Agnes and Peter, presumably to try to get well. Maybe he got liquored up, maybe drugs, won't be sure until the autopsy is complete. The crime scene photos indicate Tran committed suicide, and preliminaries suggest one gun was used."

"The neighbors heard shots and called the police," LeRoy added. "I agree with Tater. This is suspicious but maybe it's our police training. It's probably exactly as it appears."

"Where's Peter, what hospital?" I asked.

"They brought him to Lafourche general. He's in bad shape," LeRoy said.

"I've got to tell Brother Lee and the others," I said. Tater and LeRoy left by the front door and I walked to the kitchen.

The rest of the day was somber even though we were busy for a Wednesday. Everyone tried to do their best but it was evident, even on Becky and Chris. A death in the family was how they explained the mood to the customers without elaborating. Anger invaded me but was soon replaced by sadness, and then guilt for not being able to prevent this. Then more guilt for not knowing what I should have done to help.

"Travis, we can't be responsible for everything," Brother Lee said. "Most things is beyond our control. Accept it and be grateful for knowin em."

"I'm angry Brother Lee, and I can't hide it. But I'm also feeling guilty because I didn't get to ask Peter more about my Uncle Tony. It's totally selfish, but I still feel it."

"You best take a day off, go see Peter, maybe get your pregnant lady friend to go with ya. Even if he ain't awake and can't talk, it'd be good for ya to see him."

"I'll think about it," I said, continuing to wipe the same spot on the counter.

"Don't think. Do it, go on home. I got this tonight. The busses always runnin so I'll be ok."

Before I was able to argue with him Brother Lee grabbed me and hugged me tightly. The anger and self pity drained from me and sorrow for Peter and Agnes, even Tran, overwhelmed me. My eyes watered with emotion, tears running down my face. Hugging him back then releasing him I used the towel to wipe my face. "Go on, boy," he said. I walked out to the alley.

The walk home was like drifting in a fog, my mind filled with grief, questions as to why, what if, but no answers. Avoiding Bourbon Street I used the streets less traveled by tourists until I got to Governor Nicholls. It was nine o'clock when I entered the gate to the courtyard. A folded piece of paper was stuck in the handle of the door. Removing the paper I opened the door, moved inside and turned on the lamp next to the sofa.

Travis meet me at the same warehouse where we was the other night. Another girl is with me and knows something about what happened to the missing girls but don't want to talk to no one but me. Said you could come but no one else. Ten o'clock-Andi.

I placed the paper on the table and paced the room, uncomfortable and suspicious with what I had read. Maybe it was Andi, and why wouldn't it have been, but I'd never seen her write anything so I wasn't sure. The language was definitely Andi so maybe this other girl was too scared to come to my place. My suspicions waned but only slightly.

Adrenaline was pumping as I changed into tennis shoes and comfortable clothes, a loose sweatshirt and jeans. A familiar feeling came over me and it was impossible to shake it. Tater had told me to stay out of it so many times I wasn't comfortable calling him. Instead, I dialed Hard Times and asked for Rufus. It took several minutes for him to come to the phone.

"This is nothing," I said, trying to convince myself more than Rufus. "But in case you don't hear from me in a few hours or so come looking for me at the warehouse behind the French Market, at the end of Esplanade Avenue."

"Take your cell phone with you. Put my number in your phone and dial it, then it'll be in the recently called list. I'm not comfortable with whatever it is you're doing, but if anything looks shaky call my phone."

"Like I said, this is probably nothing but…"

"TRAVIS!" he yelled. "Don't take chances. Do as I tell you. Put your phone in the ankle of your left sock, not in your pocket. Make sure you can get to it. Call me as soon as you finish whatever it is you're up to."

CHAPTER FORTY-THREE

It would take me twenty minutes to walk to the warehouse. Checking the clock I noted it was nine-thirty so I had ten minutes to spare, to think about Andi and her note. Was I making a big deal out of nothing, I wondered? Andi had always been secretive and hard to read. As I stepped outside the cool, night air refreshed me, calmed me, and the adrenaline slowed.

The warehouse door was easy to squeeze through, same as before. I maneuvered my body into the darkness, the door slightly ajar behind me, and waited for my eyes to adjust, but it was too dark. The lone hint of light was near the air vents at the top of the walls, close to the ceiling. Uneasiness fell over me and I paused. I wasn't alone, and whoever was here was watching me as I entered through the door, aware I wouldn't see them. "Andi," I called out.

Ten seconds passed but seemed longer. I was about to call out to Andi again when I heard, "TRAV...mmmm." Andi's attempt to answer became muffled. Jumping to the side to get out of the door I crouched and duck walked along the wall, hoping to catch the movement of a shadow. The beam of a flashlight jumped at me from across the warehouse hitting me in the face. I froze, realizing I couldn't run away once the light was on me. Squinting and turning my head to the side, I stood up and waited.

"Eh la bah, Chef T." The voice was familiar but I couldn't put a face with it. "Or do you prefer the old New Orleans, 'Where ya at', greeting." A response wasn't necessary. "Or maybe," he said. "The simple, hello mes ami."

"Move the light out of my eyes," I said. "And I doubt we're friends."

"Walk toward the light, not too fast, and watch your step. No telling what you might stumble over."

The beam of light moved down from my face, focused on my feet and illuminated a small area about two feet in diameter. It was enough light on the warehouse floor for me to see my steps, but nothing else. I crossed the railcar tracks that ran down the center of the warehouse, following the circle of light. When I was about ten feet from the person holding the flashlight the beam stopped moving and focused on the legs of a body, motionless on the floor. He wanted me to stop, and to look at the body. The holder of the light moved the beam over the body. A young girl lay on her side, hands bound behind her back, mouth gagged, alive, and panic in her eyes.

"Where's Andi?" I said.

She appeared in front of me, pushed from out of the darkness. Her hands were tied behind her and she had also been gagged, the reason her calling out my name had become muffled. Andi fell to the floor on top of the other girl before I could catch her. All the training Mr. Chin had given me was useless. There was no way to tell in the dark how many were watching me, if they were armed, although I presumed they were, where they were in proximity to the light, and more importantly, what I should do next. Closing my eyes I focused, listened and gained a sense of there being at least two of them. If there were more I was sure they weren't in the building.

"Who are you?"

There was silence for a moment then the beam of light turned up, illuminating his face. "Degas, from the marina in Empire. But," he said, "not at your service. In fact, you are at my disposal. That *is* the key and operative word, *disposal*." He trained the light on my face again, blinding me before I closed my eyes.

"I remember you," I said. "You were helpful, so what's this all about? None of it makes sense."

"Agreed," Degas said. "It makes no sense someone as young as you would be so damned nosey and persistent. You should have left Maximilian and Agnes alone, but you *had* to know about Tony. Yeah, I suppose that's where you got your nosiness from. Tony wouldn't leave well enough alone either, and wouldn't look the other way, even for a price. Too bad, because I liked Tony."

"You're talking in riddles," I said. "Uncle Tony died in a boating accident years ago. This sounds like nothing but a load of bullshit to me. And who the hell is Maximilian?"

"Maximilian, Pierre, Peter? All the same person. It's amazing what someone will tell you when they have a gun to their head, but more amazing is what they'll confess when the gun is to the head of their loved one. Be still for a minute and let Ducky secure your wrists together."

"Ducky?"

"Yes, Ducky. Perhaps a silly name to you, but one that stuck with him. He loved to hunt ducks as a young boy and never understood why he had to wait for the season to open or why there were limits on how many were legal to shoot. Always took what he wanted. A valuable asset, someone who doesn't let the law get in the way of having what he wants."

The other person positioned himself behind me and I instinctively moved away. "STOP!" Degas yelled, shining the powerful beam of light into my eyes. "I do have a gun but would hate to use it, at least not yet. I'm not gonna tell you again, put your hands behind your back and let Ducky secure your wrists together." The beam of light dropped to my chest. Reluctantly I moved my hands behind my back. "Don't pull on the cable ties," Degas said, after my hands were secured. "It will make the binding tighter. Better than handcuffs, and you'll never break them loose." A strong blow to the top of my right shoulder sent me to my knees and throbbing pain coursed through my upper body.

Wincing, my shoulder numb from the violent hit, I managed to balance upright on my knees. Andi and the other young girl lay still three feet from me. Too dark to see, and with my hands tied together I didn't have a next move. I was defenseless and helpless.

"Slide the door open," Degas yelled over his shoulder. The large door behind him on the river side of the warehouse creaked as it opened, pushed by yet another person which meant there were at least three of them. The moon was half full and visible rising over the river. It cast light into the warehouse and a clear image of Degas was visible. I watched Ducky join the third man standing next to the rolling warehouse door he had opened. Beyond the open door was a large boat tied up to the wharf. A quick look around confirmed there were three of them.

"You have a problem," I said. "Peter isn't dead. He's in critical condition but still alive." Degas paused and I tried to buy more time. "He survives and it changes things when he tells the police what happened."

"A minor problem Ducky can handle by visiting an old friend in the hospital, assuming what you say is true. They think it's a murder/suicide, and I made sure with a note by Tran confessing what he had done, so Peter is not being protected. And who's gonna tell them differently, you? No, I think not Chef T. You have cooked your last meal."

Andi lifted her head and I caught her movement in my peripheral vision. Glancing at the fear in her eyes I looked back at Degas and asked, "What about the girls?"

"The young ones are my weakness so you don't have to worry about me hurting them as long as they cooperate. And eventually they all cooperate," he said. "They will simply disappear and no one will care or come looking for them. They never do."

"Where are you taking them?"

"You ask too many questions and you're wasting my time." Degas walked toward me and then said to Ducky, "Get the two girls into the boat. Then we'll deal with Chef T."

Ducky pulled Andi to her feet and then reached for the other girl. As he lifted the girl to her feet I said, "Take the gag away so I can at least say goodbye." Ducky looked at Degas who nodded. He yanked the gag down.

"Travis I'm sorry, they used Cat, you know, Kathleen from Baton Rouge? They used Cat to get to me and then used me to get ya to come here. I shoulda figured somethin was up. I'm sorry Travis," Andi said. Tears were running down her cheeks.

"Relax and listen," I said. "The important thing is to do what they say. They've killed people and they'll do it again so don't fight them."

"He's right," Degas said. "Now be good girls and follow Ducky."

"What happens to them?" I asked.

Degas leered at me, anxious to tell me. The sick, perverted ones always want to brag and Degas was sure he was safe. "You want all the details?" he asked. "Sorry, but I don't have time. Let's just say they will be taken care of. They'll join the other girls at my camp near Venice. It's comfortable, and accessible only by boat. Six bedrooms and each girl gets her own. There are two others down there now. Think about it Chef T, my choice of young girls, whenever I want, whatever I want them to do, and anytime I want. It's almost more than I can comprehend sometimes. When I get tired of them I move them offshore to an abandoned oil platform, sell them to the drug dealers bringing cocaine up from Columbia, or the warlords of Mexico. They trade in anything that will produce money, drugs, girls, black market, you name it. They hate Americans and gladly pay me for a chance to abuse white girls. One like Kathleen can bring a hundred grand easy. This one here," he said, pulling on Andi's arm, "she's a little thin. They'll negotiate down to about fifty thousand. But don't worry, they're worth more alive. In another year they'll wind up in Asia somewhere giving toothless blowjobs for five dollars." He chuckled and said, "It *is* a cruel world."

"This makes no sense," I said. "All this over some girls. Are you really that sick?"

Degas slapped me as hard as he could and I fell back to my knees. "The tip of the iceberg you arrogant piece of shit!" Ire belched from his mouth as he kicked me in my stomach.

"Stop before you kill him right here!"

LeRoy moved out of the shadows. "Sorry Travis. I wish there was some other way but you wouldn't let it go," LeRoy said. "I tried to steer you away but you wouldn't quit. Why'd you have to keep pushing about Tony, and then insisting on Peter and Agnes being helped? It made things worse. It was only a matter of time before they talked."

Degas had calmed down and reached to help me up. "The situation is never as we think, is it Travis? Peter had too much to hide, but even he would eventually talk."

"It's… getting clearer," I said, gasping for breath, my stomach aching. "Besides the girls… you run the black market too, don't you. LeRoy helps keep you safe."

"LeRoy was a little harder to convince. He was getting too close to the truth while investigating Tony's death. He didn't buy the accident either because Tony was too good in a boat. I gave him a little cash, extra for keeping us all safe. That led to a little more cash, and then one day a freebie with a young girl. Pretty soon he came to expect it. Been on the payroll ever since. Women and money, the downfall of most men."

"How much do you get, LeRoy? Enough to make… murder worth it?" I said through clenched teeth, wheezing between words.

"I wasn't in on the killing. But yeah, it's worth it. I'm in too deep to back out."

"Besides," Degas said. "LeRoy don't wanna give up them young girls. Plus, a nice cut of the action helps with his retirement. The state doesn't pay as well." Degas moved in front of me and said, "If it wasn't us it would be the Vietnamese Mafia. It isn't a matter of stopping it, but rather a matter of who controls it."

"You still talk in riddles," I said, my stomach still aching from the hard kick, but my breathing under control. "What mafia, and who is Maximilian?"

"Well not actually a mafia, but there is a small group of the Vietnamese that don't like playing by the rules. Most of the Vietnamese are extremely honorable. They stay to themselves, take care of their own, don't mingle too much with Americans. But there's always a few, and these few help me by fishing the sharks. I supply the boat and they do the work. They get their cut and I handle getting it out of the country and into Asia. It's big money, millions over the last ten years alone, not to mention years ago before we realized how big this would become. Tran was mixed up in it so he became easy to manipulate, most drug users are. He kept me informed on what they were doing and I kept him out of jail. As for Maximilian well, Tran helped me with that too."

"More riddles. Tran was Agnes's nephew so what's he got to do with who Maximilian is?"

"Tran was not her nephew. He was an embarrassment to Agnes, but she took care of him because he was her son, her only surviving child. But she didn't want Max...Peter to know so he became her nephew. She was afraid Peter would kick her out if he found out she had a son who was a problem, especially since she had hidden it from him for so long." Degas paused. "Enough of this bullshit, get the girls in the boat," he yelled to Ducky.

"Why would LeRoy tell me about the black market and set up Peter and Agnes for an arrest? This is insane," I said.

"I told you about the black market but never told you how big it is," LeRoy said. Tens of thousands of sharks have been taken over the last couple of years. I needed to make sure you didn't know anything, and you didn't. Arresting Peter and Agnes was to keep them quiet, scare them, and with you in the mix I was sure Peter would never trust you to tell you anything."

"So what happens to me?"

"You come with us in the boat. It's a twenty-eight foot, deep-vee hull with twin, two-fifty horsepower motors. She screams down river and no one bothers us. I've been running the river for so long the harbor police wave as I go by and never stop me. We'll be at Fort Jackson in a little over an hour. The river side of the fort is perfect to hide bodies, the sand is easy to dig and the body decays quickly."

Andi and Cat looked at me as Ducky moved behind them. Their faces grimaced simultaneously as he grabbed at the back of their heads and secured a handful of hair from each. He pushed them toward the open door. The moon had risen out of my view but still cast enough light through the doorway to see them being manhandled toward the edge of the wharf. Ducky jammed their heads together, held them tightly and spoke to them before pulling hard on their hair. He released them, pushing so roughly they almost fell and then jumped down into the boat. Reaching up he grabbed Cat's arm and pulled her down and into one of the seats at the rear of the boat. Grinning with pleasure he did the same with Andi, manhandling her much more roughly than Cat. Ducky's head was visible after he had tied Andi and Cat to the seats. Standing over them, admiring his work, I was sure he began to salivate before climbing back out of the boat onto the wharf.

"Ducky has a mean streak," Degas said as he and LeRoy watched. There was displeasure on LeRoy's face, but he said nothing.

Degas grabbed my arm, motioned for LeRoy to do the same and they pulled me toward the door while I resisted. They stopped pulling and Degas punched me again in my stomach, but I anticipated it and bent at the waist with the blow, lessening the affect. Standing erect I was sure I heard a splash before we got close to the door. Degas and LeRoy pulled me through the open door, released me and ran to the edge of the wharf, stopped and looked down. Without a sound I felt the cable tie around my wrists release while someone behind me held my hands in place and maneuvered me back into the shadows close by the door. I concentrated my focus on LeRoy and Degas as I backed up against the line of wooden pallets stacked along the outside wall of the warehouse. The narrow space between the stacks was dark and impossible to detect someone hiding there.

"Ducky," LeRoy called out. "Where are you, quit screwing around."

"Fuck him," Degas said. "If he's too stupid to keep from falling into the river he deserves to be left behind. Get Chef T and let's go," he said, motioning toward me. "We've wasted enough time and been here too long already."

"Sorry Travis, but it's time to go," LeRoy said as he approached, reaching out with his arm to grab me.

A hand shot out of the darkness behind me, lightning quick, and grabbed LeRoy by the throat, rendering him unable to make a sound. "GO!" was all I heard, but I was already leaping toward Degas and smashing him with an open palm to the nose as he turned toward me. Taking a half step back I kicked his left knee with a snapping motion. Degas went down as the cracking of bone echoed over the wharf. He was crippled instantly and had no time to pull his gun. My control was absent, and I was incensed by all I had seen and been told. I kicked Degas hard several times, grabbed his shirt and lifted his torso two feet off the ground before driving my fist through his face, smashing it as if it were made of brittle clay. Degas was unconscious but I didn't stop. Twice more I drove my fists into him before I heard the voice screaming my name.

"Travis," Robert yelled. "TRAVIS!" he screamed again, louder the second time, causing me to pause. "We don't kill," he said.

I looked down at Degas, grabbed his shirt and lifted him close enough to drive my fist into his face one more time before releasing him. He fell to the concrete in a heap, unconscious and still. "I'm not finished," I said. "But I'll stop." LeRoy was sprawled out on the wharf, also unconscious. Robert stood over him.

"Call the police but leave me out of it," Robert said. "You have all you need so make it fast. I'll find you later."

"NOT later," I said trying to calm myself. "Make it sooner. Dammit Robert, I need you to tell me what's going on." He was gone before I could take my cell phone out of my sock and call Tater.

"Two ambulances and lots of back up, and NOW," I said. "Ten minutes or somebody dies." Although I had never killed anyone, and abhorred the thought, I watched Degas and LeRoy, not sure I wouldn't have to.

Tater showed up first, running into the warehouse, gun drawn and yelling my name. It had taken him fourteen minutes. Degas and LeRoy had regained consciousness but were unable to stand. "Out here," I yelled as I moved into the door opening. "You're late." Sirens in the distance were growing louder as the back up and ambulances rushed to answer the call.

An hour later Andi, Cat, and I were at headquarters answering questions and making statements. I was thankful to have them as corroborating witnesses to all Degas had told us.

By eight o'clock in the morning the three of us had finished and needed a break. Detective Gravois took Cat, and Tater drove me and Andi home. Sitting in the back seat Andi pressed against me so tightly my shoulder dug into the door.

"Relax and ease up. You're squishing me against the damn door."

Andi ignored me and nestled up against me even harder. "Don't leave me, Tee," she said. "Please don't leave me."

We rode in silence for twenty minutes, my arm around Andi's shoulder. For years I had believed I had it tougher than most, sometimes letting self pity cloud over me and turn my days negative even though Mr. Chin had taught me better. Sitting next to Andi, a sixteen year old girl who had experienced too much pain, I had a better perspective on my life. Especially when I looked at her and she could still smile.

Alexis, Terry, and Jerry were standing in the courtyard when Andi and I walked through the gate. Tater had called and told them we would be home shortly. Terry held a tray with cups of coffee and as I reached for one Alexis exclaimed, "Jesus, Travis your hands look horrible." It was true, both hands were slightly swollen and the knuckles of my right hand were raw with broken skin caused by pummeling Degas's face. "How the hell you gonna cook with them hands?" she said.

CHAPTER FORTY-FOUR

Two days after the warehouse incident my situation had improved. I was back to cooking, Andi was safe, Cat was in child protective services, and LeRoy and Degas would certainly go to prison and never get out. It was too early to tell for sure but Ducky's body would eventually be recovered from the river, but where or when was anyone's guess. One jumper from the Mississippi River Bridge took three weeks to find, eventually turning up under a dock near Pointe a la Hache, almost forty miles downriver. Peter, or Maximilian or whomever, was still in critical condition and day to day. I called Lillian at Charity Hospital, and after talking with her I phoned Tater.

"Pull some strings, do whatever you need to do, tie it to an ongoing investigation but get Peter air lifted to Charity. Lillian told me they have the best gun shot trauma facility in the south. Tater, it needs to happen as soon as possible."

"Dammit Travis, you can't *save* them all, remember? But you'll never stop trying, will you?" Tater didn't expect an answer and I didn't give him one. "If I pull this off you'll owe me forever, understand? The rest of your life is mine," he said hanging up the phone.

Lillian answered on the first ring. "Tater will make it happen. I don't know how but he will and I need, NEED, you to call me as soon as Peter gets there. I'll do whatever you want, whenever you want, but please do what you can."

"Calm down, Travis. If he can be saved we'll do it. Let's pray it isn't too late. Now, go back to work and keep busy. I'll call you if he gets transported here."

The lunch business was slow, especially for a Saturday but supper made up for it. Every time I placed an order in the window and pulled the ticket down two more orders would be put up. I had trouble keeping up but at least the time flew by. It was almost ten o'clock before I could stop and look around the restaurant. When I slowed down my mind raced back to the last few days. Becky walked into the kitchen and grabbed me, pulling me toward the door to the dining room. "Over there, them two doctor ladies are back and asking for you. I told them it wasn't a good time and then they said, 'We're doctors, we can make it better'. I'd save you from them but somethin tells me ya don't wanna be saved, so take a break and I'll bring you some coffee."

"Well, ain't you a big celebrity," Babs said as I sat next to her. "At least in the Quarter. Chef T this and Chef T that, why it's enough to make a southern girl all giddy."

"I'm not up for any karaoke," I said. "Still recuperating, taking it easy and working."

"Perfect," Babs said. "So tell us if it's true, rumor has it you got roughed up, had to fight off a bunch of them."

"Not true," I said then stopped, remembering what Robert had said about leaving him out of it. "There were three of them, one fell in the river and the other two weren't much of a challenge." The omission of the whole truth bothered me since it made me look heroic when in actuality I had been challenged by Degas alone and minimally.

"Doesn't matter if it was one or a hundred, the story is you saved two young girls."

"Did you get checked out by a doctor?" Gwen asked.

"I'm fine, a scratch or two, maybe a bruise. No need to get checked out."

"Here's the deal, Tee. Gwen and I have a suite at the Monteleone Hotel on Royal Street. It's a short walk. We think you should come with us, let us make sure all your parts are in good working order, and if you want we'll order up a late night masseuse, then maybe the hot tub on the balcony. Why it's practically our civic duty." Babs watched me blush then said, "Travis, a true southern gentleman never refuses a lady."

"Twenty minutes," I said rising from the table. "Got a couple of things to take care of in the kitchen."

"Travis," Babs called out to me as I was walking away. I turned back toward her. "Make sure you tell them you won't be in early tomorrow."

"You two do share, don't you?" I said.

CHAPTER FORTY-FIVE

Two weeks had passed since the night in the warehouse with Degas and LeRoy. Whoever said there was no honor among thieves was right because LeRoy cut a deal with the feds and turned states evidence. The deal was doable because he wasn't involved in the murders, and not because of his service as an enforcement officer. If anything, being an agent made the deal harder to cut. But it saved the state thousands of dollars on a trial so they negotiated. The federal government was involved because of the off shore, black market poaching and the trafficking of young girls. Degas would plead guilty to all the charges except murder which would be reduced to manslaughter. The young girl found hung in the warehouse he blamed on Ducky. Even still, Degas would spend the rest of his life in Angola and LeRoy would get twenty years minimum, with no chance for early parole.

The state of Louisiana confiscated all Degas owned, the marina in Empire, bank accounts with close to a million dollars, even the large camp near Venice where he had imprisoned the girls. Two girls were rescued from the camp the day after the warehouse incident, alive but badly in need of medical attention and counseling. Detective Gravois took a personal interest in helping them because they had been taken from New Orleans.

There were no leads on the murdered girl brutally disfigured by the warehouse rats. Gwen had told me that sometimes there is no way to trace the body and it remains nameless, an unsolved case. Over time maybe someone from where the girl ran away might talk to the right person at the right time and generate a lead. And maybe DNA from a parent turns out to be a match. All mostly false hope by those involved so they can sleep knowing there's a young girl in the morgue, unidentified and unclaimed.

Christmas was five days away and I was feeling the spirit. Sal loaned me his car and I picked up Father Billy and drove to Charity Hospital. Lillian met us at the nurse's station of the intensive care unit. Lillian and Father Billy were old friends having met at Hope Haven. They hugged each other like lost relatives.

"What's the latest?" I asked. "It sounded bad on the phone."

"Follow me," she said, and led us away from the intensive care ward, down a hall to the last room. Lillian pushed the door open allowing Father Billy and I to enter before her. Peter lay in the bed, his head turned toward the window looking out. He heard us and turned to watch as we entered.

"Peter's been told what you did to help him," Lillian said. He's also been told Agnes was murdered. Travis, he asked for you but go easy, let him talk but don't upset him."

"Peter looks strong," I said, confused with the idea he still might not survive.

"He had a good chance of surviving but it was smart to move him here. There's no reason he shouldn't live, but you can understand how despondent he is. I'll be back to check on you all shortly."

"I'm sorry about Agnes," I said.

"Ya never get used to loosing someone," Peter said. "What about Tran?"

"Tran is dead, too. Degas was behind all this, but I'm not sure who killed Tran or Agnes."

"Must have been Ducky," Peter said. "He was mean, would do anything for Degas. I should a spoken up years ago. But I wanted to stay out of it, be left alone. At least Agnes can be with her son, and her other children."

"You knew Tran was her son and not her nephew?"

"Yes, for a long time. It was obvious watchin her with him." Peter looked at me and said, "Travis, Ducky killed Tony. Caught him off guard and broke his neck, then made it look like a boat accident. Tony knew what was going on and was about to arrest them. I figured it out but Degas threatened me, told me he would tell them I did it because Agnes and Tony had become involved, were having an affair. I got scared, didn't want to lose Agnes. I had already lost so much." Peter looked at me, tears in his eyes.

"Peter, I understand and I don't blame you. Uncle Tony knew the truth, and now, so do I. Nothing else matters." Peter nodded but said nothing. "Peter, I'd like to ask you a few questions, please." He nodded again.

Father Billy moved a step closer to me and said, "Not too much, Travis."

"Who is Maximilian?"

Peter looked away, staring at the ceiling for a moment then motioned for Father Billy to come close to him. He whispered into his ear, Father Billy nodded, made the sign of the cross on Peter's forehead and then stepped back. "A sort of Absolution," Father Billy said to me. "A little unorthodox but I've always bent the rules a little.

"Maximilian is my given name," Peter said. "I was born in Metz, France in 1930, an illegitimate birth, frowned upon at the time even in France. When I was ten my mother sent me to Germany to be near my father, but he wanted nothing to do with me. I didn't realize it at the time and neither did my mother. After I turned twelve they put me on a German U boat." Peter lifted the hospital gown over his shoulder exposing the crude and faded 0188. "I was told it was for experience, they said it was safe. The German U boats were having their way in the Gulf of Mexico. In a two year period they attacked seventy ships in the Gulf of Mexico, sinking fifty-eight of them, and the U.S. navy wasn't called upon to help until after most of the ships had been sunk. Only a few people today know about this but I studied it, ashamed of what the Germans had done. It was on U166 where the sailors gave me this tattoo. I was proud cause it made me feel like one of them. But then one night not long after entering the gulf the ship's first officer came to me. He told me he had orders to make sure I didn't return, said I was to be washed overboard and lost at sea. But he couldn't do it. He refused to kill me. So one day in July they surface, put me in a small raft and dropped me off on a sandy, barrier island, Chandeleur Island, but I didn't know it at the time. Soon after, U166 was sunk, the only German U boat to go down in the gulf. I was supposed to be the one to die and instead, I was the only one to survive. Minos took me away from the lighthouse and raised me. We changed the tattoo to 0188," he said holding his hand over the old tattoo. "I studied about the war, read as much as I could and became ashamed of my heritage, who I was. Minos and Agnes were the only ones I ever told, but I think Agnes was forced to tell Degas because he threatened her with Tran, but I didn't figure this out until now."

"Peter, there was nothing to be ashamed of. The war was years ago and had nothing to do with you. Why would you carry so much guilt?" I asked.

"My father wanted nothing to do with me because my mother was Jewish, which I had come to realize by the time I was ten."

"I still don't understand. There were other Jews in Germany," I said.

Peter looked down, staring at his lap and then in a whisper said, "My last name is Hitler."

I stared at Peter, not blinking, not moving for a full minute. Father Billy moved to the bedside and placed his hand on Peter's.

"I never saw my mother again," Peter said. "She was young, eighteen when I was born, and I guess infatuated with his presence. I studied about World War II in school but I read about my father, too. He was persuasive and charming before he came to power. The young people of Germany and many in Europe rallied behind him. I guess my mother was vulnerable, and he didn't realize she was Jewish, or didn't care when he met her. By the time the war started he hated the Jews and had a plan to get rid of them, even his own son."

"Do you remember your mother's name?" I asked.

Peter nodded and a faint smile appeared. "Ciera Chauvin," he said. "I remember everything about her. I'm seventy-four years old and never one day did I not remember her."

"What was the absolution about?" I asked looking at Father Billy.

"Peter wants this to remain confidential so I absolved him which binds me to confidentiality of the confessional. However, you are not bound by anything. Peter and I are asking you to keep this to yourself. It is his wish."

"It didn't seem like a confession, I mean, Peter did nothing wrong, but maybe I understand about guilt. Whatever he wants, I'll do."

Lillian knocked on the door and entered. "Not too much, remember? Peter needs to rest. He was weak when he got here. I think it's time you both should leave."

"How much longer in the hospital for Peter?" I asked.

"Another week at least, then we'll see how he is. I think he'll be released to go home by then, but he'll need care."

Father Billy gave Peter a blessing before we walked out. "I have a favor to ask," I said. "I'll tell you on the ride back to the rectory."

CHAPTER FORTY-SIX

Christmas was in two days. Alexis had decided to stay in New Orleans even though her mother objected vehemently. Andi had gone back to Mississippi to visit her mother who was still in a rehab facility. She had promised to be back before Christmas and to bring her younger sister if the foster care parents would allow it. Alexis lay on my couch and I rubbed her feet.

"You missed your chance, pal," Alexis said. "I think sex is out of the question."

I stopped rubbing her feet and looked up. "I would think so," I said. "Hell, I can see your belly moving. It's bumping and grinding more than the girls at Hard Times."

"Boy, are you smooth." Alexis placed both hands on her belly and smiled. "Here, right here, feel the baby."

Alexis took my hands, placed them on her belly and I felt the baby move. It's impossible to not smile when you feel a baby move inside its mother, and I think I grinned like a child at the circus. "If I had to guess I'd say it looks like you won't make it to the due date. I might be an uncle any minute."

"I love you Travis," she said. "I would not have made it if not for you. You need some work but you've been good to me, good for me. If it's a boy I hope he turns out as well as you. And NOT like his father."

"Guess it's right what they say about expectant mothers. They go through TONS of emotions. But thanks, and if it's a girl I'm sure she'll be as strong as you."

I attended mass on Christmas Eve at St. Louis Cathedral. I sat with Maggie and Charles, happy they were together. Alexis was too uncomfortable to come with me so I prayed for her, faithful all was as it should be. Andi had returned and with Lizabeth, her younger sister. They stayed with Alexis, excited to be with her and doting on her like two grandmothers. As mass ended I made my way to the exit at the back of the church. Robert stepped up along side of me as I went through the doors.

"I thought you weren't Catholic," I said.

"I'm not but it *is* Christmas. Aren't all welcome?" he asked.

"Always," I answered. "It's hard enough to get Catholics to go to church much less non-Catholics. But then, you are a rarity so I shouldn't be surprised." We walked into Jackson Square and continued through to Decatur Street and turned toward Café du Monde. The weather had turned cold and I had to turn the collar of my jacket up against the brutal wind.

"Time for coffee?" Robert asked.

"Don't you have family to spend Christmas with? What are you doing back here, and what took you so long to contact me?" We walked on and he ignored my questions.

Robert and I sat at a corner table in the rear of the patio, our backs to the wall separating Café du Monde from the parking lot on the other side. We watched a few people from mass at the cathedral order beignets and coffee and then leave. It was a quiet time of year, and a quiet night. The portable patio heaters were set on high, glowed bright orange with heat, and warmed the area enough to make it almost comfortable.

"No, I don't have family to spend Christmas with," Robert said. And after I talk with you, I'll be gone."

"Why no family, I mean what are the odds two of us together, each with no family?" Robert didn't respond but instead took a bite of beignet and watched me. "I guess the odds are pretty good."

Robert wiped the powdered sugar from his mouth, took a sip of coffee and then began. "My mother was a stripper and my father was an egg-head professor at Princeton. I have no way of knowing for sure but I suspect she was the only woman he had ever been with, romantically I mean. My father was a true nerd. Neither was right for the other but mom got pregnant and my father tried to do the right thing. He wanted to marry her but the bouncer at the club where she danced had other ideas. Right after I was born the bouncer killed them both in a drunken rage. He got life in prison, and is still there…I make sure to keep tabs on him." Robert looked at me, waiting for my reaction. There was none. "Just as I thought," he said. "If my mother had any family they didn't bother to find her. My father had no siblings and any relatives he had must not have wanted anything to do with the baby of a stripper. You learn these things growing up in an orphanage, but you learned this yourself. See, you and I aren't necessarily so different. I'm probably a little smarter than you, whereas you are more creative. A big advantage to you. Brains can still get you killed. Creativity will save your life, but I've done ok. I'm forty-three and mostly stay out of the danger zone."

"I'm thankful you were in it at the warehouse. I would not have made it out alive if not for you. You show up at the most interesting times," I said.

"You can thank Rufus, well, not literally. He doesn't need to know anything."

"What are you talking about?"

"I was in Hard Times, about to contact you when Rufus came up to my table. Said he was worried about you, said something was up. He told me where you said you were going. If not for him I might have missed the whole thing. I'm not a big believer in coincidence but this time it worked out. I went back to the club and told him you were ok, a little trouble but you handled it."

"Robert, can we cut out all the crap and get to the point of this?"

"I am part of a group designed to help our government. The *company*, not how we refer to it but good enough for now, was formed after the nine-eleven tragedy in New York in 2001. A few in the company came from inside government, and those who did were in other capacities. We as a group are relatively new, a couple of years old. Our selection process is very in-depth, and the criteria extremely strict, unbending in fact." Robert took a sip of coffee, placed the cup back on the table and looked out at Decatur Street. "We are involved in large issues," he said. "On a small scale."

"So you work for the government, so what? Lots of people do."

"I didn't say I work for the government. The company, *helps* the government, we don't work for them. There's a big difference."

"How is it different?" I was becoming aggravated with Robert's vagueness and could tell he sensed this.

"Travis, listen for a minute. Our government has too many groups and agencies. There's the FBI, Secret Service, CIA, Navy Seals, Army Rangers, Special OPS units, and more black ops groups than we can count. All are high profile, and absolutely undeniable. And because we have the freedom of information act, most people in this country believe they are entitled to know everything about everything. It is hard, sometimes impossible, to gather information and remain anonymous, or more importantly, to deny existence if and when necessary.

"The government was tracking Osama Bin Laden by cell phone until some reporter assumed it was his duty and right to report this. As soon as his report was published all the cell phones for Al Qaida went dead and they lost him. That's one example, there are many more, but off the immediate point."

"Why are you telling me this?"

"It's simple. You fit the criteria."

"Which is?"

"You're single, orphaned with no family, never been in the military, you're college educated, and have a profession which will take you almost anywhere in the world with acceptance and no questions asked. And the fact you can already handle yourself in a fight is a big plus. In short, you are expendable, and deniable. Cold but true."

"Plausible deniability," I said. "I've heard of it."

"No, not plausible, complete and absolute deniability, essential in our line of work," Robert said, correcting me and making his point.

"Expendable?" I questioned.

"Unfortunately, yes. You die and no one starts digging, no family to appease or compensate or worry about. Your friends would wonder, maybe ask a few questions, but they're friends, they'll let it go."

"You're right, cold," I said, finding all this hard to believe. "What about you, what's your specialty? I assume you fit the criteria."

"International banking. I can go anywhere in the world and work. Banks are everywhere and they like American educated employees. Mostly because of what we were taught about American banking, not because we understand much about their banking. Because, as the U.S. stock market goes, so go the markets in the rest of the world." Robert paused a moment as if considering what or how much he should tell me. "Currently my office is in the Cayman Islands, about as secret and protected as it gets."

"Doesn't sound like much of a future. I mean, if we don't work for the government then how do we get paid, what about retirement, other benefits?"

Robert laughed. "I have to remind myself you're twenty-six and still naive to many things. Our group is well taken care of. We have ways," Robert said.

"You're going to have to explain a little more for me to be interested," I said. "For instance, how big is the *group*?"

"Look Travis, we're interested in you joining us. When I leave tonight you'll have a couple of weeks to think about it. If you decline I won't contact you again, and as far as you're concerned, I don't exist. But think about this, I didn't have to come to your aide. We both got lucky, you more than I. I'm persistent to a point, but if you're not in one hundred percent then we say goodbye and none of this ever happened."

Leaning back in my chair, my legs stretched out, I looked across Decatur Street at Jackson Square. "I love New Orleans, I love to cook, and I love the people in my life. Maybe it was different for you but everybody here is in my blood. I don't think you understand what you're asking, to leave New Orleans, maybe never come back. It's not an easy or quick decision."

"I didn't ask you to leave New Orleans. This will always be your home and your base from which to work. Assignments can last a few weeks, but realistically a few months, to as long as a year. You'll always come back here unless you find a place you like better. It's a ten year commitment with an option for ten more. After twenty years you are retired. Assuming you live that long."

"Suppose I don't want to retire, what then?"

"Again, naive. You'll want to. Optioning for a second ten years is not guaranteed, so let's make the first ten and worry about the rest later."

"Okay," I said. "I'll think about it but naive or not, tell me how well I'll be taken care of."

Robert sat back and folded his arms across his chest, apparently considering how much more he should tell me. "Daily, we move closer and closer to being a global society, not only a U.S. society. What we do, the services we provide benefit the entire free world, although make no mistake, America comes first. You're smart enough to understand the risk that statement connotes. It works like this," he said. "Our group operates out of the Caymans, the islands of big business and *very* private banks. It's easy to get here or anywhere else from the Caymans. Our business is casinos, a multimillion dollar business and legitimate, but it's all a cover. If you sign on with us, not literally because we do nothing in writing, after training you'll take a vacation to the Caribbean, visit a couple of islands where we have our casinos, take a girlfriend with you if you like, always a nice cover, and gamble a few days with your own money."

"I'm not a gambler, and why would I use my own money?"

"Gamble with your *own* money, then on the next to last day the player card I will have issued to you, and you've been using as you play, will be inserted into a specific slot machine, predetermined by me. You'll play for about twenty minutes, drop several thousand dollars…"

"Do you realize how ridiculous this sounds?" I interrupted.

"Drop several thousand dollars," Robert repeated, "and then, with the player card still inserted, you'll hit the jackpot for, let's say, a hundred grand."

"More than ridiculous," I said. Robert didn't flinch as he stared at me. Shifting in my seat I asked, "And how can you be sure of this?"

"The casino is ours. The corporation is domiciled in the Cayman Islands and untouchable. All the games are run by the company. The slots are electronic and can be set to make any percentage of profit we want. I assure you they take in more than they pay out. But there are a few select machines programmed to pay off big for the right player's card. One of our associates is a gaming expert and electronics wizard. We leave nothing to chance, Travis, except your commitment."

"Two weeks to think it over?" I asked.

"This works if you're, pardon the pun, all in. And there is *no* quitting. I'll be in touch." Robert rose from his chair and walked away.

The walk back to my place was brutally cold by New Orleans standards. The wind accelerated through the streets of the French Quarter, pushed by a cold front gripping the city like an eagle's talons holds its prey. I turned the corner at Governor Nicholls Street and broke into a full run. The flashing lights of an ambulance parked outside Terry and Jerry's home filled the street with pulsating color.

"OOOOH, SHIT!" I heard Alexis cry as she was being wheeled out on a stretcher.

"TRAVIS! Do something," Terry squealed.

"What happened, what's wrong," I yelled at Alexis, leaning down toward her as they pushed her to the ambulance.

She grabbed my coat, yanked me close to her, and through clenched teeth she mumbled, "My water broke and the baby ain't waitinggggg! OOOOOHHH!"

"Wait. It's not time, you're not due for a couple of weeks," I said. Alexis's clenched teeth and rabid eyes stared back at me. "I'll call Babs," I yelled as they closed the ambulance door and sped away.

Terry was backing his car out of the small garage as I stood there dialing Babs's number. Andi and her sister, Lizabeth, watched as we all stood like statues, freezing in the cold air. "Come on," I said to Andi, "You and Lizabeth get in the car and we'll all head to Touro. The baby's coming whether we're ready or not."

"Jesus, Travis, calm down," Babs said. "This is not the first baby to be born, and even if it is Christmas day I promise you he is *not* the Messiah. I'll be at Touro in twenty minutes."

"He? It's a boy?"

"Yes, it's a boy but Alexis didn't want anyone to know. Hang up, damn it, and let me get to the hospital."

At 6:00 A.M. Babs walked into the waiting area of Touro Infirmary, one of the oldest hospitals in New Orleans. "The world population is greater by at least one right now," she said. "Eight pounds, six ounces, nineteen inches long, a head full of dark brown hair, almost black, and mother and baby are doing fine."

"Can we see her and the baby?" Andi asked.

"Yes, they're getting her ready and she'll be in a room shortly," Babs said.

"A private room!" Terry insisted. "Money is no object."

Terry's comment of money being no object made me think of Robert and what he had told me. As farfetched and ridiculous as it had all sounded I suddenly sensed it was all true. "Come on," Babs said. "The nursery is this way. You can see the new baby through the glass. He'll be brought to Alexis later this morning."

Alexis had asked to see me first, alone. Standing by her bed I held her hand. Through the window the first light of Christmas day was glowing. "I think my momma's already on her way here cause Uncle Terry called her. What am I gonna do, Tee?" she asked.

"You're going to be grateful, that's what. I certainly am. A new baby boy, healthy, and he needs you. What a day, huh?" The words were hard to find and harder to deliver to Alexis. I'd never considered anything like this happening in my life and I was as lost as Alexis.

"I don't even have a name picked out," she said. "What kind of mother doesn't have a name for her child? Help me Tee. I sure ain't gonna name him after his son of a bitchin' father. Ya know, he never even called one time to see how I was doing."

"Men can be cruel so let it go. You have one responsibility, which is to your baby," I said. Turning toward the window I glanced out, noticed the daylight increasing, and nodded. Looking back at Alexis I said, "Max, I like the name Max."

Alexis squeezed my hand, thought for a minute and said, "I think I like it. Max, hmmm, I do like it. Little Max, Big Max, to the Max…"

"Stop before I change my mind," I said. "The others are waiting, give it some thought while they come in and visit. I'm supposed to be at the restaurant helping Brother Lee get the food ready for his party this afternoon."

"When's the last time you got some sleep?" Alexis asked. "You look like hell. How are you gonna stay awake?"

"A little coffee and I'll be fine," I said. "I'll be back later tonight, maybe bring you a special treat." As the others entered the room I said, "Brother Lee's at two O'clock. Bring your appetite."

CHAPTER FORTY-SEVEN

The kitchen at Brother Lee's was in full swing when I walked in at eight o'clock. Scatback and his mother were working together, opening oysters and placing them on trays to be served raw from the buffet table. The meal was not intended to be nearly as large and varied as Thanksgiving had been. In truth, most people had been to Christmas Eve parties with too much food, then Christmas breakfast and more food. Brother Lee's party was more about people coming by, sharing the joy of Christ, and remembering what good friends and family mean to each other.

We were almost ready. I looked at the clock on the wall and realized it was almost noon. "Come see this," Brother Lee hollered from the rear kitchen door. "Don't never see this too often."

Brother Lee and I stood together and looked out on the alley. Snow had started falling and it was coming down hard. Flurries shot up the alley, pushed by wind gusts as we watched. "When's the last time it snowed in New Orleans?" I said.

"Can't remember, but it don't happen much," Brother Lee said.

"Christmas day, 2004," I said. "I'll remember this day."

The hospital lobby was quiet and at seven o'clock I entered Alexis's room. She had bathed, her hair was brushed and had a glossy sheen, and her face was radiant as she held her new baby son at her breast. "I'm trying to get him to latch on," she said. "Never thought I'd

262

have to teach a baby to nurse. But I think he's almost a natural." Alexis paused then said, "Don't get upset…I wanted to name him Travis, but I didn't know how to ask. I was hinting but you came up with Max. I thought sure you'd jump at the chance. Silly me, huh?"

"Guess I'm a little thick at times, but I like Max, short for Maximilian. I'll explain it to you one day. But right now I'm exhausted. Here," I said, holding out the bag of food I'd promised to bring.

"Put it on the table, it rolls over the bed. I'll eat later. It's his turn," she said, looking at her baby. "You look worse than before. The big chair in the corner folds down into a sleeper. I'm ok here, so is Max, take a nap. If I need you I'll wake you up."

Babs woke me the next morning at six. I had slept all night never hearing the nurses check on Alexis or bring her Max for feeding. "I take it you slept here all night," Babs said.

"Didn't intend to but yeah, guess I did."

"Hang on a minute, let me finish with Alexis and we can get some coffee," she said. "You can go home tomorrow morning," Babs told Alexis. "This is one of the healthiest babies I've ever delivered, and you look pretty good, too. I hope you stay in New Orleans so I can take care of you."

"Take that one," Alexis said motioning toward me, "and get him out of here. I expect my mother to show up any minute. I don't have the energy to explain him to her."

CHAPTER FORTY-EIGHT

New Year's Eve in New Orleans is almost as big as New Year's Eve in Times Square, New York. The French Quarter and Jackson Square were packed with people. Babs had insisted I spend it with her and Gwen. After the Fleur de Lis on top of the old Jax Brewery building dropped at midnight we managed to make our way to Bourbon Street. I tried to sneak past Hard Times but Rufus grabbed me and wouldn't take no for an answer. We wound up in the VIP section as his guests.

Rufus looked at Babs and said, "In case you're wondering, *every* night is amateur night."

"Not a chance big boy," she said. Looking at me she added, "Believe it or not, Gwen and I do have our limits."

Several days later, after the small lunch crowd had cleared out and the restaurant was quiet, Father Billy came in and asked for me. We sat at a table in the middle of the dining room and Chris brought us iced tea.

"I wanted to come see you in person," he said. "I'm coming from Catholic Charities on Howard Avenue. I went there to get the help you asked for. It took a little work and persuasion, but I was able to do what you asked." Father Billy took a deep breath and said, "Travis, you aren't going to believe this." The look on his face, the smile, promised it was good news. "We are more than ninety percent sure Peter's mother is still alive. She's ninety-two years old, is in good health for her age, and living in a retirement home in Metz. She survived the war, got married, had another baby and moved into the home after her husband died."

"Another baby? Peter has a sibling?" I said. "After all these years his mother's still alive?" I was more emotional than I expected or understood. Maybe it was the fact Peter still had family, a wish I had abandoned years ago in Hope Haven, that caused me to well up.

Father Billy took a letter from his pocket, opened it and placed it on the table. "Peter's mother married Hans Muller from Switzerland in 1948. They had one daughter, Angelis Muller in 1949. I'm not sure but Angelis might have gotten married, might have children, and if so Peter's an uncle." He placed his hand over mine and said, "Travis, this is such a good thing. I'm not sure where we go from here, but we must find a way to reunite Peter and his mother, introduce him to his sister, and right away."

Lillian had apprised me of Peter's status almost daily. There was no imminent danger and he would be released soon. The drawback was, released to do what, go back to Cut Off, to the house of the murders? It wasn't much of an option, and if Peter never wanted to step foot in the house again it was understandable. "Will the church let you have time off? Can you escort Peter back to France?"

"I imagine so but Travis, there are passport issues and much to be considered. What name is he to use? I mean, we know the truth but he doesn't want it out."

"Give me a couple of days to get things in order, maybe a week. Clear your schedule and brush up on your French."

"I don't speak French," Father Billy said.

"Well then, brush up on something. I'll be in touch."

CHAPTER FORTY-NINE

The terminal of the airport was moderately busy. People scurried to check their bags, arrange flight changes, grab a quick bite in one of the many eateries, or browse the gift shops. Peter walked with a cane for balance, still weak from the ordeal of being shot twice, the loss of blood, and the excitement of what waited for him. Father Billy carried a bag with essentials for both of them in case their luggage got lost, and did his best to steady Peter. The security check point was as far as I was allowed to go. Holding out my hand to shake with Peter I was caught off guard when he wrapped his long arms around me and drew me into his chest, squeezing with the strength of a man half his age.

Stepping back from Peter I took his hand and placed a piece of paper into it. "I did some checking on the internet the last couple of days. It's amazing what you can find with a little bit of diligence," I said.

Peter looked at the paper. I had written July 30, 1942; U-166; 28 degrees-37'N and 90 degrees-45' W; Located in 2001 at 5000'. "What does this mean?" he asked.

"A company searching the floor of the gulf for new pipeline locations came across the wreckage of the Robert E. Lee, a steamer ship carrying over 400 passengers and crew sunk by U-166," I said. "And in the same area they found U-166. It was in two pieces several hundred feet apart, but they were able to identify it. After U-166 fired upon the Robert E. Lee she surfaced and watched the Lee sink while passengers and crew flailed in the water. Twenty six of the passengers died. A U.S. navy patrol cruiser was escorting the Lee and fired depth charges at U-166. The submarine went down at the same time as the Lee. Those coordinates are where they found her at five thousand feet, the blackest part of the gulf, too deep for surface light to reach."

Peter folded the paper and put it into his wallet. Shaking my hand he thanked me again. "I wonder if I'll ever be back," he said.

"You'll be back," I said. "And we'll take a boat ride out to the coordinates; maybe throw a wreath in the gulf for your ship mates." Peter stared out the windows of the concourse. "Peter, even though I hate what the German sailors did, I am grateful for what the human beings on the submarine did in letting a young boy live. Hopefully they can rest in peace," I said.

"Evil never rests in peace," Peter said, putting his arm around my shoulders and hugging me again. Turning, he steadied himself with his cane and started through the security line.

"I'll see you in a couple of weeks," Father Billy said. "I'm taking a side trip to Rome, the Vatican, after I get Peter situated in his new home. Too bad you're not coming with us."

My heart ached with the thought of reuniting with a mother after all those years, knowing it would never happen for me. "I can only imagine," I said. "Bring back pictures, and tell the Pope hello for me."

For ten minutes I stared down the concourse watching them get smaller and smaller with each step. Why is the gate always at the end? Father Billy had asked rhetorically. Not having ever flown, or traveled abroad I had no answer for him anyway.

Stepping outside from the terminal I paused. "Normally I wouldn't give someone an extra week to decide, but I made an exception in your case," Robert said as he joined me.

"I needed the extra week, and you needed it to get done what I wanted."

"Passports usually take longer, but sometimes we can make things happen fast. It's the nature of our business," he said. "And we're connected to the right people."

"I suppose you're looking for an answer."

267

"Well it certainly got tougher for you to make a decision. Peter gave you his house, his camp, his truck, and whatever else he had. You're pretty well set, but there's still the issue of money."

"Did I ever tell you my parents left me a trust fund? I was five when they died and it wasn't that much money, twenty five thousand dollars at the time. It's grown into a hell of lot more, but I can't touch it until I'm thirty which is four more years."

"Four years is a long time. A man can make a small fortune in four years," Robert said.

"And tons of enemies, too. Could even get killed," I said. "Robert, it's not about the money. Another character flaw of mine perhaps, but money isn't everything, necessary of course, but not what I live for."

"June first in Costa Rica," Robert said. "Three months of intense training while you cook at Martha's American Café. Nice front, and a natural for you." Robert stepped to the cab line for a ride back to the French Quarter. He turned toward me and said, "I need an answer by tomorrow, Travis. We're flexible, but this has gone too long already."

"Robert," I said walking toward him. "Wait for me. I'm in, One hundred percent, no quitting." Robert nodded but said nothing. "This better be good," I added.

EPILOGUE

After much deliberation and arguing with myself I decided not to tell anyone until May first. And when I did tell those who mattered I realized it was best I had waited. Brother Lee was the most upset, and the one it hurt the most to disappoint. But after realizing Scatback would replace me and do an even better job Brother Lee became less difficult, although at times I would catch him watching me as I worked. He was wondering why it had come to this, what should he have done differently. Brother Lee had saved me and there was nothing he could have done better. Even with a ten year commitment I would be back and take care of him.

Scatback, while visibly sad I'd be leaving, was excited about the opportunity my leaving presented for him. For effect, because it wasn't necessary, I leveraged his excitement to make him promise to keep working with Maggie, finish his high school requirements and enroll in the culinary classes at Delgado. He would have promised anything, but since it was for his own good I didn't feel bad about manipulating him.

Becky played it as big as the others telling me, "I almost made an exception in your case, almost gave in to temptation."

I shrugged and told her most sincerely, "Bullshit, and you and I know it." The tear she shed gave me second thoughts about her confession. At times it was more like a funeral home around the restaurant than a place to eat and be content. I promised them I'd be back, and my leaving was temporary, but it didn't help. It would pass but take all I had to not change my mind.

Alexis cried and Andi threw a fit and walked out, but came back two minutes later and ran up to me sobbing, hugging me, and begging me not to go. Andi scared me and I hoped she would not run back to the street blaming me for abandoning her. The toughest lesson for me to learn had been what I was told many times, and had finally admitted. Maybe you can't save them all. Time would tell with Andi.

Sometimes a man has to make promises and I made more than I would be able to keep, but with a little luck I might be able to pull off most of them. The big promise was impossible. Alexis made me promise to come back and marry her if she hadn't found a man up to her standards for Max. At least I had some time.

Tater was less understanding than anyone else. The detective in him could sense I wasn't being totally honest, and I hated not telling him the whole truth, but he wouldn't have believed me anyway. And more than this, I hadn't been told the whole truth. Like the others, he would get over it. Tater and I ate at Dave's, in the dining room, and remembered where we had come from together. "Damn, New Orleans gets in your blood," I told him. "You might not know the whole truth, but you know I'll be back."

"Coming back is not the problem," Tater said. "It's the leaving. I expect to hear from you on a regular basis, and if I don't I'm comin lookin for ya."

The last week of May and my affairs were in order. Robert had shown up unannounced and unexpected. Typical for him. It turned out New Orleans had gotten into Robert's blood as well. New Orleans has a way of claiming what she wants, be it a way of life, a mispronounced street name that becomes accepted as correct, a non-native daughter or son, and occasionally a lost soul. His visit was mostly social and personal, but he took the chance to make sure I was still in, had purchased my ticket, taken care of all my affairs per his earlier instructions, and would show up as planned. I was learning, whatever I was jumping into, Robert was thorough.

As expected the ones I would have the least amount of trouble with waited for me in a suite at the Monteleone. No strings and no guilt were their specialties, and they gave the term "free spirits" a new definition. I wouldn't miss them the most, but I was sure I'd miss them often. They made sure of it.

THE END

LAGNIAPPE

(Pronounced lan yap)
A French term used in Louisiana meaning a little extra for free

The following are a few of Chef T's favorite recipes.

TAI CHI W/ A TWIST

A MIXED DRINK RECIPE
1 OZ. OLD NEW ORLEANS RUM
1 OZ. COCONUT RUM
2 OZ. GREEN TEA W/ GINSENG
1 OZ. PINEAPPLE JUICE
1/2 OZ. MINT INFUSED SIMPLE
SYRUP
1/2 OZ. BLUE CURACAO
1 ROUND SLICE OF A SMALL BLOOD ORANGE

MIX ALL INGREDIENTS TOGETHER EXCEPT THE CURACAO AND ORANGE. POUR OVER CRUSHED ICE. DRIZZLE BLUE CURACAO AROUND EDGE OF GLASS. CUT EDGE OF ORANGE, TWIST AND PLACE ON TOP OF GLASS. ADD 1 OR 2 DROPS OF TABASCO. DO NOT MIX.

EASY SHRIMP APPETIZER

1 BAG FROZEN SHRIMP, PEELED AND DEVEINED (1 LB BAG)
1-1/2 TBS. EMERIL'S BABY BAM (RECIPE ON HIS WEB-SITE)
2 TBS. BUTTER
1/2 CUP GRATED ITALIAN CHEESE (PARMESAN OR 5 CHEESE BLEND)

THAW SHRIMP IN COLD WATER (TAKES ABOUT 10 MINUTES) RINSE AND DRAIN. MIX SHRIMP AND SEASONING IN A BOWL MAKING SURE ALL SHRIMP ARE COATED. HEAT BUTTER IN 12" SKILLET AND WHEN HOT ADD SHRIMP AND SAUTE UNTIL COOKED, ABOUT 4-5 MINUTES. REMOVE FROM STOVE, ADD CHEESE AND BLEND. TRANSFER TO DISH AND SERVE WARM WITH FAVORITE CRACKER, MELBA TOAST, OR FLATBREADS.

CAJUN FRIED RICE

4 TBS CANOLA OIL
1 CUP OKRA, CROSS CUT INTO CIRCLES
1 CUP ONION CORSELY CHOPPED
1/2 CUP CELERY CORSELY CHOPPED
1/4 CUP EACH OF GREEN, RED, AND YELLOW BELL PEPPER
1 TBS GARLIC FINELY CHOPPED
1 TSP SALT
1/2 TSP EACH OF BLACK, WHITE, AND RED PEPPER
1/2 TSP THYME
2 BAY LEAVES
1 LB ANDOUILLE SAUSAGE
3 CUPS COOKED RICE
1 TBS TABASCO
1 TBS WORECESTERSHIRE SAUCE
2 TBS PARSELY FINELY CHOPPED

IN A LARGE SAUTE PAN (BIG ENOUGH TO HOLD ALL INGREDIANTS) HEAT 2 TB OIL. ADD OKRA AND FRY OVER MED HEAT TURNING OFTEN. WHEN OKRA IS COOKED THROUGH ADD ONION, CELERY, PEPPERS, GARLIC AND ALL DRY SEASONING. SAUTE TIL ONIONS ARE SOFT AND TRANSLUCENT. REMOVE FROM PAN AND RESERVE. CLEAN PAN AND ADD REMAINING OIL. WHEN OIL IS HOT ADD ANDOUILLE AND FRY TIL LIGHTLY BROWNED ON EDGES. ADD RICE AND TOSS WELL. WHEN HEATED THROUGH ADD REMAINING SAUTEED VEGETABLES, TABASCO, WORCESTERSHIRE AND PARSLEY. TOP WITH SLICED GREEN ONION.

NEW ORLEANS STYLE BARBEQUE SHRIMP PIZZA

1 CUP BUTTER
4 TBS FLOUR
1 CUP SEAFOOD STOCK
1/2 CUP BEER
2 TSP SALT
1 TSP RED PEPPER
1 TSP BLACK PEPPER
1 TSP WHITE PEPPER
1 TBS GARLIC FINELY CHOPPED
1 TSP THYME LEAVES
1 TSP ROSEMARY, FRESH IF AVAILABLE
1/2 TSP OREGANO
1/2 LEMON
1 TBS WORECESTERSHIRE SAUCE
2 TBS PARSELY FINELY CHOPPED
1 LB SHRIMP 21-25 COUNT, PEELED AND DEVEINED
1/2 CUP PARMESAN CHEESE FRESHLY GRATED
1/2 CUP GRUYERE CHEESE FRESHLY GRATED
1 LARGE PIZZA CRUST PRECOOKED

FOR SAUCE

IN MEDIUM SAUCEPAN MELT BUTTER. WHISK IN FLOUR AND COOK OVER MEDIUM HEAT 2-3 MINUTES. WHISK IN SEAFOOD STOCK AND BEER UNTIL FULLY INCORPORATED. SAUCE SHOULD BE SLIGHTLY THICK. ADD REMAINING INGREDIENTS (EXCEPT CHEESE) AND SIMMER 3 MINUTES.

TO PREPARE SHRIMP

ADD SHRIMP TO SAUCE AND GENTLY SIMMER 3-5 MINUTES TO JUST PINK. DO NOT OVERCOOK. USE SLOTTED SPOON TO REMOVE SHRIMP AND SET ASIDE FOR PIZZA:

SPREAD PARMESAN IN EVEN LAYER ONTO PIZZA CRUST. ARRANGE SHRIMP ON TOP OF CHEESE. SPOON SAUCE OVER SHRIMP. TOP WITH GRUYERE CHEESE. BAKE IN OVEN AT 425 DEGREES FOR 5-7 MINUTES UNTIL LIGHTLY BROWNED AND CHEESE IS BUBBLY.

GRILLADES AND GRITS

1/2 CUP PREPARED ROUX
4 OZ. BUTTER
1 CUP ONIONS CHOPPED
2 TBS GARLIC FINELY CHOPPED
1/2 TSP THYME LEAVES
2 EA. BAY LEAVES
2 CUPS BEEF STOCK
1-1/2 CUPS CRUSHED TOMATOES
1 TBS WORCESTERSHIRE SAUCE
1 TBS TABASCO
2 TBS PARSLEY CHOPPED
1-1/2 LB BEEF ROUND
1 TSP CAYENNE PEPPER
2 OZ. CANOLA OIL
SALT AND PEPPER

FOR SAUCE

IN 1 GAL. SAUCEPAN HEAT BUTTER. ADD ONIONS, GARLIC, THYME, BAY LEAVES, SALT AND PEPPER. SAUTE TIL VEGS. ARE TENDER. ADD ROUX AND FULLY INCORPORATE. ADD BEEF STOCK AND CRUSHED TOMATOES-SIMMER TIL DESIRED CONSISTENCY IS REACHED. ADD TABASCO AND WORCESTERSHIRE SAUCE. ADD SALT AND PEPPER TO TASTE AND SIMMER.

FOR GRILLADES

CUT BEEF ROUND INTO 2" SQUARES. LAY MEAT SQUARES ON CUTTING BOARD, SEASON WITH SALT, PEPPER AND A PINCH OF CAYENNE. USE A MEAT MALLET TO POUND SQUARES UNTIL VERY THIN. HEAT 2 OZS. OIL IN LARGE 16" SKILLET. LIGHTLY FLOUR EACH SQUARE AND ADD TO SKILLET BROWNING ALL PIECES AND SET ASIDE. DEGLAZE PAN WITH 1 CUP OF BEEF STOCK AND ADD TO SAUCE. ADD MEAT TO SAUCE AND SIMMER TIL COMPLETELY TENDER ABOUT 1-1/4 TO 1-1/2 HOURS.

FOR GRITS

2 CUPS HEAVY CREAM
2 CUPS WATER
1 CUP INSTANT GRITS

HEAT CREAM AND WATER TO A SIMMER. WHISK IN GRITS IN A STEADY STREAM. ADD SALT AND PEPPER TO TASTE, COVER AND SIMMER 5-6 MINUTES.

SPOON GRITS INTO A BOWL AND LADLE SEVERAL PIECES OF MEAT WITH SAUCE ON TOP.

RUFUS' BUTTER BEANS

2 LBS. BUTTER BEANS (LARGE WHITE LIMAS, NOT GREEN)
1 LB PICKED PORK (BONELESS)
1 LB SMOKED SAUSAGE (PREFERABLY LOW SODIUM, LOW FAT)
4 RIBS CHOPPED CELERY (OR 1 CUP)
1 LARGE, YELLOW ONION (ABOUT 2 CUPS)
4 LARGE BAY LEAVES
½ TSP. CAYENNE
1 TBLS. BLACK PEPPER
6 CUPS LOW SODIUM CHICKEN BROTH
6 CUPS WATER

RINSE BUTTER BEANS AND SOAK FOR ONE HOUR. CUT PICKLED PORK INTO LARGE, BITE SIZE CUBES AND SAUTE IN LARGE POT (AT LEAST 8 QUARTS) FOR 4 TO 5 MINUTES, ADD SLICED SAUSAGE AND SAUTE FOR 5 MORE MINUTES. ADD CELERY AND ONIONS AND SAUTE FOR 5 MINUTES. ADD BUTTER BEANS, BAY LEAVES, CAYENNE, BLACK PEPPER, CHICKEN STOCK AND WATER. STIR AND BRING TO A BOIL. COVER POT AND REDUCE HEAT TO LOW, WHILE MAINTAINING A SIMMERING BOIL. STIR OCCASSIONALLY AND COOK FOR TWO HOURS.

NOTE: TASTE AND ADD SALT AS DESIRED. THE STOCK AND THE MEAT HAVE A LOT OF SODIUM SO DO NOT ADD ANY SALT UNTIL BEANS ARE COOKED. ADD SALT IF DESIRED AND COOK FOR 20 TO 30 MINUTES. SERVE OVER RICE.

BROTHER LEE'S SMOTHERED COLLARD GREENS

1 LB FAT BACK (ALSO KNOWN AS SALT PORK) REGULAR BACON
1 BUNCH (OR 2-16 OZ BAGS) COLLARD GREENS CLEANED AND CHOPPED
1 MEDIUM CHOPPED ONION
1 OZ (5 TO 7 CLOVES) MINCED GARLIC
2 JALAPENOS, SEEDED AND CHOPPED

FRY FAT BACK IN A 4-QUART POT AND REMOVE FROM POT AND SET ASIDE WHEN COOKED. ADD ONION TO POT AND SAUTE FOR 3-4 MINUTES, ADD GARLIC, JALAPENOS AND SAUTE FOR ONLY ABOUT A MINUTE. ADD HALF THE COLLARD GREENS TO POT AND ADD ENOUGH WATER TO COVER GREENS. AS GREENS REDUCE IN SIZE, ADD THE REST OF THE GREENS AND BRING TO A BOIL. RETURN FAT BACK TO POT, REDUCE HEAT TO LOW, AND SIMMER FOR ONE HOUR. ADD SALT AND PEPPER TO TASTE AND CONTINUE COOKING ON LOW UNTIL GREENS ARE VERY TENDER, USUALLY ANOTHER HOUR. SERVE AS A SIDE DISH OR OVER RICE.

NOTE: FOR A MEATLESS DISH, DELETE FAT BACK AND REPLACE WITH ½ CUP OF OLIVE OIL AND FOLLOW RECIPE. VEGETABLE STOCK IS RECOMMENDED INSTEAD OF WATER FOR THE MEATLESS VERSION.

ABOUT THE AUTHOR

Houston Neal Gray is the author of *Diverted*, his first novel, and is actively writing a sequel to it as well as the next book in his Chef T series. The picturesque view of the Mississippi River from his writing room keeps him inspired. He lives in New Orleans with his wife, Jo Ann, and can't imagine ever living anywhere else.

Made in the USA
Charleston, SC
01 July 2015